# BERTIE'S THEORY OF ICE CREAM

OTHER TITLES IN THE
44 SCOTLAND STREET SERIES

*44 Scotland Street*
*Espresso Tales*
*Love Over Scotland*
*The World According to Bertie*
*The Unbearable Lightness of Scones*
*The Importance of Being Seven*
*Bertie Plays the Blues*
*Sunshine on Scotland Street*
*Bertie's Guide to Life and Mothers*
*The Revolving Door of Life*
*The Bertie Project*
*A Time of Love and Tartan*
*The Peppermint Tea Chronicles*
*A Promise of Ankles*
*Love in the Time of Bertie*
*The Enigma of Garlic*
*The Stellar Debut of Galactica MacFee*

ALEXANDER McCALL SMITH

# BERTIE'S THEORY OF ICE CREAM

*A 44 Scotland Street Novel*

Polygon

First published in hardback in Great Britain in 2025
by Polygon, an imprint of Birlinn Ltd

Birlinn Ltd
West Newington House
10 Newington Road
Edinburgh
EH9 1QS

1

www.polygonbooks.co.uk

Copyright © Alexander McCall Smith, 2025

The right of Alexander McCall Smith to be identified as
the author of this work has been asserted in
accordance with the Copyright, Designs
and Patents Act 1988.

All rights reserved. No part of this publication may be
reproduced, stored, or transmitted in any form, or by
any means electronic, mechanical or photocopying,
recording or otherwise, without the express written
permission of the publisher.

ISBN 978 1 84697 716 9

*British Library Cataloguing-in-Publication Data*
A catalogue record for this book is available on
request from the British Library.

Typeset in Sabon LT Pro by The Foundry, Edinburgh
Printed and bound in Great Britain by Clays Ltd, Elcograf S.p.A.

*This book is for Neil Skidmore.*

# 1

*Ceilings, Gesso, Dinner Parties*

We all get different things out of looking up at ceilings. For Angus Lordie, owner of the dog known as Cyril and an accomplished portrait painter, a ceiling was a blank canvas on which the mind could paint whatever it wished. Ceilings were finished with plaster, of course – at least, ceilings in Georgian buildings in that part of Edinburgh were – but he thought it might just as well be gesso: that thick white paste of chalk and binding agent that artists slapped on a canvas before applying paint.

Angus had learned to make traditional gesso at art college, and still used those materials rather than acrylics. Acrylics were convenient, but they lacked the *feel* of the old ingredients, and, importantly, they did not smell. Angus liked things to smell, believing that if something smelled, it was in some deep sense more natural than something that did not. So, for his own gesso, he used rabbit-skin glue mixed with warm water and old-fashioned chalk – a combination with a very characteristic pungent smell. Then, ideally with early Italian music playing in the background, he would roll up his sleeves and apply the resulting paste to the naked canvas. Also audible in the background at such times would be the complaining voice of Domenica – "Angus, that disgusting smell! Is it *really* necessary?"

Looking up now at the broad white expanse of his ceiling on Scotland Street, he imagined how Poussin might have filled it from cornice to cornice. Nicolas Poussin liked sky, with stray cumulus, a horizon of hills as often as not, and a foreground of unhurried figures. There was more than enough sky in Scotland to satisfy Poussin. He would have approved, too, of Drummond Place, of the railings and the tall trees that swayed in the wind that blew in from the Forth or the Pentland Hills. He would have understood the Scottish weather, with its changes and challenges. He would have felt at home with the classicism of Edinburgh.

On the other side of the kitchen table, Domenica Macdonald, anthropologist and wry observer of life, who had married Angus some years previously, rescuing him from paint-spattered bachelordom, saw that he was staring at the ceiling and asked him what he had been thinking about. You do not have to know what your spouse is thinking all the time – and sometimes it is better not to – but Domenica occasionally liked to enquire.

"I was thinking of how Poussin would have painted our ceiling," he replied. And then, without revealing any further thoughts, he said, "And you?"

"Friends," she said. "I've been thinking about how long it is since we had anybody in for dinner. Or lunch, for that matter. Or coffee . . ."

Angus frowned. "Really? Didn't we have . . ." He faltered. He thought there had been somebody, and it was not all that long ago, but now the recollection escaped him. Had it been Matthew and Elspeth? Or that woman from Melrose who had bought one of his paintings, and who turned out, as often happens in Scotland, to be a cousin of his second cousin's husband?

Domenica remembered these things. "I can tell you exactly," she said. "It's five months since I cooked dinner for anybody apart from us. I bought a leg of lamb and I used five cloves of garlic. I remember it very clearly. There was a moment of indecision before I chopped the third clove, but then I decided to throw caution to the winds."

"And yet we have those evenings when we invite everybody," said Angus. "The regular crowd, including Stuart downstairs . . . Speaking of whom, I saw wee Bertie the other day, and that little friend of his—"

"Ranald Braveheart Macpherson," prompted Domenica.

Angus smiled. "Yes, that's him." He returned to the question of dinner parties. "Yes, we have those suppers for friends, but not nearly often enough."

Domenica looked thoughtful. "I think social habits have changed. People aren't going out so much to other people's houses – at least, not in the formal way they used to. The dinner party's dead, I think."

Angus considered this. It was a resounding statement: *the dinner party's dead*. It was rather like announcing the end of the Age of Baroque or the Mesolithic period. Yet, it was probably true, he thought. There had been a time when on most Fridays or Saturdays there would have been an invitation to go to dinner at somebody's house. The evening would follow a set pattern – drinks beforehand, and then the set-piece: a three-course meal, with conversation running along well-worn tracks. He smiled at the recollection.

"Something amusing?" asked Domenica.

"I'm thinking of the topics that were discussed at Edinburgh dinner parties," he said, adding, "in the days when people still had them."

She waited.

"Firstly," he said, "those who were not there. They would *always* be discussed – sometimes with a distinct lack of charity."

Domenica grinned. "This city has always been a bit—"

"Brittle?" Angus offered. He remembered what the poet Ruthven Todd had said in one of his poems about his native Edinburgh. It was, he said, a city where "dry minds grew crusts of hate, like rocks grow lichen". Ouch. Did Todd really think that? And was it true? Perhaps, he decided – at least, in the days when the city was so stratified. But not now, even if Edinburgh was still a bit . . . how might one put it? Disapproving? Yes, that was it, and the times when disapproval might be shown were at these dinner parties when absent friends – or absent *rivals*, perhaps, were being discussed.

But there were other topics for the dinner table. House prices. Schools. Books that everybody was reading, or at least thinking of reading. He remembered an occasion when an author who had been read by nobody at the table had nevertheless been roundly dispatched by all present. It took a certain style to do that – and Edinburgh had it.

What had happened? Was Domenica right in saying that the Edinburgh dinner party was no more – or was it simply that he and Domenica were not being invited to such dinner parties as were taking place? That, he thought, was a distinct possibility. It was even quite likely that there were still plenty of dinner parties being held – but it was other people who were gathering round the tables. They could even be happening right there – in the flats on their common stair; right there at 44 Scotland Street, and they knew nothing about it.

He thought of the flats in question. There was Stuart downstairs – formerly Stuart of Stuart and Irene, but now Stuart and his mother, Nicola, and of course, Bertie and his little brother, Ulysses. Did Nicola act the hostess and invite friends to dinner while Ulysses wailed in the background? He was so unlike Bertie, that child. And he was so malodorous. It was wrong, Angus knew, to blame a child for that, but Ulysses really was so . . . Angus put the matter out of his head. He was wondering now whether he and Domenica had a sufficient number of friends. But what was the right number when it came to friends?

"Have you heard of the Dunbar number?" he said, rather suddenly.

"What?" Domenica asked. There were so many numbers to be remembered nowadays – was this Dunbar number yet another one?

# 2

## *The Categories of Friendship*

"Robin Dunbar," said Angus. "I'm reading his book. You've seen it. It's the one Matthew lent me. He got it from Big Lou. Dunbar's an evolutionary psychologist. It says that on the back cover. Do you know what that is?"

Domenica knew. She was an anthropologist; evolutionary anthropology was an important branch of her own discipline and took much the same approach. "Evolutionary psychology," she explained, "looks at how our behaviour and dispositions have been moulded by our survival instincts. If we do something, it's because it helped evolutionary survival."

She hoped she did not sound too pedantic. It was sometimes difficult to deal with complex ideas without sounding as if one was delivering a lecture, but it was hard to see how one could otherwise describe evolutionary psychology. It was like trying to illustrate the double helix without using one's hands.

But Angus understood. "That's why he spends so much time studying friendship. Is it all to do with survival?"

Domenica nodded. "Ultimately, everything's to do with survival if you're an evolutionary psychologist – friendship's no exception. I haven't read him on the subject, but I imagine your Professor Dunbar says that the reason we have friends is that if we don't, we perish."

"Yes," said Angus. "I think that's his approach. I'm only on chapter four, though."

"And his number?"

"The Dunbar number," Angus said, "is one hundred and fifty."

Domenica smiled. "We're always keen to find a number that explains everything," she said. "What's the number in *The Hitchhiker's Guide to the Galaxy* that explains everything? Forty-two, I seem to recall. That's the answer to the question, although nobody actually remembers what the question was."

Angus brought up the Golden Ratio. That was *his* number, he felt. Other people could have forty-two or one hundred and fifty: he would stick to 1.618, or *phi*. "I've always believed in *phi*," he said. "One of our tutors at art college swore by it. He told us that if we wanted to understand beauty, we had to be able to detect *phi* in whatever it was we were looking at. A beguiling face. A shell we've picked up on the beach. An example of Palladian architecture." He paused, and gestured towards the window. "That window. The ratio between its height and width is *phi*. That is, 1:1.618. Much of the Edinburgh New Town is the embodiment of that ratio. *Phi* is ubiquitous."

"All very interesting," said Domenica. She and Angus had discussed *phi* before; you could not be married to a person for long before discovering their views of *phi*. "But why one hundred and fifty?"

"That's the number of friends we can have," said Angus. "Not close friends, of course – we have far fewer of those – but friends we'd actually describe as friends rather than—"

"Acquaintances?" suggested Domenica.

"Yes."

Acquaintance was a rather *cold* term, thought Domenica. To call somebody a mere acquaintance implied that it was unlikely that they could be something closer – that they would remain something barely above stranger. It was preferable, though, to the term she had heard one of the students in the downstairs flat using: *randoms*. That suggested a profound separation – even an indifference. Some terms were destined, she thought, to remain the property of the young – and *random*, in that sense at least, was one of them. These were words that wore their baseball caps backwards. Not, she thought, with an inner grin, that I am in any way hostile to neologisms . . .

"How did Professor Dunbar arrive at a hundred and fifty?" she asked.

"Because it's always been there," Angus replied. "If you look at the size of human communities – in all sorts of societies – historically the basic unit was around a hundred and fifty. For a very long time, there were about a hundred and fifty people in villages. When the population became bigger, new settlements were created. And plenty of other human associations recognise this. Companies do. Armies, too. They organise themselves administratively in collections of about that number of people."

"But why?"

Angus smiled. "Try talking to more than a hundred and fifty people."

Domenica looked thoughtful. "Yes, I can see that. You won't know the people you're talking to if there are—"

Angus completed the sentence: "Too many of them. We only trust people we know – or people we feel we *could* get to know. One hundred and fifty, it seems, is a natural size for a human community."

"Big groups then—" Domenica began.

"Don't work," Angus interjected. "People are unhappy in big groups."

"Nations?"

Angus hesitated. Then he said, "They work best if they're

small: Singapore, Switzerland, Denmark. You do know, by the way, that the Danes are the happiest people in the world. Empires are inherently unstable. States that are made up of reasonably manageably sized units are less shaky." He closed his eyes for a moment. He wished the world at present was just a little less shaky . . . He continued, "But what really counts is being part of something much smaller. That's why people in large cities create villages within the metropolis. Then they tell others, rather proudly, that their city is made up of villages." Angus paused. "But I shouldn't be telling you this. You're the anthropologist, not me."

Domenica smiled. "I knew it, I suppose. But you're the one reading the book – obviously. I'd heard of Professor Dunbar, though. Doesn't he have other numbers?"

"Yes," replied Angus. "There's 1.5. We have 1.5 *intimates*. Then there's five. That's the number of *close friends* we can manage. After that, it's fifteen, which is the number of *best friends* we have – followed by fifty *good friends*."

Domenica was silent. She was thinking of best friends – and of the letters she had to write, if she was to keep her friendships in good repair, as we were advised to do. And, as it happens, so was Angus. He thought of his friends from art college – they were *good friends* on the Dunbar scale. They had been through so much together, and yet he only saw one of them now. And his friends from the Scottish Arts Club. He had let so many of them slip away, as one does, simply by forgetting, or by not doing what he and Domenica clearly should do, which was to invite them round for a meal. Break bread with those you loved – you had to do that, and yet we did not do it enough because . . . why? Because of the pace of the life we led now; with all the things we had to do; with all the information we had to absorb; with all the moments we lost when we might otherwise think of our friends, or sit with them and hear them say the things they always said and that we had heard them say so many times before.

# 3

## *Sister Maria of the Rhododendrons*

Angus and Domenica's discussion of friends might have gone on longer than it did, had Cyril not made it clear that it was time for his walk. He could put up with fairly long periods of inaction, as Angus and Domenica sat at their kitchen table, but there were limits to canine patience, and now they had been reached.

"I think he needs his walk," said Angus, as the first whines drifted up from under the table.

Domenica looked down. "Probably. I'd offer, but . . ."

"No, but thanks anyway. I could do with stretching my legs."

That was true, but there was another reason. Cyril had been with Angus before he and Domenica married, and although, with the natural stoicism of his species, he had accepted the change in his domestic circumstances, his principal loyalty was to the one who smelled of paint and turpentine – and that was Angus. Cyril identified the human world by smell. Big Lou, into whose coffee house Angus took him regularly, smelled of bacon rolls, and was highly popular with dogs for that reason. Matthew, whom Cyril met from time to time at Big Lou's, had a more complex smell, as he lived in the country and brought into town each morning olfactory layers of heather and sheep and silage, just as a wine will be redolent of its *terroir*. And then there was Bertie, who had that very particular small boy smell of pencil shavings and rubber bands and Scottish tablet.

Cyril, whose private catalogue of smells was as broad in its scope as any encyclopaedia, remembered each of these with complete precision and effortless discrimination. There would never be any mistaking the waft of Domenica – Earl Grey tea, Waterman inks, marmalade – or that of Sister Maria-Fiore dei Fiori di Montagna – votive candles, old editions of the *Corriere della Sera* and, occasionally, Edinburgh Gin.

Angus knew that although Cyril was prepared to go for a walk with Domenica, he would only do so out of politeness, in a half-hearted manner, and would, as if working strictly to rule, stop at every lamppost, until tugged away and obliged to continue. Now, of course, Cyril had seen Angus retrieving the lead and was waiting eagerly at the door, his pink tongue extended in enthusiasm, his single gold tooth, installed by a retired dentist in the Scottish Arts Club, glinting in the shaft of evening sunlight that came in from a window.

With the lead attached to Cyril's collar, Angus made his way down the common stair to stand in the doorway of 44 Scotland Street. On the other side of the cobbled road, a furtive black and white cat – an intruder from Cumberland Street, at the very limits of his territory – slunk away to safety. Cyril noticed, but did not dignify the cat with a response. One day scores would be settled with the cat world, and that would be a dreadful day of judgement, but not now. And the same went for squirrels, too, who were, in their way, even more of an irritant to dogs than cats. They would be shown no mercy either, but realistically a reckoning was unlikely, and would, for the time being, remain nothing but a canine daydream. But at least such a dream was something to live for.

Angus began to walk up Scotland Street. It was late May, a time of year when, at 56 degrees north, give or take a few minutes, the evening sun seemed reluctant to disappear altogether. It was 8.15 – he and Domenica would not sit down to dinner for at least another half-hour – and the sky above the city was cloudless and full of light. Warm sunshine still touched the hills of Fife with gold, visible from only a few blocks away, where Dundas Street dipped down towards Canonmills. It was a time of glowing stillness; a time of little traffic and not much human movement. From an open window somewhere, perhaps at the top of the street, there came, barely audible, the faint notes of a piece of music that always made him stop where he was, as if rooted to the spot. This could be heard now, and he stood quite still, as did Cyril, who sensed the moment too, although music was nothing to him. Music has no smell, as Auden pointed out in one of his poems, and so was of no account to Cyril.

It was the trio from *Così*, the song which the trusting women sing to their departing lovers: "*Soave sia il vento*" – may the breeze that carries you on your journey be a gentle one. Angus had always loved it, and remembered the precise moment that he first heard it, when the music teacher at school had played it to him on vinyl and he had found himself on the verge of tears, so struck was he by the sheer beauty of Mozart's music. And the teacher had said to him that he should never be ashamed to cry, and that if Mozart or Puccini or whoever moved one to tears, then that was a sign that one had a soul, and that was something to be grateful for, rather than to be embarrassed about.

He listened to it now, and glanced down at Cyril, who looked back up at him with complete and unwavering love. For Cyril had a soul, too; of course, dogs had souls, as any dog owner knew – you had only to look into a dog's eyes and you would see it. Love was the mark of that soul's existence, and could be recognised, Angus felt, not only in dogs but in other creatures. A mouse, he thought, which could show love for its murine family, had a soul, even if only a very small one.

Burns saw that when he disturbed that field mouse, and was moved to one of the greatest of all nature poems.

The music faded; the window out of which it had been drifting was closed. Angus continued with his walk, and was soon in Drummond Place Gardens, where he let Cyril off the lead, slightly against the regulations, but keeping him walking to heel, in a nod towards the garden committee. Cyril's instinct was to rush off, but he knew that this would bring displeasure, and so he complied.

They walked round the path widdershins rather than deasil, which they would do tomorrow. Nobody else appeared to be using the gardens, and the leaves in the trees were quite still. Cyril kept his nose up, sniffing at the information-laden air. Squirrel, but not recent; the scattered crumbs from a ham sandwich that somebody had eaten while sitting on one of the benches, but now carried off by a gull; the sharp smell of grass that had been mown that morning and was still strong in the air; and something else . . . Edinburgh Gin, still here, and not far off. Cyril stiffened and sniffed again. No, there was no mistaking it. He looked up at Angus, as if to warn him, but Angus had already seen the movement in the rhododendron bushes and was preparing to greet Sister Maria-Fiore dei Fiori di Montagna, who emerged from the bushes brushing soil off her hands.

She did not seem surprised to see Angus and Cyril. "Well," she said, "what an evening! For a moment or two, earlier on, I thought I was back in Tuscany."

Angus smiled. Dear Sister Maria-Fiore dei Fiori di Montagna. He would not ask her what she was doing in the rhododendron bushes. She was capable of any eccentricity, he thought, and in the scale of possible eccentricities, this was not a major one.

# 4.

*Bowdlerising Babar*

While Angus and Domenica were discussing friendship and evolutionary psychology, out at Nine Mile Burn it was Matthew's turn to prepare the triplets for bed. Elspeth was a believer in the immutability of the boys' bedtime – Matthew, by contrast, was prepared to take a more flexible view: the difference between 6.30 and 7 p.m. was, in his mind, a matter of little significance. For Tobermory, Rognvald and Fergus, though, half an hour was a semi-eternity to which, by careful manipulation, a further ten minutes could sometimes be added. And if that happened, it was only deep into injury time – 7.30, perhaps – that the bedroom light would eventually be extinguished and the day brought to a close.

"You shouldn't let them get away with it," said Elspeth. "They'll play us off against one another. Children do."

Matthew shrugged. "You don't want to be too strict."

Elspeth was having none of this. "Children need structure," she said. "They need predictability."

Matthew sighed. "You wouldn't want me to be Captain von Trapp. Remember him? He blew a whistle and expected the children to snap to it and line up. You don't want that."

Elspeth defended herself. "Of course not. But they still need structure. We all do. If we don't have rules as children, we grow up as lawless adults. That does nobody any favours. Civilisation collapses."

Matthew laughed. "Surely bedtime—"

She interrupted him. "No, Matthew, look at where we are. Just look."

He was puzzled. "I'm not sure what you mean."

"I mean, look at the lawlessness. The cyclists who ride through red lights all the time – and I mean, all the time. Go to town and you'll see them."

Matthew looked doubtful. Elspeth seemed to be suggesting that civilisation was collapsing about their ears. People were always suggesting that – it was part of, well, of civilisation that there should be those who said it was all coming to an end – that society was collapsing. He was not at all sure that his allowing the triplets an extra half-hour playtime in the evening would hasten that process of collapse. And yet, and yet . . . civilisations *did* collapse, and it may be the causes of their collapse were to be found in the small things – the growth of dishonesty at the personal level, the loss of respect for legitimate authority, the weakening of belief in anything.

He thought about something he had seen that morning, when he had driven into town to go to work in his gallery. He had been driving through Tollcross and had stopped at the traffic lights outside the King's Theatre. A young man had been riding his bike behind him, and as Matthew stopped the cyclist had sailed past him. With only the most cursory glance down the road to the left, he had ignored the red light and shot across the intersection. A motorist coming from the left had braked hard, only narrowly avoiding an accident. The cyclist, although he had seen the avoiding action taken by the motorist, was completely indifferent to it. He did not slow down; he made no apology; if anything, he increased his speed.

Matthew had felt a surge of resentment. It was a small thing, a little incident of a sort that would be repeated countless times that day, but he found himself fuming at the fact that the cyclist showed so little concern for other road-users. Did he think himself entitled to behave like this? Did he consider himself above the law?

Matthew's anger at witnessing this example of anti-social behaviour gave way to a feeling of depression. If there were people like this, how could anybody feel sure about anything? We all depended on one another to obey the rules, or life together would become impossible – but that simple fact seemed to be beyond the comprehension of so many.

He found himself fantasising what he would do in response. He imagined himself running down the lawbreaker with his car – knocking him off his bicycle and saying: *There, that's what happens.* He imagined himself grabbing him and shaking him while at the same time delivering a message about how nobody can be above the law. He imagined throwing the offender's bicycle into a metal-crushing machine and proclaiming, "There!"

He did nothing, of course. But now that he thought about it again, it struck him that perhaps that small incident was rather important after all, and that from it there could be extrapolated something far bigger. Perhaps this is what it felt like – to be at the end of something, to be in the final days of the Roman Empire, when the old gods died and you didn't even have them left to believe in. Which was where we were, he thought. God had gone, some said, and we were left with just ourselves, and a few of us – no, rather a lot of us – didn't care very much about what happened to others.

But now he had to attend to the boys, who were insistently asking for a story. They wanted Babar, who had gone from Africa to Europe and was being fitted for a green suit and felt hat – the pernicious accoutrements of Western civilisation, the critics claimed: signifiers of the French values that were being imposed on the Land of the Elephants. Tobermory, Rognvald and Fergus were not much bothered about that, but they were watchful of any attempt by Matthew to censor the tragic parts. Babar's mother is shot: that was the harsh truth as described by Laurent de Brunhoff, and any attempt to skip the page on which that occurs had been met with reproach from the boys. "Don't miss anything out," warned Rognvald. "We want to hear everything."

Reluctantly, Matthew had agreed, and had read out the offending section, his voice lowered in sympathy. Somewhere in Africa this was actually happening: real baby elephants were being abandoned by the corpses of the mothers from whom poachers had gouged the tusks. The world's pain was utterly real.

"You should speak louder," said Tobermory. "We can't hear you, Daddy, if you mumble the bits that hurt."

# 5

## *Japanese Knives*

Every evening, after the boys were put to bed, there was a period of half an hour or so when Matthew and Elspeth would sit in the kitchen and talk about the day's events. It would come to an end when something needed to be done about dinner, but before that, there was that blissful feeling of not having to do anything very much other than talk. That evening, though, was different, as they had invited their new neighbours in for a meal, and although Elspeth had prepared vegetarian haggis tartlets for the entrée, Matthew was in charge of the main course, which was mushroom risotto.

Elspeth sat at the kitchen table, a glass of white wine before her, as Matthew chopped the mushrooms for his sauce. He was good at knife skills, she thought, as he had spent a day at a cookery school in Queen Street learning how to chop things. Not that chopping mushrooms involved much skill: mushrooms never *resisted*.

For making the effort to go to the cookery school, she had rewarded him with a set of Japanese chef's knives. These had come in a personalised case on which the words *Matthew's Knives* had been embossed.

He had appreciated the present, although she had been surprised to see his face fall slightly as he unwrapped it.

"Something wrong?" she had asked. "I thought that after your course you'd like to have a proper set of knives—"

"Yes," he said quickly. "I mean, no, nothing's wrong. Yes,

of course I'd like a set of proper knives. Who wouldn't?"

"You looked a bit . . . a bit taken aback."

He hesitated. "I was thinking of a silly thing."

"What silly thing?"

"My granny," he said. "She told me something." He paused. "But she was really superstitious. It's nothing."

She asked him to tell her. "You can't just say it's nothing. You looked . . . well, you looked *doubtful*."

"My gran said that you should never give a friend a knife – it cuts the bonds of friendship."

Elspeth stared at him. "Really?"

"Of course, I don't believe that. There are all sorts of ridiculous superstitions about knives."

"Such as?"

He remembered one. "When I was a boy – when I was seven or eight, we used to think that if you cut the bit of skin between your thumb and your forefinger, you got lockjaw. I really believed that."

Elspeth smiled. "You waited to feel your jaw getting stiff?"

"Yes. And if you got lockjaw, you died. Everybody knew that."

Elspeth remembered another childish belief. "There was a girl in my class called Mary McTaggart. Her parents made her wear white socks with everything, even to the school dance. We teased her – and I feel really bad about it."

"That's what children do," said Matthew. "We can't carry that burden for the rest of our lives."

"No, maybe not. But she believed that if you put blotting paper in your shoes you would faint. We laughed at her and challenged her to show us. She eventually did."

"And?"

"She fainted."

Matthew smiled. "Psychosomatic. She told herself she

was going to faint, and she did."

Elspeth took a sip of her wine. "I still feel bad about Mary McTaggart."

Matthew frowned. "You shouldn't."

"It was bullying. We wouldn't have called it that, but that's what it was."

Matthew sighed. "Listen, how old were you?"

"Fourteen, fifteen. Old enough to know better."

Matthew disagreed. "That's far too young," he said. "Nobody's responsible at that age. I wasn't. I was a complete pain until . . ." He paused. "Until about twenty, I think. I was opinionated. I thought I knew everything, whereas I really knew nothing – or next to nothing."

Elspeth said, "I would still have liked you."

"That's kind, but you wouldn't."

She looked at him fondly. She loved Matthew, and she knew that he loved her. Their marriage was fine, she thought, but she found this discussion of change unsettling. Here was Matthew saying that his younger self was very different from his current self – from what he was today. But if we could change like that, then there was nothing to stop the future self from being, in its turn, quite different again. That suggested, she thought, that we were not one self, but were, rather, a series of selves, existing over time. And if that was so, then was it not possible that she might find herself at some future point married to a stranger?

"Thinking?" asked Matthew.

She nodded.

"About?"

She hesitated. But then she said, "I was thinking about how people may grow apart."

He frowned. "Who in particular?"

She did not want to say that she had been thinking about

themselves, because that would imply that she thought this was happening, and it was not. So she quickly thought of an instance. "I was at school with somebody . . ."

"Not Mary McTaggart?"

"No, not her. A girl called Debbie Russell. I don't think I've ever told you about her. She was very attractive. The boys all loved her. She came to Edinburgh to do a course at Queen Margaret in occupational therapy. She didn't finish it. She married a rugby player. They were both twenty. He came from a farm down near Selkirk. You know how they love rugby down there."

Matthew nodded. He had been at the rugby sevens in Melrose. He'd felt as if he had been a pilgrim visiting a holy place.

"I couldn't believe it when I heard they were married. She was my age, for heaven's sake. What was she doing getting *married*?"

"Physical attraction?"

She said, "That came into it, I suppose. But that doesn't always last, does it? He had a knee injury and had to stop playing rugby. He put on a lot of weight. He started to look a bit like a rugby ball."

"Oh . . ."

"Yes, and she drifted away – inside, that is. She didn't want to be married to a rugby ball. She grew up. He carried on thinking about rugby and beer and the things that he thought about when he was twenty. She started to read – something she had never done before. She learned French. She became bored."

"The moral?" asked Matthew.

"No moral. Just an observation. Well, maybe there is a moral. Don't marry too early. Wait until you've done your growing up."

Matthew looked thoughtful. "But biology dictates otherwise, doesn't it? Aren't we more suited to having young children when we're in our early twenties? We have more energy. We can cope with it. Later on . . ." He paused, and looked intently at Elspeth. "Do you really think we're different people at different stages of our lives?"

She did not answer immediately. But then she said, "Yes, I do."

"Are you a different person from who you were when we met?"

"Yes, I think I am." She smiled. "Hadn't you noticed?"

# 6

## *The New Neighbours*

Matthew had already met the new neighbours, Robert and Maureen, even if briefly, on the day after they had moved in. He had mail for them that had been mistakenly put through his door, and delivering this had given him the opportunity to welcome them to the neighbourhood.

"You'll like it here," he said, handing over the letters. "It's a friendly neighbourhood. Let me know if there's anything you need to know about the area."

Introductions were made. "We lived in Biggar for a few years," said Robert. "Near the Gasworks Museum. You probably know it."

"It's the only working gasworks in the country," said Maureen.

"They made gas from coal," explained Robert. "They still make gas – just to show how it was done in the past."

Matthew nodded.

Maureen spoke with a pronounced Glasgow accent. "Before that, it was Glasgow," she said. "We were six years there. Bearsden."

Matthew nodded politely. "Nice," he said. It was a reply to anything, he thought, and he often said it when he could think of nothing else to say. In particular, when people said something about themselves, *nice* always worked as a response.

"Then I got a job in Edinburgh," Robert continued.

"The people in Edinburgh approached him," said Maureen, giving Matthew a knowing look.

Matthew waited.

"I'm in investment," Robert said at last.

"Investment," echoed Maureen, as if to explain.

"Investment?" said Matthew.

Robert fixed Matthew with a defensive look. "Footprint-free investment. We invest only in companies that have a negative footprint."

"Which means no footprint at all," explained Maureen. "That's what Robert does. He's the leading footprint-free expert in Scotland."

Robert gave her a modest smile. "Come now, Maureen. There are others."

"None with your reputation," said Maureen.

"Oh, I don't know." Then he added, "I do my best, I suppose."

Matthew was not sure what footprint-free investment was. He asked Robert to explain.

"Not many people know much about it," Robert began. "The idea is to restrict investment to companies that have no footprint at all – that make the minimum impact on our world."

Matthew said that this sounded like a good idea. "So, no oil. Nor tobacco . . ."

"Definitely not," said Robert. "But no building companies either. Buildings *impose* on the world. All construction companies are out."

Matthew frowned. "Railways? Bus companies?"

Robert shuddered.

"Manufacturing?" asked Matthew.

"Manufacturing involves the use of non-renewable resources," replied Robert. "Manufacturing is bad – no question about it."

"But surely we have to have at least *some* things."

Robert shook his head. "We've already got more than enough stuff," he said. "The world is groaning under the weight of all the things we've made. We need to repair and repurpose the things we already have."

Suddenly Maureen turned to Matthew. "How many shirts have you got?" she asked. "I mean, how many actual shirts do you have – ones that you wear?"

Matthew glanced at her in astonishment. Her tone was accusing, and he felt that if he declined to answer, the situation might rapidly deteriorate. "I'm not sure," he said mildly. "Not all that many, I think."

Maureen was not going to give up. "A rough estimate, then."

"Twelve," said Matthew. He would try to make light of his answer – in the hope that it might draw heat out of the exchange. "Some of them need buttons and I don't use them very much."

He realised almost immediately that this was the wrong thing to say.

"Buttons are easy," said Maureen. "Anybody can sew on a button. Even a man."

Matthew looked sheepish. "I know. I must get round to it. No excuse."

"No," she said. "Robert has three shirts. Two of them have had their collars turned." She saw Matthew's blank expression. "That means, they're turned round. You can prolong the life of frayed collars that way."

"Oh," said Matthew.

"You need water to make cotton shirts," said Maureen. "That's why it's wasteful to have more than you need."

I may need more than three shirts, thought Matthew. How

would *you* know how many shirts I need?

Matthew was silent. He was not sure what to do. Instinctively, he wanted to bring this conversation to an end. He wanted to walk away. There was not going to be any prospect of friendship with these new neighbours. How could he sit down with somebody who had become so immediately confrontational? At the same time, they were neighbours, and in the countryside it was difficult to be stand-offish.

He hesitated, but then he reached a decision. He should not rush to judgement – he had barely met these people, and they were, after all, their neighbours – and they were right, anyway: we had to conserve the world's resources. He would issue the invitation that he and Elspeth had discussed in advance.

"We wondered if you would like to come over for dinner," he said. "Informal. Kitchen supper."

Maureen accepted without hesitation. "We'd love that."

Elspeth had given Matthew a date to propose. It suited Robert and Maureen. Now Matthew asked, "Is there anything you don't eat?"

"We're vegan," said Maureen.

"Fine," said Matthew. "Both of you?"

Robert nodded. "Both. Are you all right with that?"

"Of course," said Matthew quickly. It should not have been unexpected. After all, it was footprint-free investment in which Robert was involved – not unethical investment. People in unethical investment presumably ate everything, with a preference, perhaps, for endangered species.

"We can bring something, if you like," said Maureen. "Sometimes, if people aren't familiar with the vegan diet, they get a bit confused."

"We had to turn down a cheese soufflé the other day," added Robert. "You'd think people would know."

There was a scratching at the door.

"That's Ralph," said Robert. "Could you let him in, Maureen?"

Maureen got up to open the door. Into the room came a large brown dog wearing a bright green collar. He cast a baleful glance at his owners and then at Matthew, who saw that he was extremely thin.

"This is Ralph," said Robert. "He's quite a character."

Ralph pointed his snout in Matthew's direction and sniffed at the air. Then he sat down and stared at the ceiling.

"You see," said Maureen. "Ralph is always thinking."

Matthew said that Elspeth was expecting him back at the house and he would have to leave. He looked forward to seeing them for dinner the following week. Robert accompanied him to the door and then to the drive outside, where Matthew had parked his car. He had called in on his way home from work.

"The garden's going to need some work," said Robert. "I don't think the last people did much with it. I've made a start."

Matthew looked around. Already there were signs of gardening activity.

"I'm planting an organic lawn," Robert went on.

Matthew said nothing.

"Are you organic?" asked Robert.

Matthew was unsure. "Our garden's nothing special," he said. "Elspeth grows some vegetables. She likes carrots. And we grow a lot of potatoes."

"Do you put anything into the soil? Fertilisers?"

Matthew shrugged. "Maybe."

"Then you're not organic," said Robert.

"Perhaps not."

They reached Matthew's car.

"Diesel?" asked Robert, looking at it critically.

Matthew nodded.

"I see," said Robert.

There was disapproval in his voice. Matthew looked away.

# 7

## A Task Ahead

It was not much more than a hundred and fifty miles away, but it was nonetheless in a very different world that, as Matthew and Elspeth entertained their new neighbours to dinner at Nine Mile Burn, Irene Pollock sat down for her supper of fish and mashed potatoes. It was an unexpected set of circumstances that had brought Irene to the fisherman's table in the Aberdeenshire coastal town of Peterhead: had she not plunged into the North Sea in her pursuit of the benefits accruing from cold water therapy; had she not then been caught in a strong rip tide which had swept her away from the beach; had she not been rescued by a passing fishing trawler, then she would still have been in Aberdeen, pursuing her PhD studies under Professor Hugo Fairbairn, formerly her son Bertie's therapist in Edinburgh, but now the holder of a chair in psychology at the University of Aberdeen.

But all of those things had happened, and here was Irene, sitting at a well-scrubbed pine table, gazing at the skipper who had pulled her out of the water just as exhaustion and cold were beginning to get the better of her. It is easy, perhaps too easy, to fall for those who snatch one from the jaws of death, and that was exactly what Irene had done. Those who go out to sea in fishing boats are often possessed of a certain rough charm, and that was the exact quality that appealed to Irene, whose fall was sudden and complete. The library and the seminar room were one thing, but this was raw life;

this was authenticity; this was an uncomplicated life of fish-filleting – for which Irene had shown an unexpected talent – and of so many things that seemed to be absent from the life she had led in Edinburgh. Edinburgh was all very well, but was it *authentic* in the way in which the towns and villages of the Scottish hinterland were authentic?

The calm atmosphere of the home into which Irene had been welcomed by those who had saved her from drowning had prompted her to reconsider the life she had been leading since she had left Edinburgh. She knew that there were those who were surprised by the move to Aberdeen, who openly suggested that she had only gone there because she and Hugo Fairbairn were lovers. There were even those who went so far as to criticise her for the choice she had made. That was an unusual experience for Irene, who was accustomed to being the source of criticism rather than its target. In her view, she had been presented with no real alternative. For years she had tried to make something of Stuart – but had eventually decided that he simply lacked the spark that she needed. It was not Stuart's fault that he was middle class, she told herself: you do not decide upon the bed you are born in. Yet, whatever the source of his attitudes, the fact remained that he was typical, she felt, of the self-satisfied Scottish bourgeoisie – content to live what it thought of as a well-ordered life, free of the challenge and excitement of commitment to change. Scotland was full of such people; people who did the same things day after day, who embodied a couthy social conservatism, and who even belonged to golf clubs. That, thought Irene, was the reality of Scotland – and so many other countries besides – and she was not prepared to accept it. She wanted to live with the wind of freedom in her hair. She had given up on stuffy Edinburgh and would find, in this life of fish-filleting and shopping in the local Co-op, something that her previous existence had lacked. This was her D. H. Lawrentian moment; this was her Jean-Paul Sartrean experience: in the arms of this virile fisherman, she would cultivate delight in the things that really mattered in this life. She would, quite simply, *become*.

Of course, she would not forget that she had family obligations. When she had moved to Aberdeen, she had only agreed to let Bertie and Ulysses remain in Edinburgh because of the need that children had for continuity in their education. Bertie was happily enrolled at the Steiner School, and Ulysses was now settled at Neo-Georgian Kids, a New Town nursery school. Stuart's mother, Nicola, for whom Irene had little time, was helping with the children – in her middle-class way – even if she was, in Irene's view, a thoroughly reactionary influence. Irene disapproved of much of what Nicola did, including her letting Bertie watch films such as *The Sound of Music* and *Mary Poppins*, in her view both insidious artefacts of patriarchy. *A spoonful of sugar* indeed! The whole cultural meal was drenched in saccharine – not that Nicola, with her limited perspective on life, could ever hope to understand that. There would be time to undo all that in the future, even if at the moment Nicola was needed to cook and do the children's laundry.

It is rare for any of us to see our life's path clearly mapped out before us, but that is what Irene now saw as she contemplated her future. She would live her new life in the north-east of Scotland while at the same time she would allocate two or three days a week to Edinburgh and to the boys. She had a mission there on that stark northern coast: although she admired the life led by the extended fishing family into which she was being so warmly received, and although she relished the authenticity that was demonstrated in their everyday activities, there were some aspects of life in the fishing town that needed attention.

The extent of the task ahead of her had been revealed when she had first ventured into the local newsagent's shop. It had been a fine morning, with a bracing breeze coming off the North Sea, bearing with it the smell of fish, nets and diesel oil. Irene had made her way to the small rack of publications on offer, and had been struck by both what was there and what was missing. She quickly passed over the *People's Friend* and the *Scots Magazine,* coming to the newspapers. There was the *Press and Journal* and the *Courier,* alongside that day's *Scotsman* and *Herald.* She glanced at the *P&J* headline: *Turriff man buys new tractor,* it proclaimed. Irene shook her head. Where was the *Guardian,* she wondered, and stepped forward to ask this of the man behind the counter.

He looked at her, and adjusted the glasses at the end of his nose. "Eh?" he asked. "Where's the *what?*"

Irene closed her eyes. There was so much work to be done.

# 8

## *Pies for Protestants*

Bertie, of course, was as unaware as any seven-year-old boy would be, of the extent to which he was the centre of more than one universe. For his father, Stuart Pollock, a statistician formerly employed by the Scottish Government but now working for an independent consultancy called Facts and Figures, Bertie provided the main reason to get out of bed in the morning. Stuart was a good parent in that he showed no favouritism between his two sons, but Bertie had been part of his life for longer than had his younger brother, Ulysses, and had borne the brunt of Irene's ambitions for longer. It was not surprising, then, that Stuart felt a particular sympathy for him. Ulysses seemed more robust in his dealings with his mother, and had managed to deal with her excessive management by being copiously sick during the music lessons begun shortly before his second birthday. It had been apparent to Stuart that this must reveal an antipathy on the infant's part to hot-housing strategies, but Irene herself had never seen it that way. She had taken Ulysses to a paediatric gastroenterologist, who had examined him and pronounced his infantile stomach to be perfectly normal. The doctor, in fact, having been assailed by a barrage of suggestions from Irene, based on her reading of the online medical literature, had correctly identified the problem as psychosomatic, but had only been able to suggest that Ulysses perhaps be given a "bit more space". This had not gone down well.

Stuart was determined to do his best by Bertie and Ulysses, and accepted that this meant that they should see their mother regularly. He stuck to this policy, even when Bertie had suggested, with his characteristic politeness, that he would not mind too much if Irene came to the flat in Scotland Street less frequently.

"I don't want Mummy to feel that she *has* to come to see us, Daddy," he had said. "She must have lots to do up in Aberdeenshire – even just keeping warm. We can talk to her online, you know. It's just as if she was in the room with us, and we can always . . ."

He did not finish the sentence. He had been on the point of saying "and we can always turn her off if we need to". He was too loyal, and too good, to say that, as was Stuart, who, coincidentally, had been thinking exactly the same thing.

The resulting arrangement had worked well for everybody. Irene came down to Edinburgh once a week, and during these visits she practised Italian *conversazione* with Bertie, started Ulysses on his Greek alphabet, and read to the boys from the *Ladybird Book of Carl Gustav Jung*. While Irene was in Edinburgh, Nicola kept well out of the way. Although she and Irene were civil to one another, theirs was a relationship edged with ice. Irene disapproved of Nicola, who returned the sentiment with interest.

"There's nothing wrong with Irene," Nicola said to Stuart, "except that she's crazy and you should never have married her. Other than that, she's just fine."

"Oh, Mother," said Stuart.

"However," Nicola continued, "Irene, as they say, is now history. You have risen above her. You are free."

Stuart shook his head. "Not entirely," he said. "We may have separated, but she still comes here each week for the boys. And they need a mother, you know."

"Stuart," said Nicola, her voice becoming firm, "the boys have me. I am their granny. I can give them everything they need in terms of female affection."

Stuart inclined his head. "You've been wonderful, Mother. I'd never underestimate how important you are in their lives, but—"

"No buts, Stuart," said Nicola. "They have everything they need. I'm here for them every day. We have a wonderful routine."

Stuart had to admit that his mother was right. The boys were unquestionably happier under the regime she had established for them. He himself was more content, too – and Nicola was in no doubt of that. His previous demeanour, best described by the Scots expression *hauden doon*, had been replaced by an air of contentment – the sort of expression one sees on the faces of those who have successfully navigated their way past submerged rocks and are now in the clear water beyond.

There was nothing in Nicola's current life that did not suit her. Her marriage to Abril Tamares de Lumares, the Portuguese wine producer, was now well in the past, and was not much regretted. Her former husband had given her a generous settlement on their divorce, and her financial position had been further improved by the inheritance she had received from a childless aunt – a pie factory in Glasgow. When she inherited it, this business had been called Pies for Protestants, but this nomenclature had been deemed to be somewhat old-fashioned, and it had been renamed Inclusive Pies. The company that had overseen the renaming, a Glasgow PR agency, had gone further, and had come up with a mission statement that was now printed on the wrappers of all the factory's products. "We sincerely hope," it said, "that our pies will be enjoyed by all, irrespective of who they happen to be. Every pie we make is made with that objective. Every pie we make is made with *you* in mind."

On assuming ownership of the factory, Nicola had quickly restructured the company to allow staff participation in the management and in a share of the profits. In so far as she now exercised any control of Inclusive Pies, this was done with the lightest of touches, and it was rare for her to intervene in any of the day-to-day decisions affecting the company. Usually, she supported the decisions of the managers on the spot, although a recent initiative had caused her to question a novel line that the Glasgow managers planned to introduce. This was a new pie, an accompaniment to the factory's celebrated Scotch pies, that would consist of a filling composed entirely of fat. This would be given the name The Wee Glasgow Pie, a marketing strategy that they had been assured would be highly successful. Nicola had understood the commercial argument, but had felt compelled to argue for a health warning to be printed on the wrapping of The Wee Glasgow Pie. Her suggestion had been accepted, with the result that on each wrapper there appeared, in very small type, the message, *Dinnae eat this pie.*

The warning went unheeded – which was exactly what the factory manager had anticipated.

"Folk don't like to be told what to do or not to do," he said. "Some Scottish politicians seem not to have worked that out yet, but I ken it fine."

# 9

## *The Specialness of Friendship*

There was another universe in which Bertie played an important part – that of his friend, Ranald Braveheart Macpherson. Ranald and Bertie had come into one another's lives at a time when, for different reasons, they were both in great need of a friend. At school, Bertie was not unpopular – anything but. In the classroom, if anybody was required to pick a partner for any particular activity, it was almost always Bertie to whom people turned. Unsurprisingly, there was considerable competition among the girls to claim Bertie as their special friend. For some time, the leader amongst such claimants was Olive, a girl in Bertie's class, who had, at an early point, identified Bertie as the boy whom she would in due course marry. "I know that my twentieth birthday is a long way off," Olive announced. "But that doesn't mean that one can't plan ahead. And I can tell you now, if you're interested, that Bertie and I are engaged to be married when we are both twenty – in thirteen years' time. That's official."

Bertie had remonstrated with Olive, pointing out that he had never agreed to an engagement. He was polite, as he always was, and said that if he ever were to consider being engaged to anybody, then he would certainly think of her.

This cut no ice with Olive. "That's not the point, Bertie Pollock. It's very kind of you to say that you would think of me, but it's far too late for that now. You already have thought of me. You made a promise, and everybody knows that you have to keep your promises."

Olive turned to her trusted lieutenant, Pansy, for confirmation. Bertie had noticed that wherever Olive was, Pansy could be expected to be close at hand. He had read about aides-de-camp, and that, he thought, was exactly what Pansy was to Olive.

Pansy was quick to agree. "You have to keep your promises," she said. "Olive's right. If you don't keep your promises, your tongue swells up. Everybody knows that."

Bertie was doubtful. "Who told you that, Pansy?" he said.

Pansy ignored this. That was her usual reaction to anything Bertie said to her.

"Pansy knows a lot of things you don't know, Bertie," interjected Olive. "Getting a swollen tongue is just the first thing that happens to people who don't keep their promises. You can be sued for breach of promise, Bertie. Had you thought of that? No, I don't think you have."

Bertie had not pressed the matter. There was no point in arguing with Olive, and so he remained silent whenever she referred to him as her fiancé. He hoped that sooner or later she would forget all about it, although he was concerned that there seemed to be little sign of that just yet. What was apparent, though, was Olive's determination to pick Bertie's friends for him.

"I don't want you to think I'm interfering in your life, Bertie," she said. "But I'd be failing in my duty as your fiancée if I let you play with unsuitable people. You do understand that, I hope. I have your best interests at heart – you know that, don't you?"

There were some members of the class whom Olive did not rule out as friends for Bertie, even if she otherwise had little time for them. Tofu, although despised by Olive, was approved of as a friend for Bertie, principally because Olive believed that Tofu was so self-centred that he would never have much time for Bertie, or anybody else for that matter. This was largely true, as Tofu's main aim in his dealings with others was to extract as much as possible from them. He was known for his greedy behaviour when it came to cakes and confectionary, and if any marbles, football cards or stickers went missing, they were more or less certain to be found in Tofu's school bag.

Then there was Larch, who was widely regarded as dangerous. Larch and Tofu were allies, and from time to time ran a numbers racket in which members of the class were cajoled into buying tickets for an undisclosed lucky number. The numbers sold to others never seemed to win, and Larch and Tofu pocketed the proceeds. If challenged, Larch would hint darkly that things could easily go wrong for anybody who complained. "I'm not saying how they could go wrong," he'd mutter. "All I'm saying is that things could go badly wrong."

The other boys were not much better. Socrates Dunbar had not been at the school for long, but had acquired a reputation for impulsivity and deeds of daring. It was Socrates who famously had put ice cream in Olive's hair at Ranald Braveheart Macpherson's birthday party, and hidden a live mouse in Pansy's schoolbag. He was on a triple-underlined warning from the school authorities and was believed to be trying to reform, but was finding it difficult.

"If you want to play with Tofu and Larch," Olive said, "that's quite all right with me. I wouldn't play with them personally, but then I'm a girl, you see, and I know better. But if you want to play with them, Bertie, please feel free to do so." She paused. "I don't think you should have anything to do with Socrates Dunbar, though."

With Olive and Pansy watching his every move, Bertie

found it hard to develop friendships. For this reason, when he first met Ranald Braveheart Macpherson, it was as if the clouds had suddenly parted and a promised land of companionship had revealed itself to him.

At first, Olive failed to notice that Bertie and Ranald seemed to be spending time together, but when Pansy reported to her that Bertie appeared to have a new friend, she immediately took charge of the situation.

"I see that you've been talking to that new boy, Bertie," she said. "I believe he has a ridiculous name, like Rob Roy MacGregor, or something like that."

Bertie's response was cautious. "He's called Ranald Braveheart Macpherson, Olive."

Olive laughed, and Pansy immediately joined in and laughed too. "Ranald Braveheart Macpherson?" Olive said. "Have you ever heard of such a stupid name, Pansy?"

Pansy shook her head. "Never," she replied. "If I was called Ranald Braveheart Macpherson, I'd lock myself away and cry. I could never face the world with a name like that."

"You wonder what his parents were thinking," said Olive. "We have to remember that grown-ups do stupid things. Anyway, I have to warn you, Bertie: I think that making friends with Ranald isn't a very good idea."

Bertie decided to stand up for himself. "Why not, Olive? What's it got to do with you, anyway?"

Olive was patient. "It has everything to do with me, Bertie. People judge you by your friends – everybody knows that. If you're friends with Ranald, who's really sad, then people will think that *you're* sad. And how will that reflect on me, Bertie? Have you even thought of that? No, you haven't, have you?"

# 10

## *Ranald and His Father*

For Ranald Braveheart Macpherson, meeting Bertie was the fulfilment of a long-felt wish – a wish that we all have for a particular friend; for one who sees things in much the same way as we do; for one who helps us feel that we are not alone in this world. These things apply to the friendships we make throughout our lives, but they have particular force when we are young and when our sense of self is still inchoate. Who does not remember the sheer exhilaration of meeting a new friend when one is young? Suddenly the world is transformed by the prospect of sharing our experience of it.

Ranald was an only child. His father, George Balerno Macpherson, was an only child, too, as was his wife, whom he called, from the day of their marriage, Mrs Macpherson. This was not an affectation, nor an instance of Victorian formality that had somehow survived into the twenty-first century. It was, rather, a combination of a fond nickname and a sign of wonder at the sheer fact of marriage – that a human institution, so common and practical in many of its implications, could have, at its heart, the mystery of union, the pretence that two could become one. She, in turn, occasionally addressed him as Mr Macpherson, or referred to him as such when talking to others, and did so out of equal fondness.

They had married relatively late in life, he being forty and she thirty-six. By that time, Mr Macpherson had recently become a director of a small financial firm that specialised in the backing of start-up companies. This was a high-risk area of finance – it was much safer to be involved in dull, unadventurous commercial concerns – but in his case the firm, Forward Projects, had backed several companies that had gone on to exceed their founders' wildest dreams. One of these was a device that stopped rugs from moving and becoming crumpled when they were placed on top of existing carpeting. This problem of travelling rugs was one that had long defeated human ingenuity. There were rolls of two-sided sticky tape one could buy, the idea being that strips of this adhesive tape applied underneath the rug would prevent it from moving. That was the idea, but it did not work. Rugs still travelled, in spite of the adhesive tape. Then there were small pieces of plastic fitted with tiny teeth, like the flattened jaws of infant piranhas. These worked slightly better, but did not completely solve the problem. Then along came a young man from Dundee, a graduate in industrial design who, for his fourth-year honours project at Napier University, had designed a product that stopped sliding Persian rugs in their tracks. This worked, and had been given the protection that intellectual property affords to keep it from the encircling sharks. That protection had been funded by George and his colleagues, and they were now enjoying the benefits of its worldwide success. A much greater slice of bourgeois humanity than anyone could have imagined, it seemed, had been exercised by this problem, and were prepared to pay for relief from it.

There had been other entrepreneurs who had been successfully assisted, including a company that made software apps that it seemed everyone wanted to possess, including a game called Mindless that attracted a widespread international following. Once again, the early involvement of George's company ensured a steady stream of income from the game.

This enabled them to back other projects that were worth supporting, but that fell at one of the hurdles that prevented so many good ideas from getting anywhere. A robotic sheep dog, operating on all-terrain wheels and painted in the livery of a real Border collie, proved to be an idea for which the world was not yet ready – in spite of its ability to move into position almost as quickly and efficiently as a real sheepdog. Nobody was able to work out why this idea should not work, until it was discovered that sheep could tell the difference. Sheep may not know a great deal – in fact, sheep know next to nothing – but one thing they are able to do is to distinguish between a small device issuing a recorded bark, and the real thing.

Mr Macpherson may have described himself as an innovative financier, but the description to which he most ardently aspired was that of patriot. From an early age he had been fascinated by the more stirring reaches of Scottish history. He admired Robert Bruce; he idolised Wallace; he mused endlessly on the glories of the Battle of Bannockburn and the humiliations of Flodden and Culloden. He liked to say, "Scotland will rise again", and he believed that with unshakeable fervour. It was taking a bit of time, though – he admitted that – but in the affairs of nations, time is an abundant quality.

"Scotland will come back," he remarked to Ranald when he took him to see a Jacobite display at the National Museum. "We all know it: Scotland will come back."

Ranald looked puzzled. "Where's it gone, Daddy?" he asked.

"That's the point, Ranald. Scotland never went away."

"Then how can it come back if it never went anywhere?" asked Ranald.

"It's a manner of speaking, Ranald. It's hard to explain. I

could say to you that it's a question of cultural survival, but I have to bear in mind that you're only seven."

For a few moments Ranald was silent. Then he asked, "Is England the problem, Daddy?"

His father looked over his shoulder. "Some say that, Ranald."

"But do you?"

Mr Macpherson smiled. "I have nothing against the English, Ranald. You mustn't dislike any group of people simply because of who they are."

"So they can't help it?"

"Well, Ranald," came the reply. "You might put it that way."

Ranald considered this. He knew that history was a live issue for his father and that he was a member of a battle re-enactment society. He knew that he and his friends dressed up as soldiers and pretended to fight Bannockburn and Prestonpans and other great battles. He had been taken to see one of these re-enactments, and had enjoyed the spectacle. He had relished the shouting and the whooping. Scottish history, it seemed to him, was full of shouting and whooping.

There was something about his father's re-enactments that puzzled Ranald. In their version, the Scots always won. That was nice, thought Ranald, but was it actually true? Surely the English must have won a battle from time to time even if these days they did not seem to win the football or the cricket very much. Ranald felt sorry for the English. They were nice people, he thought, and they deserved to win at least sometimes. He suspected, though, that his father thought otherwise. That was the problem with grown-ups, thought Ranald: they weren't consistently fair. Of course, they explained to children that life wasn't always fair. But, Ranald wondered, whose fault was that?

# 11

## On This Tiny, Spinning Planet

As Angus Lordie walked back with Cyril from Drummond Place Gardens, he was unaware of the fact that he was being observed from a high window in Scotland Street by his neighbour, Stuart. There was nothing unusual in the sight of Angus and his dog walking along Scotland Street – Cyril was given several walks a day – and now Stuart barely noticed them. He was deep in thought as he looked out over the street – he was expecting Nicola at any moment. He had just spoken to her on the phone and she had told him that she had left Big Lou's café and would be back in the flat in fifteen minutes or so.

"No hurry," said Stuart. "The nursery people say that we can collect Ulysses any time before six."

"You wanted to discuss something?" Nicola asked.

"Yes," replied Stuart. "I've had a call from up north."

Nicola knew what that meant. *Up north* had become their way of referring to Irene, the sobriquet having been coined by Nicola, and often accompanied by a slight wince that she hoped Stuart would not notice.

"What did she want?" asked Nicola, stopping for a moment as she walked down Dundas Street.

"I think we need to talk about it," said Stuart.

"Give me an idea."

"No," said Stuart. "It's tricky."

Nicola did not press him. She was suddenly filled with

dread and was not so sure that she wanted to hear what he had to say while she was walking along the street. Irene sometimes made her want to tear her hair and stamp her feet in frustration, and she thought that might not be appropriate out in the open, in Dundas Street. Stuart and Irene now lived separate lives, but Irene was still there, with her visits to Edinburgh to see the boys. Nicola could have coped with that – she accepted that as their mother Irene should continue to be a presence in their lives – but that did not mean that she wanted her to be a part of Stuart's life as well.

Stuart was weak. He was a kind man – a good man, really – but when it came to standing up to Irene, he had never managed to draw any lines. He had been dominated, right from the beginning, by a woman who could not help herself from trying to shape the lives of those with whom she came in contact. Irene was a shrew – it was as simple as that. She was a termagant.

Nicola put her phone back in her pocket and resumed her journey. She glanced up at the sky; the forecast had spoken of rain, but it seemed clear enough. In the distance, over the roofs of Canonmills and Trinity, the hills of Fife were bathed in afternoon sun. A woman walking up the road passed her on the pavement, and their eyes met briefly. The woman smiled, and her lips moved in a whispered, inaudible *good afternoon*. Nicola smiled back, and the two women shared a transient moment of mutual recognition – *we are together on this tiny, spinning planet*. Nicola looked back up at the sky, at infinity. We're all lonely; we're all shipwrecked on this planetary rock; all we have is one another, and then only for the briefest moment in all these countless billions of years that make up time. Why spend that time fretting? Why spend that time grumbling about one another? Or worse, when we should be cherishing one another; when we should be trying to relieve the pain of this world; when we should be extracting from each of our precious minutes such joy and happiness as we can.

So arresting were these unexpected thoughts that Nicola stopped and, for a few minutes, stood where she was, indifferent to passers-by, to the number twenty-three bus that laboured uphill past her on its southwards journey to Morningside, almost unaware of the cyclist who had stopped on the other side of the street when a bag of potatoes he had been carrying in his rucksack spilled out onto the road. Some of the potatoes had started to roll down the steep gradient of that section of Dundas Street; others had already been crushed by passing cars. But Nicola thought nothing of that: her mind was on charity and on the fact that she was showing a marked lack of that quality in the way she thought about Irene. Yes, she was unbearable, but was that her fault? Every woman had a potential excuse for her shortcomings, just as every man had. The causes were different. In the case of women, it was often what had been done to them by a male-dominated society, by insensitive or exploitative men. In the case of men, it was often because of damage wrought by a vision of masculinity to which they had to aspire. That was a problem in Scotland – a big problem that had been there for centuries and was still unresolved.

She pulled herself together. You could not stand in Dundas Street and think about such issues while people about you were getting on with their ordinary lives. It would look odd, and none of us liked to look odd – although on occasion there was every reason for us to stop and look up at the sky, and think about how we get through life, from one day to the next, and how at many times we fail, even as we try to do better. And how at times, if we are honest with ourselves, we just want to sit down and cry.

Now she noticed the cyclist. He had picked up some of his potatoes and was dusting them off before replacing them in his rucksack. She wondered about that. In general, she was an adherent of the three-second rule: if you pick food up within three seconds of its falling to the floor you will be all right. There was no truth to that rule, but she followed it because it was one of those rules that made life easier – and rules that make life easier are worth believing in, even if you have your doubts.

But dropping things in the street was another matter altogether. The gutters were insanitary – even in Edinburgh – and she was concerned that the young man replacing his potatoes could pick up something rather nasty. But was she his keeper? Were the potatoes of others strictly their own affair?

On impulse, she crossed the street.

"I don't think you should eat those potatoes," she said. "You never know what . . ."

He looked at her in surprise. He was a man of about her age – somewhere in his late fifties, but of athletic build: he was evidently a regular cyclist. She saw that he had blue eyes. She saw that he was wearing a red bandana.

"They'll be all right," he said.

Nicola shook her head. "Let me buy you some more. There's that shop down there. They sell potatoes."

# 12

## A Whole Country to Love

The cyclist looked at Nicola with astonishment. He brushed a lock of hair from his forehead. She noticed that this left a smudge: his hands had been dirtied by picking up the potatoes from the ground.

"I'm sorry," he said. "What did you say?"

"I offered to buy you some potatoes."

She looked at him, uncertain whether she might have offended him. People had their pride, and some found it difficult to accept gifts – especially from complete strangers.

Then he smiled. "I thought that's what you said." He shook his head – not in refusal, but in puzzlement. "Why?"

"Because I saw you lose . . . well, not lose all of them, but quite a few. And because I don't like the idea of anyone eating potatoes that have been in the gutter. Germs—"

"But why you? I mean, we don't know one another, do we?"

She shook her head. "We don't. I'm called Nicola, by the way . . . and I'm just a . . . well, I suppose I'm just a passer-by in this particular situation."

He smiled again. "I'm David. And I suppose I'm just a cyclist who stupidly spilled a whole lot of potatoes on Dundas Street."

"I'd really like you to let me do this," said Nicola. "And, if you do, we can put the dirty potatoes in the bin. Please let me."

She looked at him again. It suddenly occurred to her that he might think she was trying to pick him up; that she was one of those women on the lookout for men, who would not hesitate to accost a stranger. Such things happened. She blushed at the thought, and decided that she should end the encounter now.

But then he said, "That's very kind of you – if it's what you really want to do."

"It is," she said. He had given in quickly, and she sensed that there was something vulnerable about him – some sadness.

He wheeled his bicycle beside her as they walked to the small grocery store a few hundred yards down the street.

"This rucksack's ancient," he said. "One of the straps has perished. That was why the potatoes spilled out."

"I like rucksacks," said Nicola. "I find them convenient. You don't feel the weight so much if it's on your back."

He seemed to consider this. Then he said, "Yes, you're right. I use it to take stuff to work."

"Which is? I mean, what do you do? If you don't mind my asking."

He assured her that he did not mind. "I work in a spectacles lab," he said. "I'm part-time now. Coasting down to retirement, I suppose. I make up the prescriptions."

"You make lenses?"

"Yes. The machines do a lot of the work now. But you have to have humans checking everything. It gets fiddly."

They reached the grocery store, and went inside together.

"I can't believe you're doing this," he said, as she took a bag of potatoes to the counter.

"Well, I am."

She handed the bag over to him. He looked at her with bemused gratitude. "Then you must let me buy you a cup of coffee next door. There's that deli. They serve coffee."

She thought of Stuart, who would be waiting for her. She looked at her watch. "I'll have to get on in fifteen minutes or so. My son's waiting for me. He wants to talk to me about something important – although I don't know what it is."

He looked apologetic. "Sorry, I don't want to keep you."

"No. I've got the time."

They went into the deli, where he bought them both a cup of coffee. When he came back to the table, carrying the two cups on a tray, Nicola said, "Do you enjoy your work? Making all those glasses."

David placed a cup of coffee in front of her. "It's all right. I've been doing it for years. I'm not qualified to do anything else."

Nicola smiled. "I've got no qualifications myself. Or none that are much use." She thought, but did not say, *but I own a pie factory:* you don't need paper qualifications if you own a pie factory.

"Qualifications," mused David. "My dad had none . . ." He trailed off.

"Your dad?"

"My dad had no qualifications."

"People didn't – in the past. But he probably did all right, did he?"

David nodded. "He did, yes. He was a miner, you see. He was one of the last of his generation to go down the pits. Bilston Glen. He was sixteen when he went down, and then the mines closed, and he was left high and dry. Maggie Thatcher. He never forgave her. His whole world ended, you see. The community he lived in. All the history, the ties. A whole chunk of working Scotland. Finished."

"I know," said Nicola.

"He was a hard-working man, my dad. He was typical of a certain sort of old-fashioned Scotsman. He ended up working on a farm. He became a tractor man." He paused. "We lost him last week. He was eighty-seven."

She hesitated. "Just last week?"

"Yes," said David. "Last Tuesday."

She caught her breath. "Oh, I'm sorry . . ."

He inclined his head. "We all have to go sooner or later. I hoped that he might have lasted a little bit longer than he did, but it wasn't to be. He was ill for quite some time, you see. Then I went to see him on the Monday and he was really frail. They said to me that if there was anything I wanted to say to him, I should say it. They were giving him this morphine syrup, you see. You know when they do that, that it's not going to be long."

He looked at her, and she reached out to take his hand in hers. He looked down at her hand on his, but did not resist.

"I loved him very much, you know. He could be a bit prickly at times, but that came from being in the mines, I think, and everything that went with that. And he felt that he and the men he worked with had been let down."

"They weren't the only ones," said Nicola.

"I loved him," said David. "We don't have enough time to love people, do we? And often we don't get round to it—"

"Until it's too late."

He had lowered his gaze; now he looked into her eyes. "Do you have somebody that you love? Or maybe I shouldn't ask that question."

She told him that it was a question we should not be afraid to ask – or be asked.

"I was married. I loved him. But then I stopped. That was abroad. That was Portugal. Then I came back to Scotland and there were people to love here. My two grandsons. And my son." She paused. "And a whole lot of other people, I suppose. A whole country, if one thinks about it."

# 13

*Pommes de Terre Liberées*

Stuart said, "Where have you been? You said ten minutes."

The irritation broke through his voice, and he immediately felt guilty. His mother was giving up her life, more or less, to look after the boys, and here he was berating her for taking half an hour off for purposes of her own.

He apologised. "I'm sorry, Mother. Your time is your own affair. I'm really sorry."

She reached out to take his hand. "No apology needed. If any apology is called for, it's from me. I said I'd be with you, and I wasn't."

He was relieved. But mothers, he had long realised, forgave everything. Their sons were simply trying their best, even when they invaded neighbouring countries or started regional wars.

"I was helping a cyclist," Nicola said.

He looked puzzled.

"He was called David," she went on. "He had very blue eyes and looked a bit, well, sad. The rucksack he was wearing gave way and scattered potatoes all over Dundas Street, just past the Fine Art Society gallery. Some of the potatoes rolled down the street."

"Oh," said Stuart. "That must have looked odd."

"A passer-by might have thought they were an art installation," said Nicola. "It's the sort of thing to which they give the Turner Prize. *Pommes de terre liberées. The liberation of the couch potatoes.* That sort of thing."

Stuart laughed. "Angus Lordie would agree, I suspect. He has strong views on the Turner Prize."

"Well, it wasn't that," said Nicola. "As it happens."

"You helped him pick up the potatoes?"

She shook her head. "I bought him a fresh bag from that place down the road – next to that deli. And he bought me a cup of coffee."

Stuart smiled. "Meeting men in the street now, Mother? Buying them bags of potatoes?"

Nicola told him how David had revealed the recent loss of his father. Stuart looked apologetic. "That was kind of you."

"I felt so sorry for him," said Nicola. "He looked so bereft."

"I'm sure it helped – just talking to you."

"Maybe," she said. And then continued, "But that's not what I wanted to talk about. When you called me, you said—"

"Yes. I need to talk to you about a call from Irene."

Nicola sighed. "Oh well—"

"I know what you feel," said Stuart. "I know you can't stand her."

Nicola protested. "I've been thinking. I may have been a bit harsh."

Stuart's surprise showed. "A bit harsh?"

"Yes. Uncharitable. Irene has . . . well, she has her reasons for being how she is. She means well, I suppose." It was hard for Nicola to say that. She, like Stuart – like everyone, in fact – had been on the receiving end of Irene's condescension and lecturing. Yet she felt now that it was somehow wrong to respond to such behaviour with a cold rejection, with an animus that matched Irene's own attitudes. There was a vicious circle to such confrontation, and the only way to break that circle was by embracing or forgiving the other. It was hard, but she had to make the effort.

Stuart remained silent. Then he said, "You don't think I've made a mistake? Our leading separate lives . . . bringing our marriage to an end?"

Nicola hesitated. She did not want to go too far. Irene was bad for Stuart, and he would never be happy if she returned to Scotland Street and everything was as it was before. She did not want that.

"No, you did the right thing," she said at last. "And remember: she wanted to go. She was the one who wanted to go up to Aberdeen to do that PhD with Dr-whatever-his-name-was."

"Fairbairn. Hugo Fairbairn."

"Yes, him." She might have said, "with that man who looks so like Ulysses", but did not. She had her doubts there, of course – or rather, she had her convictions – but she did not want to hurt Stuart. So, she said instead, "She precipitated the separation. You went along with it, but if there's any blame to be laid at anybody's door – and I don't think there is – then I think it's not at yours. You did your best, Stuart, but oil and water, you know – sometimes a relationship just doesn't work out."

Stuart listened. Then he said, "You know, of course, that she's shacked up with a fisherman up there? She's with the chap who fished her out of the sea when she was swept off Aberdeen Beach."

Nicola nodded. Stranger things had happened – but not many. The idea of Irene, of all people, living with a fisherman, and gutting fish for him, was so bizarre as to be almost unbelievable. But it was, apparently, quite true. "I suppose," she said, "that there are precedents. People sometimes go for their opposites. Some people like a bit of rough." She apologised for the expression. "Sorry to use that term, but you know what I mean."

"He could be very sensitive for all you know," said Stuart. "Let's not stereotype, Mother."

Nicola looked incredulous. "Do you seriously suggest that a deep-sea fisherman in that part of the world is likely to be in touch with his feminine side?"

Stuart shrugged. "The old categories are being challenged. There are probably plenty of sensitive fishermen. Artistic, even."

"Nonsense," said Nicola. "How many pastel-coloured fishing boats are there?"

"You're very old-fashioned, Mother," said Stuart. "The world has changed, you know." He remembered something. "However, you might have a point . . . There's a fishing boat over in Stornoway called *The XY Chromosome*. I read about it in the *Scotsman*."

"You see," said Nicola. "But anyway, what did she say?"

"She wants to spend a bit more time in Edinburgh. She wants to be a bit more hands-on with the boys."

Nicola repressed an urge to groan. She had to be positive. She had to try to be charitable. So she confined herself to saying, in as neutral a tone as possible, "I see."

"She's proposing to come down on a Friday and to spend Friday night and Saturday night here. She'd go back up north on Sunday morning."

The groan that Nicola had suppressed would now be contained no longer. "Oh," she said. "Well, I suppose—"

"She has something in mind for Bertie."

Nicola drew in her breath. The figure of Charity, briefly at her side, now turned her back and left the room. Faith and Hope remained, but they were clearly aghast. In a small voice

Nicola said, "She's had Bertie projects in the past. The Italian *conversazione* classes. The yoga. The psychotherapy in Queen Street. *Yoga for Tots* down in Stockbridge . . . What now?"

Stuart looked grave. "She wants Bertie to get an Irish passport," he said.

# 14

## *Irish Grandmothers, Passports, Identity*

It took Nicola a few moments to recover her composure. It was challenging enough to think of Bertie with a passport – how could anybody think of taking Bertie away? – but why should it be Irish? Not that there was anything wrong with Irish passports, which were ideal for Irish people, but Bertie was Scottish, and if he were to have any passport – which was completely unnecessary at present – then it should be one that was appropriate for a Scottish person. Until such time as Scotland changed its constitutional status, that meant a United Kingdom passport, of the sort that Nicola herself had, and Stuart too – not that Stuart ever went anywhere very much.

"An *Irish* passport?" Nicola stuttered.

Stuart closed his eyes, and made a gesture of resignation, of hopelessness in the face of some unfathomable mystery. "Yes. He's eligible, apparently. Irene's mother was Irish, and that means Bertie has an Irish grandmother. The holy grail of so many who want to avoid the queues at European Union airports. An Irish grandmother."

"Oh."

"Grandmothers, of course, are significant when it comes to certain matters. A Scottish grandmother is useful if you want to play professional rugby for Scotland. Discover your Scottish granny and suddenly, hey presto, you're Scottish for sporting purposes." He paused. "There are hundreds of Scottish grannies offering their services to those without one.

You see them at the rugby matches at Murrayfield – rows of grannies watching their grandsons playing. Sometimes they need to be reminded which one is their grandson. It's quite touching."

Nicola smiled. "Speaking as an ancestor . . ."

Stuart laughed. "An ancestor? I suppose you are – from Bertie's perspective. But getting back to passports, there are lots of paper Irishmen these days. Some of them have never crossed the Irish Sea, but that's no problem."

"That's generous of the Irish Government."

"Yes. And Irene wants to take them up on the offer."

Nicola was thoughtful. "I don't suppose it can do any harm. He won't lose his current citizenship just by becoming Irish, will he?"

"No. You can be British and Irish – or Scottish and Irish, if you will."

Nicola wondered why Stuart had been anxious. "Is that all you wanted to talk to me about?"

Stuart shook his head. "Unfortunately, there's more to it than that. You know how Irene is . . ."

She did.

"Well," Stuart continued, "Irene feels that if Bertie is to become an Irish citizen, then he needs to acquire some sense of Irish identity."

Nicola rolled her eyes. They had been there before, she thought. There had been that long campaign on Irene's part to make Bertie aware of Italian culture. There had been the *conversazione* sessions. There had been the trips to the National Gallery on the Mound to see the Florentine paintings. Bertie had been too small to see them properly, and had needed to be lifted up physically to view the pictures. He had been unaware of the looks of sympathy that this spectacle had elicited, and had, in fact, taken in much of what he had been exposed to, but in Stuart's view it had all been a bit much. Bertie was a small boy, and small boys should not spend too much time on the Renaissance. He had been unable to sway Irene on this, though; she was in charge of Bertie's education, she insisted, and it was not helpful if Stuart sought to interfere.

Now Nicola asked how Irene planned to instil in Bertie a sense of Irish identity. And why, anyway, should this identity be necessary? A passport might be useful, of course – she could see that, but did identity make any difference? How could you make a small boy Irish? Dress him in green? Teach him the language? Bertie already had Italian to contend with, and a smattering of Gaelic that his teacher at school, Miss Campbell, having Hebridean roots, was attempting to teach the children in her class. That had met with mixed success. Ranald Braveheart Macpherson had done quite well, having been encouraged by his father, for political reasons, to read *Tintin* in Gaelic; Tofu had somehow learned a number of colourful Gaelic swear words; but most of the class now knew little more than the Gaelic words for ambulance (*ambaileans*) and police (*poileas*), terms they picked up from passing vehicles. Olive had managed to master Gaelic numerals up to three, while Pansy struggled to count up to two.

Stuart now disclosed what Irene had told him over the phone about her planned identity programme. She had been in touch, she said, with an Irish postgraduate student in Edinburgh, Eamonn Flynn, who was working on a thesis on the playwright, John Synge. He had agreed to act as Bertie's Irish culture tutor, and would give him a two-hour tutorial each Saturday morning – at the flat in Scotland Street.

"He's promised to cover all the main aspects of Irishness," Irene had announced. "History, art, folklore – everything that makes Irish culture what it is." She'd paused, and then added, "I assume you're happy to pay. He's not going to charge much."

Stuart had been silent.

"Are you still there, Stuart?"

"Yes, but—"

"It's a wonderful opportunity for Bertie, you see. He'll end up with an Irish passport and an ability to live in Ireland at some stage in the future should he desire to do so. What's not to like about that?"

"Yes, but . . ." Bertie had never expressed any interest in going to Ireland. He wanted to go to Glasgow when he was eighteen: there was no psychotherapy in Glasgow and virtually no yoga. Glasgow was freedom.

"I don't see any downside," said Irene, with the air of one bringing a conversation to an end.

"But he's only seven, for heaven's sake," protested Stuart. "He's still learning how to be Scottish. First things first, Irene."

"Being seven is the whole point of this," snapped Irene. "Remember the Jesuits."

"What have the Jesuits got to do with it?" asked Stuart peevishly.

"I'm surprised you don't know this," Irene began, "but the Jesuits said, *Give us a child until the age of seven and we'll have him forever*. Or words to that effect. They knew the power of—"

"Of fear?" suggested Stuart.

"Perhaps. I don't see eye-to-eye with the Jesuits, of course, but they knew that one is never too young to learn. Look at Mozart."

Stuart groaned. "Mozart's father was a bit pushy, don't you think? He put Mozart on a piano stool when he was, what? Two?"

Irene sighed. "Stuart," she said, "I thought we'd got beyond all that sort of thing. Let's not argue. The arrangement is made and I think you should just accept it. Eammon said that he'd send details of his bank account. I suggested he direct them straight to you."

# 15

## Bruce Steps Out

Bruce Anderson, surveyor, owner of a desirable New Town flat – with its original Georgian cornices – and lightning-strike survivor, looked in the bathroom mirror. He approved of what he saw, but then he had always liked the image mirrors reflected back to him. You might as well be honest with yourself, Bruce thought: if you're good-looking, then there was no reason to deny it. Accept it; celebrate it.

In many respects, Bruce, like many attractive people, had led a charmed life. People were drawn to him because of his looks: there is something about physical presence that entices people, moth-like, to its flame. And just as moths may be consumed by the heat generated by light, those who fall for a beguiling face run a high risk of being singed, or worse. Bruce was not indifferent to those who fell for him, only to face disappointment, but he could hardly respond to all of them. "There are so many women," he said to a friend, "and only one of me."

He had been brought up in Crieff, in surroundings of soft hills and comfortable, beckoning glens. He had been educated at Morrison's Academy, where he was encouraged to develop his talents, without being put under too much pressure. Bruce coasted along comfortably in the middle of his academic cohort. He was good at sports, particularly at rugby, and was a considerable social success. At school dances, he was besieged; it was his destiny, he decided, to be the object of female admiration, and if girls chose to break their hearts over him, then that was hardly his fault.

After studying land management at university – a subject that was particularly popular with the surplus sons of farming families – Bruce became a surveyor in Edinburgh. He had a good eye for property, and for the potential of houses and flats that were suitable for development and resale. That was the direction he saw his career going in when, quite suddenly, his life was turned upside down by a bolt of lightning that descended on Dundas Street at the very moment Bruce was walking past Queen Street Gardens.

The effect of lightning on the human body can range from negligible to catastrophic. If you are struck by lightning when you are wet – as you might be, for instance, after being caught in a rainstorm – your chances of survival are much greater than if you are completely dry. The reason for this is that the electric current travels to earth through the moisture without penetrating the internal organs. In Bruce's case, he did not have the protection of damp, but the lightning nonetheless did no internal damage, simply lifting him off his feet and tossing him into the middle of the road. He became unconscious, but not for long, and was soon discharged by the hospital to which he was admitted. But unknown to the doctors who examined him, Bruce's brain had been affected by the massive charge of electricity that had enveloped him, and he underwent what appeared to be a profound change of character. This led to him seeking admission to Pluscarden Abbey for a period, and divesting himself of a substantial proportion of his worldly goods.

Had the effect of the lightning strike been permanent, then Bruce might well have remained at the Abbey and eventually taken his vows as a monk. He had been well received there, and visitors had been intrigued to see such a handsome young postulant joining the ranks of the mostly middle-aged monks who inhabited the monastery. But the effect of the lightning proved to be impermanent, and slowly Bruce's original character reasserted itself. His memory was restored, as were most of his mannerisms. He returned to Edinburgh, faintly horrified by the extent of his generosity during what he came to describe as his "high voltage" period. Now, it seemed to those who knew him and who had been puzzled by his apparent change of personality, the old Bruce was back. The use of clove-scented hair gel, such an enthusiasm of the earlier Bruce and so suddenly abandoned during the lightning/monastic period, started once more, as did the general preening. Under the influence of the lightning, he had disposed of a lot of his clothes to his flatmate, Borthy Borthwick. Now Bruce began to ponder how he might get his clothing back. Broad hints were dropped to Borthy to the effect that sometimes things were given away that should not be given away, and that it was wrong for people to take advantage of those suffering from concussion or, purely for purposes of illustration, lightning strike. Sufficiently embarrassed, Borthy had voluntarily returned a number of shirts, while Bruce secured the return of the rest by the simple expedient of removing them from the tumble dryer, into which they had been placed by Borthy, and putting them back in his wardrobe.

Pulling himself away from the mirror, Bruce took the shower with which he liked to start each morning. Then, with body butter and facial moisturiser applied, he dressed himself for the day. Since his return from Pluscarden, he was unsure of his next career move. He could always go back to surveying – one of the big estate agents had already approached him with an attractive offer. They were keen for him to take over their Edinburgh residential division as he had, they thought, the right social skills to drum up new business. Bruce had the reputation of being good with female clients, and that was a side of the firm's activities they wished to develop. He himself was not so sure: buying and selling houses had its challenges, but he felt that he was cut out for something bigger. Bruce was aware of the ticking of the clock: his looks would not last forever, and there would come a time – not all that many years away – when he would wake up and discover that he was *thirty-five*. The thought appalled him. Thirty was bad enough, but thirty-five was on the downward slope to forty, beyond which it required little imagination to see the decline of middle age. No, he would have to look for something more interesting than writing reports on the state of roofs and wall cavities. There would be something – he was convinced of that – but how did one connect with one's more exciting future? How did one get the message out to those who could do something about it?

He went back to the mirror and smoothed his hair. There was the agreeable scent of cloves. There was the reassuring sight of features as yet unaffected by gravity: gravity was such a tragedy for so many. He felt cheered. He would go round the corner to Big Lou's and treat himself to a bacon roll with his latte. One bacon roll would not make a difference. If you survived being struck by lightning, then bacon rolls would surely not do any harm.

He took a final look in the mirror. "Gorgeous," he muttered.

# 16

## *Like, Like, Like*

The busiest time in Big Lou's day were the hours between eight and ten in the morning. During this time, the coffee bar filled up with those on their way to offices in the city centre. On fine mornings in the summer, these regulars would be joined by the occasional resident of that part of the New Town who had started the day with a walk in the Queen Street Gardens, or sometimes further afield, and now wanted a cup of coffee before returning home. The later regulars, of whom Matthew and Angus formed the core, usually arrived shortly after ten. By that time, Big Lou would have cleared up from the earlier rush, and would be ready, from behind her well-polished counter, to join in the conversation.

Matthew, of course, was more than a mere customer. A year or so previously, he had stepped in to help Big Lou financially, and had acquired, in the process, a majority interest in the coffee bar. Not that Matthew would have dreamed of exercising any control over Big Lou; she was perfectly capable of running the business herself and had, in fact, made a considerable success of it. But the cost of running a small business in an expensive part of town was always there, revealed in the accounts in a painful column headed *overheads*. Business rates, the property tax paid to the City Council, were a constant drain and enough, in many cases, to make small businesses untenable. It seemed to Big Lou that the fundamental principle that lay behind them was all wrong: local taxes should be levied on the basis of income, and calculated on a sliding scale, so as to make those who earned the most pay the most. By basing such taxation on the value of property, an arbitrary burden was placed on businesses irrespective of their profitability.

But taxation was not the only burden with which Big Lou and people like her had to contend. There were insurance and energy costs, the latter being a particular issue for businesses like hers, which used electricity to boil water for the coffee, to bake the cheese scones that she liked to offer her customers, and to fry the bacon that went into her celebrated bacon and haggis rolls. Then the coffee bar had to be heated: people could not be left to shiver while they sipped their lattes and flat whites. That meant that Big Lou had to fuel a small gas boiler at the back of the premises to provide hot water for the radiators. All that gas had to be pumped in from the North Sea or from further afield, and all the people working on the rigs or sailing the giant tankers had to be paid, as did the coffee growers in distant West Africa or South America – even though Big Lou insisted on buying Fair Trade beans, these people still seemed to get rather little for all their hard work. *I'll never know them*, thought Big Lou. *I'll never know these faraway people with whom I'm joined in our daily labours.*

The coffee bar worked, though, and Big Lou made an income from it that was adequate for her needs. She owned her flat, having bought it with her share of her parents' estate. They were tenant farmers, and hard-working ones at that, and in a lifetime of careful farming they had saved enough to give Big Lou and her brother, Jock, a start in life. Jock had gone to Dundee, where he trained as a plumber, and had done well enough to buy a medium-sized plumbing supplies business. Big Lou had initially worked in the Granite Nursing Home in Aberdeen. When she was left a legacy by a grateful patient, she used it to set herself up in Edinburgh, and had settled in Canonmills, at the far end of Dundas Street, in a flat that was large enough for her and her adopted son, Finlay.

Finlay was now settled as a weekly boarder in the ballet school in Glasgow. He had shown a talent that the school authorities were confident would guarantee him a place in Scottish Ballet in due course. Big Lou was proud of him, not only for his dancing talent but also for his equable temperament. There was a gentleness and kindness about Finlay that was immediately apparent to anyone who met him, as well as good manners of a sort that were rare in a narcissistic and indulged teenage culture. Finlay had been taught to speak politely to adults, to look them in the eye, and to listen to what they had to say to him. This made him a rarity – but a much appreciated one. Big Lou had also succeeded in discouraging Finlay from uttering the word *like* before every noun, or using it to describe any state of mind or report any act of speech. Finlay never said *I was like*, when he wanted to say how he felt or communicate what he thought. Angus had noticed this when he had encountered the boy helping Big Lou in the café one Saturday morning.

"He speaks beautifully," he later reported to Domenica. "He was telling me about the ballet school over in Glasgow, and never once did he use the word *like*."

"A miracle," said Domenica. "It's a form of infectious verbal tic now. I heard a couple of student-age women talking on the bus the other day. You should have heard them. *I was going to like the supermarket, and I saw like this guy who was like standing there, you know, and I was like Wow! And he was like doing nothing, just standing, and then he was like 'Are you like a friend of Jemma's?' and I was like . . .*"

Angus winced. "It's awful. *Like* awful, in fact."

"Is nobody teaching people how to speak well-constructed

language any longer?" asked Domenica. "Probably not. The theory is that children should express themselves however they like. Nobody believes in teaching them to speak clearly. Nobody tells them to open their mouths and articulate. I assume that nobody teaches them to recite poetry any longer."

"I suspect not." Angus sighed. "Scottish education," he said. "Remember when it was so highly regarded? And now? Down we plummet in all the tables. And as we descend, we deny it."

Domenica looked out of the window. "We have to be careful about saying that everything is in complete disrepair or in crisis. *Anno domini*, remember . . ."

"Even if it is?" said Angus.

Domenica did not answer, and so Angus said, "There used to be a country called Scotland. There used to be a place where . . ." He stopped. There was so much that had been lost. But Domenica was right: one should not dwell on that. Dr Pangloss, perhaps, had a point.

# 17

## An Address on Heriot Row

Bruce was the first of the regulars to arrive at Big Lou's that morning, preceding Matthew and Angus by a quarter of an hour. There were no other customers when he came in through the door – what Big Lou called the early shift had come and gone: the office workers to their offices in St Andrew Square, the staff from the National Portrait Gallery to theirs, further up the hill, and the three hairdressers from George Street had left for their first appointment of the day, fortified by Big Lou's croissants and coffee.

"Busy, as usual, Lou," said Bruce as he surveyed the empty tables.

Big Lou gave a dismissive snort. She did not dislike Bruce, but she treated him as she would have treated any young farm hand back at Snell Mains when she was a girl. Those young men were called *loons*, a word used in that part of Scotland to describe young males, and that was all Bruce was, for all the stuff he put on his hair and his expensive jeans and jackets – he was a loon from Crieff, or wherever it was, and she was not having any of it.

"If you got yourself up at a reasonable hour," she said, "you would ken fine how busy this place is. Honest folk dinnae lie in their beds till ten o'clock, Bruce."

Bruce laughed. "How do you know I haven't already been to the gym, Lou? Or gone for a run?"

"Because you're not the type," said Lou. "Anyway, the usual?"

"Double bacon this morning, Lou, if you don't mind."

She gave him a sideways look. "Hard day ahead?"

Bruce sat down on one of the stools at the counter. "I'm looking at a flat."

Big Lou started cooking the bacon. Bruce drew an appreciative breath. "That's the way to start a day," he said. "If only they made an aftershave that smelled of frying bacon."

Big Lou wrinkled her nose in disgust. "You shouldn't need to plaster yourself with all those things, you know. What's that stuff you use? I can smell it from here. Cloves, is it?"

Bruce smiled. "Women like it. They've told me."

"Well, I don't."

Bruce smiled again. "Sorry, Lou, it's not meant for you."

She ignored this. "Where's this flat?"

"India Street," replied Bruce. "It's right up at the top – at the Heriot Row end. A basement."

"And?"

Bruce leaned forward. "I'm going to put in an offer, Lou. Keep it to yourself, but I'm putting in an offer."

She knew that Bruce renovated property for resale. "To sell on, I take it?"

Bruce nodded. "For a big profit, Lou."

Big Lou turned over the sizzling bacon. "What I don't get, Bruce, is how simply decorating a place, maybe changing a few things in the kitchen, can make such a big difference to the price."

"Well, it does," said Bruce. "But this time I've got even bigger plans."

"Such as?"

Bruce glanced over his shoulder, although there was nobody else there. He lowered his voice. "The value of property depends to an extent on the address," he began. "You understand that, I take it?"

She gave him a scornful look. "I'm no' that daft."

"Just checking. Well, if your flat down in Canonmills is worth four hundred thousand, what would it be if the exact same place – same number of rooms, same matching avocado bathroom set—"

"Dinnae condescend tae me, Bruce," warned Big Lou.

"Only joking," he said quickly. "No offence. Nothing wrong with avocado-coloured bathroom sets, if that's what you like."

"My bath is white," snapped Lou.

"Good colour, Lou. You can't go wrong with white. Anyway, the point I was making is this: if your flat . . . with its matching white bathroom set and all . . . were to be further up the hill – say in Fettes Row or St Stephen Street, it would be worth four hundred and fifty thousand pounds. Same flat, different address. Location, Lou. Location."

Big Lou nodded. "We all know that."

"Indeed," said Bruce. "So, tell me, Lou, what's the best address on this side of Princes Street?"

Big Lou buttered a roll, to be ready for the bacon. "The best address? Ann Street? Isn't that pretty pricey?"

Bruce nodded. "It is. Small houses, though. I remember there was a lawyer who said of Ann Street – 'awfully difficult houses to get a coffin out of'. Very funny, that."

Lou smiled. She liked jokes that reminded Edinburgh not to get above itself. She returned to Bruce's question. "Moray Place?"

Bruce considered this. "Moray Place is certainly a good address – and prices reflect that. It's not cheap."

"That's where they have their office," she said. "Those two who come in here from time to time and sit at that table over there. You've seen them. The ones who always wear their Watsonian ties. They were in the other day."

Bruce frowned. He was not sure who Big Lou was talking about.

"One of them is the chairman, and the other is the secretary – of the Association of Scottish Nudists."

"Oh yes," said Bruce, remembering now. "Them. They always look so miserable."

"Aye," said Big Lou. "And wouldn't you? If you were a Scottish nudist and had to cope with our weather? And the midges? Midges *love* nudists. But it's not just that. They're always fighting with the Glasgow members of the Association. They have this big battle that's been going on for years."

"But you're right," said Bruce. "They have their headquarters in Moray Place. And that'll be worth a bit. But it's not the best address, not quite. There's Heriot Row, you see."

Big Lou agreed. "They're awfie expensive, those houses. Ridiculous. You could buy a farm for the price of one of those places."

"Precisely," said Bruce. "And you see, Lou, this basement flat in India Street has a window that faces Heriot Row – below the level of the street, of course, but there's a set of steps that goes down from the pavement on Heriot Row. It connects to this little space down below where there was a coal bunker in the old days."

"So?"

"So," said Bruce, with the air of a conjuror pulling a rabbit out of a hat, "I buy that flat – current address, India Street – and I knock the window out and make it into a door. First result, an address on Heriot Row. Second result, the value of the flat goes up by twenty-five per cent – minimum."

"You're going to do that?" asked Big Lou incredulously.

Bruce winked. "I need that roll, Lou. The bacon's ready."

Big Lou turned away. Was turning a window into a door legal? Heriot Row was listed – the buildings were in a conservation area. Was Bruce serious?

# 18

## Constancy, Loyalty, Lion Tamers

Bruce was hungry. Wolfing down his bacon roll, he was just finishing it when Matthew arrived, closely followed by Angus, with Cyril on his lead. The dog looked around appreciatively: this was familiar territory, laden with positive scents and, in the particular way in which the canine mind preserves memories, closely linked with recollections of ankles encountered on previous visits.

Cyril had no idea why he was in Big Lou's coffee bar. His understanding of the world was a simple one. He did not know why the world was as it was: it simply was there, just as he was. Angus was at its centre – that was the foundation of his conception of things – and all that Cyril wanted was to be with him. It was that straightforward. Angus was God. His will was absolute. It was the sun. It was the rain. It was the wind that blew in from the North Sea. It was everything. Without the benefit of language, in his devotion Cyril enacted that fundamental precept enshrined in the catechism of so many human religions: submission to a spirit outside and beyond us. In so far as dogs had an ontology, that was it.

Matthew and Angus were surprised to see Bruce. Although he had been a customer of Big Lou's over the years, his attendance at morning coffee was sporadic. They had both been alarmed by the lightning strike in Dundas Street, and were relieved that Bruce survived relatively unscathed. The outcome, Angus pointed out, could have been so very different. Few of us might know people who have been struck by lightning, but Angus had a friend who was hit by a bolt on a golf course during a freak storm, and who had not survived. There was, however, something about Bruce, a breezy confidence, that made his survival less surprising. It was often the case, he thought, that those who survived any setback did so because it never occurred to them that there would ever be any other outcome.

Both Matthew and Angus had their reservations about Bruce. Matthew had frequently been irritated by Bruce's self-centredness.

"In Bruce's view," he once remarked to Elspeth, "it's all about him."

She had not disagreed; at times she found Bruce insufferable. How could he be so unaware of others? And yet, it seemed to her, there were plenty of self-centred people. Indeed, weren't we all ultimately at the centre of our individual universe? There were those who devoted themselves to others, those saintly figures who worked tirelessly for the greater good, but even these people put their concerns centre stage. Those concerns might be noble, altruistic ones, but they were still *their* concerns, and they might be all that mattered to them. Which meant, of course, that there was no such thing as pure altruism: the good we do for others may at the same time be good we do for ourselves. If you feel good doing good, then you are acting for your own benefit.

Elspeth wrestled with this. "Yes, Bruce thinks only of himself," she said. "But then who doesn't think of himself or herself? Ultimately, that is."

Matthew did not hesitate. "You," he said firmly.

Elspeth had not expected this. "That's very kind," she said. "But I'm as selfish as anybody else."

Matthew shook his head. "No, you aren't. Definitely not.

Who do you think of first all the time? I'll tell you. The boys. Right from the time they were conceived, you've thought of them. You've put their interests first."

Elspeth was silent. It was true. Fergus, Tobermory and Rognvald were at the centre of her universe. And Matthew, too, even if to a slightly lesser extent.

"And you," she said. "I think of you a lot."

"I know you do. There are so many women who are just like you, Elspeth. They think of their children and their husband."

"Or partner . . ."

"Yes, all right, their partner. They think of them and would do anything to protect them."

Elspeth looked thoughtful. "Men do too. You think of us, don't you?"

"Of course," said Matthew. "But it seems to me that there's something different about a woman's love. Women are protective in a more absolute way. Or most of them are. Some, maybe not so much."

He thought of Irene. Stuart had drawn the short straw when he married her all those years ago. That was one case of somebody who did not think of family first and foremost.

"I might mention one exception," he said. "Irene. I'm not sure whether she's the best example of maternal love. Look at the way she went off to Aberdeen. She left those two little boys . . . how could she?"

Elspeth sighed. "She's a case apart," she said. "It's very unusual for a woman to desert her children. But it does happen. You see it occasionally."

"Have you?" asked Matthew. "I mean, have you ever seen it – apart from in Irene's case?"

She had. "There was somebody I worked with once. She was called Janet. She was a fantastic skier. I met her on a skiing holiday. I did only the very easy runs, but she went off on the black ones – and off-piste too, which can be pretty dangerous."

"Foolish," said Matthew.

"They run terrible risks, those people. They disturb the snow and suddenly there's an avalanche, and that's it. Anyway, there were fifteen of us in the party – staying in this terrific ski lodge. I got to know her then. She was engaged to a chap called Dominic, whom I vaguely knew. They got married two years after that trip, and she had a couple of children. Dominic was an orthopaedic surgeon – a nice, uncomplicated sort of guy. I liked him."

Matthew did not like the way the story was going. Nice, uncomplicated orthopaedic surgeons had no part in a story about passions. "What happened?" he asked.

"You're not going to believe this," said Elspeth. "But I promise you, it's true. She met a lion tamer."

Matthew burst out laughing. "I *don't* believe that."

"It's true. She had to go to Honduras for some business reason. She had carried on working, you see. She was an accountant. She had to go to those places from time to time because there are so many companies registered out there. She met a lion tamer in a circus. He was twenty-five. She was just short of thirty. She sent a message back to Scotland, saying that she wasn't coming back. She actually did that. She asked her husband to look after the children. Just like that."

Matthew shook his head. "Poor guy. Poor children."

"She came back, though," said Elspeth. "Six months later."

Matthew waited. Surely not. "The lions—"

"No," said Elspeth. "The lions were innocent as those in that Edward Hicks painting . . ."

Matthew's eyes lit up. "*Peaceable Kingdom*? I love that painting. All the animals clustered together . . . none of them contemplating eating the other."

"Exactly," Elspeth continued. "He fell for a trapeze artist from Panama City. He wasn't the faithful type."

"Swings and roundabouts," said Matthew.

# 19

## *Every Bacon Roll Takes Its Toll*

But now, in Big Lou's, Matthew and Angus joined Bruce at his table while Cyril found a comfortable spot on the floor – one that gave him a good view of Matthew's ankles but that was not so close as to allow temptation to get the better of him. He had once given Matthew a nip under the table and still remembered the retribution visited upon him. There would be no recurrence, but it involved a considerable moral effort on Cyril's part.

Bruce brushed the last crumbs of bacon roll from his lips. "Oh, well," he said. "Another day, another bacon roll . . ."

"Those are definitely not good for you," said Angus. "Every bacon roll you eat takes six minutes and thirty seconds off your life – or something like that. The University of Michigan found that out, apparently."

Bruce grinned. "You'd think they'd have better things to do."

"I don't know," said Angus. "Six and a half minutes may mean nothing to you. But at my stage in life—"

"It would mean much more to Cyril," said Matthew. "What's the multiplier for dogs? Seven? Doesn't one year make seven dog years – or something like that?"

Matthew glanced at Cyril, who looked back at him, wagging his tail briefly in acknowledgement. "Does Cyril know that he's mortal?" he asked.

Bruce laughed. "Cyril doesn't know anything. A dog's

brain is just a sort of switching mechanism. Food. Smells. Run. Bark. That's all there is in there. It's a sort of sophisticated sausage."

From behind her counter, Big Lou overheard this. Bruce was as bad as René Descartes. He thought dogs were just machines. "You've obviously never met a real sheepdog, Bruce," she interjected. "You've seen those dogs? You've seen them working? You haven't, have you?"

Bruce shrugged. "They go where you tell them – sure. But do they know why they're doing it? They don't. Pure conditioned response."

Big Lou muttered something. She disagreed. Bruce was just an ignorant loon. Nothing had changed since the lightning strike. She busied herself pouring coffee for Matthew and Angus.

Angus spoke mildly. "I think you underestimate what dogs feel, Bruce," he said. "They have an intense emotional life. They have feelings – just as we do. They feel sad. They feel elated. They grieve."

Big Lou brought the coffee over to the table. "Angus is right," she said. "Animals grieve. If a chimpanzee loses its child, it may carry it around for some time. Dolphins and whales do the same. They show every sign of sorrow."

Bruce looked sceptical, but said nothing, and Big Lou returned to her counter. Matthew looked at Bruce, and then exchanged a glance with Angus.

"We haven't seen you for a while, Bruce," Matthew said. "How are things?"

"Just fine," said Bruce. "Busy."

Angus took a sip of his coffee. "It's best to be busy. One doesn't want to hang around."

Bruce smiled. "Yup," he said. "And you, Angus? What are you up to? Painting anybody?"

"A straightforward portrait," said Angus. "Nothing special."

Bruce nodded. "You could always do me, you know."

Matthew grinned. "You, Bruce? A portrait of you?"

"Why not?" said Bruce. "Somebody said to me the other day – you should have your portrait painted. I said, 'Well, you've got a point.'"

Matthew stared at Bruce. The old Bruce was back. This was *vintage* Bruce. He wanted to laugh. Matthew was modest to the point of being self-effacing: he found it hard to imagine how anybody could want to have their portrait painted. Why? Why should one want to preserve one's image on canvas? Why should one feel that one was of interest in that way to others? He would be happy to have a portrait of Elspeth, or one of the boys, but that was different. Portraits should be willed by others, not by oneself. Unless you were a narcissist like Bruce – and he *was* a narcissist; he had to be.

Angus was eyeing Bruce over the top of his coffee cup. He was avoiding catching Matthew's eye. "If I painted you, Bruce," he said, "how would you like me to do it?"

"In oils," replied Bruce quickly. "Life size, maybe."

"No," said Angus. "What I meant was: how would you like to be portrayed? In what setting? Doing something, or sitting, or standing perhaps? There are plenty of options."

Bruce looked thoughtful. "I could be outside?"

Angus explained that anything was possible. He had once painted somebody, a keen mountaineer, against a background of Ben Lawers. "He was one of those Munro baggers. He climbed Munro after Munro and so he said that he would like to have Ben Lawers in the background. It worked quite well. He was wearing his climbing kit with those metal clips hanging from his belt – you know those things – what do you call them?"

"Metal clips," said Bruce.

"Yes, metal clips. And a rope. He had a coil of rope at his feet."

Matthew frowned. "You don't want too much in the picture, do you? Some accoutrements are all right, but you don't want to detract too much from the—"

"From the face," interjected Bruce. "You want to get the face."

"Yes," said Angus. "That's important."

"But there's so much more," Bruce said. And then continued, "Could I have my shirt off?"

Matthew's eyes widened. Angus looked embarrassed. He had not agreed to paint this portrait. "Possibly," he said. "If—"

Bruce cut him short. "It's just that I do go to the gym," he said. "And you get results if you go to the gym."

"Results?" Angus muttered.

"Yes," said Bruce. "I don't like to boast, but some people think I don't look too bad with my shirt off. You know how it is."

"I'm sure you look great," said Matthew. "But—"

Bruce was staring at him. "But what? Why should guys be ashamed of how they look? Women aren't. They love telling other women how nice they look. Haven't you noticed? Yet we never say things like that, do we?"

Matthew looked away. Cyril, thinking that Matthew was looking at him, wagged his tail again. The dog's mouth was slightly open and exposed his gold tooth. The problem with narcissists, thought Matthew, was that they had no insight into the effect that their self-obsession had on others. Bruce had no idea – none – that others might feel distaste at his fixation on his appearance. And yet, the point that he made was an interesting one. Many men *were* reluctant to comment on the way other men looked – or even to talk about why they wouldn't talk about it. Taboo, thought Matthew. It was all to do with taboo, and the fear of male intimacy. For many men – most men, perhaps – this was dangerous territory – an area of deep repression. Or was it simple lack of interest, which was not necessarily the same thing?

# 20

## *Livestock Relocation in the Borders*

Nicola was a believer in routine, especially in the lives of children. Since she had begun to assist in the day-to-day care of Bertie and Ulysses, she had taken great care to ensure stability and predictability in their young lives. Bertie had been no problem, of course, as he was a compliant and uncomplaining child. He had survived seven years of Irene, which had made him philosophical about virtually anything that came his way. He had put up with yoga and psychotherapy; he had tolerated endless Italian *conversazione* sessions – his Italian was now fairly good, and he was able to watch the Italian television news bulletins with almost complete comprehension; he had accepted without demur the need to sit quietly while Irene attended her Carl Gustav Jung Association meetings. All of this he had managed without any discernible signs of resentment. In his view, his mother was problematic, but he was confident that he would eventually turn eighteen and would then be able to go and live in Glasgow, where there was no psychotherapy, precious little *conversazione* and, by all accounts, barely detectable incidents of yoga.

He had taken in his stride his mother's departure for Aberdeen. This, he thought, was, on the whole, a good idea, as it would take the pressure off him and would also make her a bit happier. He wanted his mother to be happy and it seemed to him that Aberdeen might be a better place for her to be happy in. He liked his grandmother, and when Nicola moved in to look after him and his brother, he made it clear to her that she was welcome.

"I'm so pleased you're here," he told Nicola. "And Daddy will be pleased too, I think. Mummy never ironed any of his shirts. He always looked so crumpled."

Nicola smiled. "Daddy could have ironed his shirts himself, don't you think, Bertie? Men can do things like that these days."

"Oh, I know that, Granny," said Bertie. "Daddy did all the ironing, though. He ironed Mummy's clothes, you see, and I thought that she might sometimes have ironed his shirts. Not all the time – just sometimes. Mummy said that she would not iron anything. She said that it was a matter of principle."

Nicola suppressed a smile. *A matter of principle...* She had always been astonished by the range of Bertie's vocabulary – and by the reading that he did, even at his tender age. And yet he remained at heart such a wonderful little boy – utterly unspoilt. Bertie, she thought, was a survivor.

Ulysses potentially posed more difficulties for Nicola when she took over. He was unlike Bertie in many respects, not the least of which was his physical appearance. Bertie took after Stuart – strikingly so – whereas Ulysses was – well, there was no point in being coy about it – Ulysses was the image of the psychotherapist with whom Irene had been so friendly. His ears were the same and if you looked at him from the side, there was the same bone structure. She wondered whether Stuart noticed this. He must, she thought – it was so glaringly obvious.

Ulysses had not been an easy baby, but once Irene moved to Aberdeen, he seemed to settle immediately. Now as an infant, and old enough to be enrolled in Neo-Georgian Kids, his behaviour was vastly improved, and although not as amenable as Bertie, he was nonetheless much more settled.

He was showing considerable ability at art and would spend hours drawing highly coloured birds, covering sheet after sheet of paper with his efforts. Neo-Georgian Kids, which was always on the lookout for signs of prodigious talent in its charges, had been delighted by this artistic promise shown by Ulysses, and had even arranged a small exhibition of his work, *A Wee Audubon Comes Amongst Us*, which they mounted in the reception area of the nursery. The press had been invited to attend an opening, at which marshmallows and cupcakes had been served, but they had not come. Nor had anybody else, and the drawings had shortly thereafter fallen off the wall.

The routine that Nicola introduced seemed to suit everybody. Stuart was an early riser, and he was happy to get Ulysses ready for nursery while Nicola prepared Bertie's breakfast and did twenty minutes of reading with him. This was rather different from the more usual reading that parents and grandparents did with their grandchildren. Bertie had already worked his way through Robert Louis Stevenson, and had, in fact, read *Kidnapped* three times. Now they were on Walter Scott, and were halfway through *Rob Roy*.

"Rob Roy was jolly brave, Granny," Bertie observed as he and Nicola travelled to school on the twenty-three bus. "Mummy said that he was nothing more than a cattle thief, but I think that's unfair."

"Everybody stole cattle in those days," said Nicola. "Rob Roy wouldn't have been the only one. There were all those Border Reivers."

"They stole cattle from the English, didn't they?" asked Bertie.

"Yes, they did, Bertie. And I'll tell you something. Do you know that some of your ancestors were reivers? Did Daddy ever tell you that?"

Bertie shook his head.

"It was on my side, you see. I was born down there in the Borders. We had people called Armstrong in our family. They were famous Border Reivers. And we also had Elliot cousins – they were also well-known down there. We used to refer to them as being involved in livestock relocation. That was a polite way of putting it."

Bertie was thrilled. "They must have been very brave, Granny. You had to be brave, I imagine, because there was always the chance that the English would catch you – and give you probation, or a community payback order."

Nicola laughed. "They could be a bit more severe than that, Bertie."

Bertie looked thoughtful. "Ranald's father has a community payback order, you know."

Nicola was intrigued. "Does he now, Bertie?"

'Yes," said Bertie. "Ranald says that his daddy has to do one hundred and fifty hours of Scottish country dancing because of something naughty he did."

Nicola laughed. "Interesting."

"Do you think he stole some cattle, Granny?"

"Unlikely," said Nicola. "I seem to recall that he got into a bit of trouble over some business matter." She paused. "But I don't think we should talk to Ranald about it. The company law offences of the father, you see, should not be visited on the children."

Bertie was silent. Their bus journey was coming to an end. They would soon be getting to the point where they would alight – outside Hughes' fishmongers in Bruntsfield. Thereafter, there would be a short walk down Spylaw Road to school, where Olive, Pansy and others would be lying in wait. Bertie sighed. How much better to have been born a reiver, all those years ago, when one could look forward to hours of excitement as one raided the north of England for what was Scotland's rightful property, or for what would soon become her rightful property.

# 21

## Olive's Book Group

Dropped off by Nicola at the school gate, Bertie cautiously made his way into his classroom. He hoped that Ranald would already be there, and he was, waving to Bertie from his seat near the window. Bertie began to cross the room to join him but was intercepted by Olive, who had been talking to a small knot of girls near the class library shelf.

"Not so fast, Bertie," said Olive. "Don't think you can come in just like that and ignore me."

"I wasn't ignoring you, Olive," said Bertie. "I've just arrived. I was going to put my bag down. That's all."

Olive gave him a knowing smile. "I wasn't born yesterday, Bertie," she said. "You were going to talk to Ranald Braveheart Macpherson, weren't you?"

Bertie glanced across the room at Ranald, who was following proceedings with dismay.

"You see, Bertie," Olive continued, "I know that you're completely dependent on Ranald. It's really sad to see somebody like you in that position. My auntie's a psychiatrist, you know, and I've spoken to her about you."

Bertie frowned. "About me, Olive? Why?"

Pansy now joined Olive, standing beside her leader, while looking challengingly at Bertie.

"I was just telling Bertie about my auntie," Olive explained to Pansy.

Pansy nodded. "Your auntie who looks after mad people?"

"Yes," Olive said sagely. "She's a psychiatrist, Bertie, and she says that she's known plenty of people like you."

Bertie stared at the ground. The school day was barely five minutes old, and he was feeling miserable.

"I told her about how you always seem to want to spend time with Ranald Braveheart Macpherson," Olive continued. "I told her how you don't seem willing to face up to your responsibilities."

Bertie bit his lip. "What responsibilities, Olive?"

Olive sighed. "I really shouldn't have to spell it out, Bertie, but you have certain responsibilities in this life, you know."

"Yes," said Pansy, fixing Bertie with an accusing stare. "You have responsibilities, Bertie, and you just stand there and deny them all the time."

"I don't, Pansy," protested Bertie. "I'm not denying my responsibilities. I promise you."

"Oh, it's very easy to promise things," said Olive. "Promises cost nothing, Bertie. Everybody knows that."

Bertie said nothing. Olive would eventually become distracted by something else, but in the meantime she simply had to be borne.

"Yes," continued Olive. "She – that's my auntie – she says that there are some people who rely on others because there's nothing inside them. She says these people are empty. She says that they live through other people. She says it's really sad."

Pansy nodded her agreement. "Really sad," she said.

"But she says that it's always possible to help people like that," Olive went on. "She says that they can use electric shock treatment. Have you heard about that, Bertie?"

Bertie continued to stare at the ground.

"In case you haven't heard about it, Bertie," said Olive, "I'll tell you about it. They put an electric wire in one ear and then another wire in the other. Then they turn on the power."

"It makes your hair stand on end," said Pansy. "Then when they turn the power off, your hair goes down again."

"They get quite good results," Olive continued. "My grandfather had electric shock treatment when he went all peculiar."

Pansy listened gravely. "There you are, Bertie," she said. "There's always hope, you see."

"But they may not need to do any of that," said Olive. "My auntie says that people can change if they get help from their friends." She gave Bertie a sympathetic look. "That's where Pansy and I come in."

"Yes," said Pansy. "We're here to help you, Bertie."

Bertie glanced around the room. He wondered whether his teacher, Miss Campbell, might come to his aid, but she was busy explaining something to Socrates Dunbar. He was in trouble again, thought Bertie. Why didn't Olive offer to help Socrates, rather than bothering him with all this?

Olive noticed the direction of Bertie's glance. "Yes, Bertie," she said. "Socrates is another person who has lots of issues. But we just don't have the time to help him, do we Pansy? We can't help the whole world, Bertie."

Pansy shook her head. "We can't," she said. "There's only so much you can do."

"So," said Olive, "Pansy and I are inviting you to join our book group. This will help you, Bertie. It will give you an interest. My auntie says that if you have an interest, your mind doesn't dwell on things that are bad for you."

It took Bertie a few moments to absorb this. He knew about book groups. His mother had been in one, and Ranald had told him that his mother was a member of a book group in Morningside. "They drink wine and fight about books," Ranald had said. "It's something that grown-ups like to do."

"I don't think I want to be in a book group," Bertie said,

adding, with his usual politeness, "Thanks all the same, Olive."

"I'm sorry, Bertie," said Olive. "You have to be. I'd never forgive myself if you were not able to get the help you need." She paused. "The next meeting is going to be tomorrow – at morning break. It'll be just you, me, Pansy, Lakshmi and Rose."

"Am I going to be the only boy?" asked Bertie.

"Boys are not normally allowed in book groups. It's the same with adult book groups: the mummies don't like the daddies to spoil them."

"Then maybe . . ." Bertie began.

He was cut short. "We're going to make an exception for you, Bertie," said Olive. "You can start coming tomorrow. We're going to be discussing a book called *Pride and Prejudice*. You may have heard of it."

Bertie had, but told Olive that he had not read it. "So I needn't come after all, Olive."

"You don't have to read it," Olive retorted. "We don't have time to read the books we discuss, do we, Pansy?"

"No," said Pansy. "Nobody will have read *Pride and Prejudice*. It's very long."

"It's all about some girls," said Olive. "These girls live in a house in the country. There are some boys who go to dances with the girls. One of the boys is called Mr Darcy. One of the girls wants to marry him. That's all you need to know, Bertie." She paused. "It's a very good book, Bertie, I can tell you that in advance. But you must make up your own mind, of course."

# 22

*Functionally Illegible*

Released by Olive and Pansy, Bertie made his way across the room to join his friend Ranald Braveheart Macpherson.

"What did Olive and Pansy want?" asked Ranald. "They were waiting for you. I saw them."

"They're making me join their book club," said Bertie.

Ranald drew in his breath. "Did you say no, Bertie?"

Bertie shook his head. "You know what Olive is like, Ranald. It's hard to say anything to her – she doesn't let you, most of the time."

Ranald sighed. "So you have to go to it?"

Bertie looked miserable. "I tried to tell her that I didn't want to join," he said.

"But you still have to?" said Ranald.

"It looks like it," said Bertie.

Ranald wondered whether they would let him join. "I don't think so," said Bertie. He had considered asking Olive whether Ranald could accompany him, but had decided there was no point. He knew what Olive's view of Ranald was, and he saw no point in giving her the opportunity to spell it out again.

"When are they going to have their meeting?" asked Ranald.

Bertie explained that it would be at morning break the following day. Ranald shook his head in dismay at this news. "You won't be able to get away, Bertie," he said. "Even if you tried to run away from school, they'd catch you before you got far. Pansy is one of the fastest runners in the school. Olive would send her after you and she'd get you."

"I know that," said Bertie. There was no way around it: he was defeated.

But Ranald Braveheart Macpherson had an idea. "You know that my dad likes history," he said. "You know that, don't you, Bertie?"

Bertie nodded.

"He was telling me all about the Roman emperors the other day," Ranald continued. "He was telling me about an emperor called Nero. He was a very bad man, my daddy said."

"Lots of them were bad," said Bertie. "They used to throw Christians to the lions. That was really unkind."

"I know," said Ranald. "It was really bad. But my daddy said that Nero was one of the worst. He put his mother in a boat and then deliberately sank it. His mummy had to swim to shore. She was jolly cross."

Bertie listened intently. Mothers could be troublesome, but that was definitely going too far.

Ranald had more to say. "Nero liked to act," he said. "Sometimes he would sing and play his fiddle. He made people come to his concerts. Just like the school play, but once they were in their seats, he locked the theatre doors. They had to stay."

"Even if they needed to go to the bathroom?" asked Bertie.

"Yes," said Ranald. "Nero didn't like people to leave when he was doing a show. And his shows could go on for five hours, my daddy said."

"Jings," said Bertie.

"But you know how you could get out?" Ranald continued. "If you died you were allowed to be carried out."

"I see," said Bertie.

"So, if people didn't like the show, they pretended to die. Then once they were outside, they opened their eyes again."

Bertie laughed. "And Nero never knew? That's a really good trick, Ranald."

"So," said Ranald, "tomorrow you should pretend to have a heart attack, Bertie. Just before break, pretend to have a heart attack. Then they'll call an ambulance to take you off to hospital. Olive won't be able to do a thing."

Bertie's eyes widened. "But won't I get into trouble when I get to the Infirmary, Ranald? Once they find out that I haven't really had a heart attack, won't they be cross with me for wasting their time?"

Ranald shook his head. "They won't be able to tell, Bertie. People often get better from a heart attack. They won't blame you."

Bertie was silent for a moment. "But what do I say, Ranald? How do you pretend to have a heart attack? Have you ever had a heart attack yourself?"

"It's simple," said Ranald. "I saw a film once that had a heart attack in it. A man just said, 'My heart, my heart!' Then he fell over. That's all you have to do."

"But I could hurt myself if I fell over," said Bertie.

"You could just sit down," suggested Ranald. "As long as you remember to say that your heart has stopped beating. If you say that, they'll know it's a heart attack. They won't argue with you."

Later that morning, Bertie hoped he might avoid Olive in the playground – the girls were engaged in an elaborate skipping game – but she cornered him and Ranald Braveheart Macpherson as they were about to go back into the classroom.

"I hope you won't forget about the meeting of the club tomorrow," Olive said, emphasising the word *club* to ensure that Ranald should be in no doubt but that he was excluded.

And then she continued, "Oh, there you are, Ranald Braveheart Macpherson – I almost didn't notice you. I'm so sorry. But I suppose you're used to being missed by people." She passed, and turned back to Bertie. "Remember it's Jane Austen, Bertie. Don't forget that."

Olive looked at Ranald again. "You won't have heard of Jane Austen, Ranald. She was a lady who wrote books. I don't think you will have read them, of course. I imagine you like *The Secret Seven* and that sort of thing. Don't get me wrong: nothing wrong with that, of course."

Bertie came to Ranald's defence. "Ranald has read tons of books, Olive."

Olive looked scornful. "Oh, I don't think so, Bertie. I saw what Miss Campbell had written after Ranald's name in that notebook of hers. She wrote *functionally illiterate*. I'm not saying that myself – that's what Miss Campbell wrote, and she's a teacher, so she knows."

They parted company at the classroom door, as Olive went off to join Pansy. Bertie glanced at Ranald, and he saw that there were tears in his friend's eyes.

"Oh, Ranald," he said. "You mustn't cry."

"I know," said Ranald Braveheart Macpherson, wiping his eyes. "I'll try."

Bertie put an arm around Ranald's shoulder. "I'm your friend, Ranald. You've got me. Remember that."

Ranald nodded. "Thanks, Bertie. It's just that I wish Miss Campbell hadn't written that I was functionally illegible."

"Don't worry," said Bertie. "Teachers write all sorts of things. Nobody pays any attention, Ranald. Everybody knows that."

## 23

*Gleaming White Teeth*

When Matthew arrived home that evening, he was greeted at the kitchen door by one of the triplets, Tobermory, who seized his hand excitedly. Matthew felt the sticky warmth of his son's hand: he had become accustomed to the dirty hands of small boys – that was just how they were, no matter what exhortations were made for the regular use of soap – and he smiled as Tobermory led him into the kitchen. Elspeth was standing at the other side of the room, tipping flour and yeast into her bread-maker. She turned to greet him, just as Tobermory tugged him in the direction of the living-room door.

"Let Mummy say hello to Daddy," she said to Tobermory, dusting her hands on her apron.

"But I want to show Daddy—"

"All in good time, Tobermory," said Elspeth. "Poor Daddy's been hard at work in his gallery and he wants to talk to Mummy."

"But Daddy wants to see—"

Elspeth crossed the room to embrace Matthew. "Don't be too surprised," she whispered. "We have a visitor. Quite unexpected."

Matthew said that he had no idea who it might be.

"You've met him before," said Elspeth. "But please don't make a fuss. The boys are pretty excited."

Matthew was now being tugged again by Tobermory, who

guided him into the living room. Once there, he looked about for the surprise that he believed was waiting for him. At first, he saw nothing unusual; then he spotted the dog lying on the rug in front of the fireplace. For a moment or two he was confused – had Elspeth bought a dog without telling him? – but then he recognised Ralph, the dog he had encountered when he visited the new neighbours.

Elspeth had abandoned her bread-making and was now standing behind Matthew as he stared at the unexpected visitor. "He pitched up uninvited," she said. "He's been here for hours."

Matthew crossed the room to stand directly above Ralph. The dog looked up at him with dark, liquid eyes. As he did so, his tail thumped against the floor several times – a languid greeting in canine body language. In so far as a dog's face might reveal emotion, Ralph was clearly pleased to be where he was. He was feeling gratitude, even if he seemed tired – or was it replete?

Matthew bent down to pat Ralph on the head. This brought a further wagging of the tail and what appeared to be the beginnings of a grin. Gleaming white teeth appeared briefly against black gums before the mouth was closed once more.

Matthew straightened out. He looked back at Elspeth. "He seems pleased with himself, but we'll have to take him back. They'll be wondering where he is."

Elspeth looked concerned. "I tried to get him out of the house, but he resisted."

"Resisted?"

"He dug in. He sat on his haunches, his front paws straight out in front of him. His whole poise said: *I'm not shifting.* And . . ."

She broke off. Matthew waited.

"And then," Elspeth continued, "he came into the kitchen. He hung around the fridge, and whenever I opened it, he would stare into it and then look at me imploringly. He could not have made things clearer had he opened his mouth and spoken intelligible English. Or Scots, I suppose. He might speak Scots for all we know."

Matthew smiled. "And said?" he asked.

"I'm hungry," replied Elspeth. "That's all. I'm hungry."

Matthew thought for a moment. Dogs were always hungry; it was part of the condition of being a dog. He said, "No surprises there."

"No," said Elspeth. "But I think that with Ralph there was something more to it. I think the poor creature was really, really hungry. Famished."

Matthew frowned. "Don't they feed him back there?" He nodded in the direction of the neighbours' house, separated by a wide field and a small stand of Scots pine.

"They're either not feeding him or they're giving him food he doesn't like."

Matthew considered this for a few moments. Then it occurred to him: Robert and Maureen had been at pains to impress him with their green credentials. Matthew did not object to that – in principle, he was in favour of green causes – he did not like waste or conspicuous consumption; he believed in recycling; he knew we had to act on climate change. But the tone in which their new neighbours had expressed their views – in a distinctly challenging, aggressive way – had irritated him. It seemed to him that they wanted him to feel guilty about not being vegan, about not even being vegetarian. In his view, that was a matter for him. He saw the arguments in favour of both those positions, but he did not subscribe to them – at least not at present, in his personal life – and he felt that his position should be respected, just as he respected theirs. If you should not impose carnivorism on others, then, by the same token, you should not impose vegetarianism or veganism on them. That is what he thought, and now it occurred to him that Robert and Maureen might be requiring Ralph to have a diet that no dog would choose, if given the chance. Dogs were carnivorous; we might not like that aspect of their character, but it was a fact of life that would never be changed. Dogs ate meat, just as cows ate grass. There was no point in denying this inescapable fact.

Matthew gave Elspeth a quizzical look. "Can dogs survive on a vegetarian or vegan diet?"

He was surprised to find that Elspeth had anticipated his question. "I happen to have looked that up today," she said. "We're obviously thinking of the same possibility."

"Well, can they?" asked Matthew.

"Apparently, they can," Elspeth replied. "You have to present it in the right way, but they can get everything they need from a plant-based diet. I looked at some recipes, in fact."

Matthew raised an eyebrow. "Such as?"

"Black-eyed bean stew with tofu," said Elspeth. "That was one."

Matthew was not convinced. "If I were a dog—" he began.

Elspeth smiled. "You can't imagine how a dog would think. It's impossible."

"But we can tell what they like," countered Matthew. "And one of the things that I think a dog wouldn't like is black-bean stew with tofu."

"Possibly," said Elspeth.

And at this point, Ralph opened a sleepy eye, looked at them and wagged his tail weakly.

"He agrees," said Elspeth.

"Possibly," said Matthew.

# 24

## *Dogs and Sausages*

"There's more," said Elspeth, a note of apology creeping into her voice. "Quite a bit more."

Matthew was about to ask for clarification, but it was Tobermory who spoke next. "Mummy gave Ralph sausages," he said, his high voice rising in response to the drama of the narrative. "Hundreds. He loved them. You should have seen him, Daddy. He ate all our sausages."

Elspeth smiled at the small boy. "Not exactly hundreds, darling," she said. And then, to Matthew, "Actually, he ate a full dozen. Those big ones I got from Anna at Baddinsgill. She made them for us from their own beef."

Matthew's first reaction was one of regret. He loved those sausages – a local product that a nearby farm occasionally made for friends. "*All* the sausages?" he asked.

"I'm afraid so," said Elspeth. "I started off by giving him only one, but then the look in his eyes was so intense, I just had to give in."

"You should have seen him, Daddy," contributed Tobermory. "He gobbled them down."

Matthew peered down at Ralph. The dog's stomach was definitely distended, he thought. A dozen large sausages . . .

"Then he came through here," said Elspeth. "And he's been sleeping ever since."

Matthew sighed. "I suppose he'd never had a sausage before. He must have imagined he was in heaven." That must be what canine heaven is like, he thought: Elysian fields of sausages.

"It's so unkind," said Elspeth. "One shouldn't force one's views on an animal. He clearly prefers sausages to tofu, or whatever they feed him on."

"Obviously," said Matthew. He did not begrudge Ralph his treat, but at the same time he could not be allowed to stay. You could not simply take over another person's dog just because you disapproved of the regime under which he lived.

"Can he live with us?" asked Tobermory. "Then he could have sausages every day. He'd be very happy, I think."

Matthew shook his head. "Tobermory, Ralph is somebody's property," he said. "We can't just let him move in with us. That would be stealing, I'm afraid."

Elspeth looked down at Ralph. "Poor creature," she said. "He was voting with his feet. I think he'd had enough."

"That's as may be," said Matthew. "But I don't think we can do anything about it."

"We could report them," said Elspeth. "For cruelty to animals."

"Report them to whom?" asked Matthew. And then, before Elspeth could answer, he continued, "That would be a great start with our new neighbours, don't you think? Calling the police . . ." He paused. Where were the police? They were so hard-pressed that they had no time to do anything very much – about anything.

Elspeth was not dissuaded. "We could get in touch with the SSPCA," she suggested. "They deal with animal welfare. They have inspectors – with legal powers, remember. They can get a warrant to go into people's homes. There was a radio programme about it." She paused. "And you can report animal cruelty anonymously. They have a helpline for that."

Matthew winced. "And who would Robert and Maureen

suspect had shopped them? They probably don't know anybody else around here yet, and I may have been the only person to have seen Ralph – as far as they know. It wouldn't be a good start."

Elspeth looked away. "I feel very bad about it all. I've given him a glimpse of an alternative to black-bean stew with tofu." She remembered something. "My grandad used to sing that song."

"What song?" asked Matthew.

"It was about American servicemen seeing Europe in the Second World War and then not wanting to go back to their former life. *How ya gonna keep 'em down on the farm after they've seen Paree* . . . Same thing, I think. He's tasted sausage. He won't want to go back to his vegan diet."

Matthew became purposeful. "I'll take him back," he said. "We really can't keep him."

"Don't take him away, Daddy," pleaded Tobermory. "Please let him stay."

Matthew shook his head. "Every dog has a home, Tobermory. This dog's home is next door."

Tobermory pouted, and then, quite suddenly, started to sob. Elspeth gave Matthew a reproachful look and then bent down to comfort the stricken child. Gently she led him back towards the door. "Bath time," she whispered. "Then a story. Two stories, if you're good. Let's go and get Fergus and Rognvald."

Tobermory did not look back, and Matthew was now alone with Ralph. The dog watched him through a half-open eye. Matthew thought: every act of exclusion is just as hard as this – probably harder. Dogs are not allowed to live where they choose – and neither, when it comes down to it, are people. People are excluded because there simply is not enough room for everybody to live where they would wish to live. It was hard, but that was the way of the world. And yet, who amongst us would not feel that when it came to *us*, it was different. Who amongst us would say that we would not try to find safe haven for ourselves, once the need arose?

He bent down to awaken Ralph. He put a hand on his flank, and then moved to the dog's collar. He pulled on this gently, causing Ralph to move his head and look at him with injured surprise.

"Come on now," said Matthew. "Time to go home, Ralph."

Ralph moved his head so that he could lick Matthew's hand. He made a slight whimpering sound. He clearly did not want to move.

"But you have to, old fellow," said Matthew. "Dogs must obey, Ralph. That's the way things are."

Ralph looked at Matthew. In his view, humans were restless and unpredictable creatures. They should have been so happy, knowing all that they did, and having such limitless supplies of everything, but for some reason they weren't. Dogs noticed that; they understood human unhappiness because they witnessed it, but they were powerless to stop it, and that distressed them. But they had no idea how to get through to these sophisticated primates amongst whom they lived. There was great friendship between the two species, for dogs had kept to their side of that ancient bargain, concluded by those early firesides. But there were great chasms of misunderstanding and perplexity as well. Dogs knew that there were many circumstances in which they could do little to lighten humanity's burden. They did their best, but it was hard work, and often man made it no easier for himself.

# 25

### *All the Sadness of Being a Dog*

Perhaps it was the sterner voice that Matthew employed – Elspeth might have urged Ralph, rather than ordered him – perhaps it was because dogs could tell the difference between suggestions that could be ignored and instructions that could not; perhaps this was why Ralph responded to Matthew's insistence that he should get up off his comfortable rug and follow him out into the night. But he did, and Matthew soon found himself leading the dog back across the nearby field and through the small clump of Scots pine that separated them from their neighbours' property. In the summer evening, there was no covering darkness, and he was careful to make use of the protection afforded by what vegetation there was. Had Robert or Maureen looked out of their kitchen window, they might have seen him, but his approach was to the rear of the building, and he thought he was unlikely to be spotted. Of course, if they did see him, he could merely explain what he was doing, after he had strayed into their garden. That was simple enough, but there was no doubt that Ralph looked like a dog that had just eaten twelve large sausages, and they might notice that and be suspicious.

As they approached the house, Matthew bent down to crouch beside Ralph in order to give him his final instructions.

"There," he said firmly, pointing to the house. "Home, boy."

Even as he said it, Matthew was aware of the clichéd nature

of the command. *Home, boy*, it seemed to him, came straight from a Lassie film: the urgent invocation *Lassie, get help!* had resolved so many tricky situations. But did people actually say *Home, boy* to their dogs?

Ralph looked up at Matthew. Neither Robert nor Maureen had given him much training, and the only words he understood were *sit* and *carrots*, the latter being used when he was rewarded with a carrot for some instance of good behaviour. For want of anything better, he would eat the carrot, but not with any more enthusiasm than he would sit when told to do so; you had to eat *something*, and if carrots were all that was available, you ate them. Now, he looked puzzled. He sat down.

"Don't sit down," hissed Matthew. "Go home."

Ralph was distracted by an itch that required him to scratch behind his left ear with a back paw. Then he looked back at Matthew, with the air of a soldier waiting for a superior officer to issue a command. There were things to be done, perhaps, but Ralph was not sure what they were. He was not a stupid dog, but then again he was not a particularly intelligent dog, and he had no idea of what he was meant to do. The safest thing, he decided, was to lie down, which he now did. After all, he still felt very pleasantly replete, and in so far as he had any urges at the time, to lie down and get a bit of sleep was perhaps the most pressing one.

Matthew bent down to pull Ralph to his feet. As he did so, he noticed a small plate attached to his collar. On it was inscribed a simple message: *vegan diet*. Seeing this filled him with dread. This was obviously an issue: people must have fed Ralph with illicit treats before, and the message on the collar was a request, or a warning, not to do so. So, he was right: if Robert and Maureen were to find out that Ralph had been entertained with sausages, there would be some explaining to do. Matthew had already decided that relations with this particular set of neighbours were going to be difficult enough, without any additional complication resulting from unauthorised intervention in the regime under which their dog lived.

Matthew's aim now was simply to get Ralph into close proximity to the house and then abandon him there, perhaps even tying him to something. He had brought with him a length of cord to do that, should it be necessary to resort to such a measure. Presumably Ralph would bark or whine, and that would notify his owners of his presence outside. By that time, of course, Matthew would have had the opportunity to disappear back into the trees.

Matthew stopped to think. This was completely ridiculous. Here he was, a grown man, a father of three, the owner of a prominent gallery, a paid-up member of the Liberal Democrat party, creeping about on somebody else's property, trying to avoid being spotted. How absurd: this was the stuff of fantasy, the sort of thing one read about in formulaic thrillers. He should simply walk up to the neighbours' front door, ring the bell, and present them with their dog. He should tell them that Ralph had strayed onto his property and that Elspeth had fed him a couple of sausages (there was no need to say a dozen) because he had seemed so hungry. No, she had not seen a sign on his collar. Was there a sign on his collar? My goodness, so there was – how unfortunate. That last bit would involve a certain dissemblance, but the rest was, for the most part, honest enough.

He almost stepped forward, determined to do what reason required, but then stopped. He was not sure that Robert and Maureen would be reasonable – he had found their manner rather confrontational on his earlier visit, and this suggested that the consumption of the sausages could trigger real conflict.

It would be safer, he decided, to stick to his original plan.

Taking advantage of cover provided by a large clump of gorse, Matthew managed to get fairly close to the back of the house. There he found a convenient post – a support for a drooping laundry line – and it was to this that he now tied one end of the rope, fixing the other to the *vegan diet* collar. Ralph was compliant. He was full of sausages and had no current argument with the world. Most dogs are accepting of what happens to them. They are perfect examples in the natural order of instinctive stoicism. If Chrysippus and Epictetus had kept familiars, thought Matthew, then those must have been dogs.

He muttered goodbye to Ralph, who looked up at him reproachfully. There was unarticulated longing in his eyes, Matthew felt. This was a dog who was unhappy in his little heart, he thought, no matter how stoic his soul. This was a dog who wanted to be authentically canine. In that respect, this was an existentialist dog.

"Stay!" whispered Matthew, in as commanding a tone as he could manage.

Ralph stared at him. Then he threw back his head, closed his eyes, and uttered the most heart-rending howl. It reached, it seemed to Matthew, to the sky above, to the Pentland slopes behind them, to the shores of the North Sea in the distance. In it was all the sadness of being a dog.

Matthew turned on his heels and ran; like the boy that was still within him, he ran wildly back towards the trees, scraping his knee painfully as he clambered over a low drystone dyke. Behind him he heard a commotion, but he did not turn to find out what it was.

# 26

*A Member of Muirfield*

Immediately after his meeting with Matthew and Bruce in Big Lou's that morning, Angus decided to make his way back to Scotland Street by a circuitous route. Cyril had been patient in the coffee bar, lying uncomplainingly at Angus's feet, only occasionally opening an eye to glance at the embodied temptation that were Matthew's ankles – and resisting it. Now Angus thought he would reward this good behaviour by giving him an extended walk along the gardens side of Heriot Row and then doubling back along Abercrombie Place. That would eventually take them down the steep brae of Dublin Street to Drummond Place, and then home.

It was a fine morning, and there were others about whose agenda was similar – people who might appear to be walking purposively, but who really had nowhere special to go and were simply enjoying being out and about under a benign sky. The weather could change in an instant – anybody who spent any time in Edinburgh would soon make that discovery: clouds could sweep in from the south-west, winds could knife in off the North Sea – anything could happen within minutes at the whim of the dyspeptic weather gods allocated to Scotland. Residents of Edinburgh knew this, and would seize the opportunity just to be outside, for the slightest reason, or none, if they had the chance.

Cyril enjoyed his walk, sniffing the air for information of interest to dogs, occasionally pausing to interpret the complicated olfactory messages left at the base of street lamps, but, like Angus, not bothering too much about anything in particular. From time to time, Angus would stop to exchange a few words with some friend or acquaintance. They met the postman pushing his red trolley of letters, and there was a brief conversation about the fortunes of Hearts football club. Angus knew nothing about football – he preferred rugby – but he always asked after Hearts, as one might politely enquire as to the health of a delicate relative. Cyril stood politely by until the walk resumed.

It was halfway down Dublin Street that Angus spotted Sister Maria-Fiore dei Fiori di Montagna. In fact, it was Cyril who saw her first, and alerted Angus by pulling on the lead towards the other side of the street. Angus hesitated; he would normally have crossed over to have a word with her, but something stopped him. They were walking in the same direction, but Sister Maria-Fiore was considerably ahead of him, and was apparently unaware of his presence. She was also walking rather fast, with the air of one on a mission, and that interested him. Sister Maria-Fiore usually *floated* about, as might one whose purpose was somehow on a higher plane than that of others. Now there could be no mistaking the fact that she had something important to do.

Angus glanced at his watch. A canvas awaited him in his studio, but it was nothing urgent: a portrait that seemed to be painting itself without presenting any technical challenges. The sitter had been to his studio four times already, and Angus had only a few final touches to add. These could wait. In fact, he was tempted to take the day off altogether, and to suggest to Domenica that they go out for lunch together at Valvona & Crolla, or possibly even go for a walk on Craiglockhart Hill if the good weather held. But what was Sister Maria-Fiore up to? There was something furtive about her manner

– detectable, he thought, even at this distance, from further up the street. He remembered that the last time he saw her had been in Drummond Place Gardens, when she had suddenly appeared, without explanation, from one of the bushes.

Angus decided that he would slow down, putting more distance between himself and the nun, and then, if he continued undetected, he and Cyril would follow her for a while, just to see what she was up to. And she *was* up to something, he decided. Sister Maria-Fiore had been up to something since her first arrival in Scotland some years earlier. She had come to Edinburgh as a result of her meeting in Italy with their former immediate neighbour, Antonia Collie. Antonia had told them all about that – how Sister Maria-Fiore and her fellow nuns had looked after her in their house in the Tuscan countryside when she was recovering from the unfortunate bout of Stendhal Syndrome that had come over her in the Uffizi Gallery. Later, Sister Maria-Fiore had come to Edinburgh and, to the astonishment of Angus and Domenica, and of many others, had rapidly become a social success.

Of course, there had been little competition. Edinburgh is not an easy city for the average outsider: persistence is required on the part of anybody interested in penetrating the various cliques that dominate its social landscape. As in any city, there are hidden shoals of local memory and attendant shibboleths. And behind all that lay an informal ideology of slight disapproval. "Yes, but . . ." expressed Edinburgh's reservations; or "That may well be, but . . ." Sister Maria-Fiore, though, with her exotic background, had no rivals with whom to contend. She was an Italian nun, and there were no other Italian nuns, indeed no other nuns of any description, beating at the door of the city's establishment. As a result, her rise had been meteoric.

It was not long before Sister Maria-Fiore dei Fiori di

Montagna became a regular attendee at receptions in the City Chambers. She danced away the night at Prestonfield House, and was pictured in Eightsomes, Dashing White Sergeants and Gay Gordons on the 'Social Scotland' page in *Scottish Field*, and in the columns of *Edinburgh Life*. Abandoning the black and white cloth of her order, she now sported an elegant tartan habit, unique in the history of conventual garb.

She was seen at every exhibition opening, peering at the paintings, glass of wine in hand. She attended the opening of parliamentary sessions at Holyrood. She was at the national day celebrations of every consulate-general, rubbing shoulders with the consular corps and their hangers-on. She had been made an Honorary Watsonian, a status never before conferred on anybody. She was an honorary patron of both Scottish Opera and the Royal Scottish Museum. She was appointed a trustee of the National Galleries of Scotland and was a lively presence at the chairman's annual dinner. She was everywhere.

And now, as Angus had recently heard, she had been elected a member of the Honourable Company of Edinburgh Golfers. Sister Maria-Fiore dei Fiori di Montagna was at the famous Muirfield golf club near Gullane. There was no higher peak to scale, with or without oxygen.

# 27

## *Ibi Sumus*

Discreetly lingering behind a parked car, Angus watched as Sister Maria-Fiore dei Fiori di Montagna reached the point where Dublin Street resolved into the cambered sweep of Drummond Place. The flat that she shared with Antonia Collie was in Drummond Place, but on the far, north-east side of it. That meant that if she were to go directly home, she would have to turn to her right. But Sister Maria-Fiore did not do that, and headed off to the left, to the junction of Drummond Place and Great King Street. So she did have a mission, Angus thought.

Now, even more than before, he was determined to find out what this mysterious nun was up to. If she went into a house, or into a common stair, he would note it down and work out whom she might have been visiting. He did not need to know this, of course, but it would satisfy his curiosity to find out. He and Domenica enjoyed talking about Sister Maria-Fiore – an exotic presence in their lives – and it would be good to have more grist for their conversational mill. Remarking on what other people were doing, Angus thought, even if what they were up to was of no particular interest, was one of the civilised pleasures of life.

He almost missed her manoeuvre. Drawing level with one of the gates into the gardens, Sister Maria-Fiore looked over her shoulder briefly – she did not spot Angus – and extracted a key from somewhere within the folds of her voluminous tartan habit. These garden keys, allocated only to residents on a geographical and, in a few controversial cases, historical basis, were a matter of intense local controversy. There were those who lived in sight of the various New Town gardens, but found their address was just outside the boundaries set out in the original title deeds. Generosity of spirit might have prevailed, and the residents of Cumberland Street, for example, might have been allowed to walk in the gardens, and even sit on the benches – only for a short time; say, ten minutes or so each day – but no, rules were rules, and there were steel-willed committee members to enforce them. That those who lived at the end of Cumberland Street had only to turn a corner and walk a few steps up Dundonald Street to reach Drummond Place was no grounds for any entitlement to use the gardens. Views are, in general, free – but not *close* views.

And a key could not be left to another in a will, as has been tried several times. In litigation, the courts had made this quite clear, saying that you could not bequeath property that did not belong to you. A testator might leave a legatee the Scott Monument, no less, but that would obviously be of no effect. Keys remained the property of the committee and should be returned upon the death of the temporary holder. The law of Scotland was clear on that point. But that, of course, was of no relevance to Sister Maria-Fiore dei Fiori di Montagna: Antonia Collie, hagiographer of the early Scottish saints, graduate of St Andrews and Glasgow universities, was a key-holder by dint of her ownership of a flat in Drummond Place itself, close to the house once occupied by Compton Mackenzie, author of *Whisky Galore* and sometime president of the Siamese Cat Club of Great Britain. Nobody could challenge *her* right to a key, and nobody would dare to question her entitlement to make the key available to her flatmate and close friend, Sister Maria-Fiore.

And so here was the nun slipping into the gardens, after a furtive look over her shoulder. Interesting, thought Angus, as he deliberately slowed down. At ground level, Cyril sensed that something was afoot, and raised his head to sniff at the air. But Angus whispered that he should be quiet and stay where he was, and Cyril obeyed.

Sister Maria-Fiore made her way swiftly down the path that led to the east end of the gardens. She was a blur of tartan amidst the greenery; now visible in a small glade, now concealed by a flowering shrub. Suddenly she stopped, fortunately in a spot where Angus could see her from his vantage point on the other side of the railings. She hesitated briefly, and then, bent double, scurried into the low foliage of a large rhododendron bush. Now he was able to make out what Sister Maria-Fiore was doing under the low branches of the rhododendron. A piece of stone, roughly the size of a shoebox, lay on the ground before the nun. She now appeared to be dusting this off, before extracting some sort of bag from her habit. She then picked up the stone, with some effort, and deposited it in the bag. The bag was then covered with leaves and twigs from the ground, and Sister Maria Fiore, crouching down, emerged from the foliage.

Angus quickly resumed his walk. Sister Maria-Fiore might see him at any point, he realised, and he wanted to avoid that. He had clearly witnessed something that was not intended for any other eyes, and he wanted time to try to work out what it was. A nun under a rhododendron bush? A mysterious piece of stone? There was no explanation that made the slightest sense.

He reached a quick decision. He would go into the gardens himself, on the pretext of walking Cyril, and would engage

Sister Maria-Fiore in conversation. It was possible that there was an entirely innocent explanation for all this, and she might volunteer it if he engaged her in conversation.

When they saw one another, Angus affected surprise. "Well, Sister Maria-Fiore dei Fiori di Montagna, imagine seeing you here in the gardens! And on such a fine day."

If Sister Maria-Fiore felt any surprise, she did not show it. "Dear *ritrattista*," she said, beaming as she spoke, "it is on days such as this that one remembers the Lord's beneficence in conferring these gardens on his humble creatures."

At least on such of his humble creatures as live in the Georgian New Town, thought Angus; there were others for whom the Lord's beneficence was more limited. All he said, though, was, "*Ibi sumus*," a literal, and incorrect, Latin translation of "there we are".

"*Ibi sumus*, indeed," said Sister Maria-Fiore, and then added, "Would you care to sit down on this bench with me? We can talk more comfortably if we are seated, I believe."

Angus smiled. "There is so much to talk about," he said.

Sister Maria-Fiore dei Fiori di Montagna inclined her head in agreement. "There are so many issues for humanity to debate," she said.

"And fight over," added Angus.

She turned to him. "My dear *dottore*," she said, "you must never give up. Discord exists, but it need not be our inevitable fare. There is also harmony and concord. Both of these are about us all the time – if only we open our eyes to them." She paused. "That which we do not see may exist without being seen."

Yes, Angus thought, that may well be, but what were you doing under that rhododendron bush?

# 28

## *Such Dear Souls, the Committee*

As Sister Maria-Fiore dei Fiori di Montagna and Angus sat down on their bench in the Drummond Place Gardens, a slight breeze in the trees moved the branches directly above their heads. A leaf, loosened by this, fluttered groundward, landing on the recently swept path.

"Our days," said Sister Maria-Fiore, "are but as leaves. They fall and lie forgotten on the ground. They cannot return to the branches from which they have fallen."

Angus frowned. Sister Maria-Fiore was known for her aphorisms – and they were never in short supply. But when one began to look at them carefully, when one took them to pieces and examined them, phrase by phrase, they were, as often as not, trite to the point of banality. And yet they were delivered with such assurance that rather than attract scepticism or sheer rejection, they were received with nods of approval and sighs of agreement. This was an example, he thought. Of course, leaves could not be returned to the tree once they had fallen. Nobody denied that, and yet Sister Maria-Fiore seemed to think that the proposition needed to be stated. And people, it appeared, were prepared to take her on her own evaluation, to marvel at her pithy observations, and then to confer on her every position of any consequence in Edinburgh, including, astonishingly enough, membership of Muirfield. Could she even play golf? he wondered.

"I hear," he said, "that you have been made a member of

Muirfield. I must congratulate you. I know scores of people who would love to be members there, but can't face those long years on the waiting list."

"Such dear souls, the committee," said Sister Maria-Fiore. "I hadn't thought of joining a club, but—"

Angus interrupted her. "You didn't apply? *They* asked *you*?"

Sister Maria-Fiore inclined her head. "They were most insistent," she said.

Angus struggled with this information. He imagined a delegation of senior Muirfield figures standing in a long line in Drummond Place, waiting for the chance to beg Sister Maria-Fiore to join their golf club.

"I didn't know you played golf," said Angus, trying to conceal his jealousy. Nobody had ever asked *him* to join Muirfield; indeed, as far as he could remember, nobody had ever asked him to join anything. Why should so many people beat a path to Sister Maria-Fiore's door? Was it because she was an Italian nun, and therefore a *rara avis* in these latitudes? Or was it because she exerted some sort of charismatic power over people?

"Golf?" asked Sister Maria-Fiore. "I don't see what golf has to do with it."

Angus looked at her with incredulity. "Muirfield is a golf club."

Sister-Maria Fiore looked at him with incomprehension. "Is it really? I thought it was a restaurant. How strange." She paused. "Of course, I noticed quite a few golf paintings on the wall, and there were bags with clubs left lying around, but I thought they were the property of people going off to play at Luffness, on the other side of Gullane."

Angus struggled to conceal his amusement. "You might have noticed that there was a golf course in front of the clubhouse. You might have seen the bunkers." He paused. Sister Maria-Fiore was looking confused. "Bunkers are sand traps," he explained. "You don't want to get your ball into them."

Sister Maria-Fiore looked thoughtful. "I thought they were flower beds," she said.

"Well, they aren't," said Angus. "And yes, Muirfield is a golf club – a very distinguished one." It was astonishing: Sister Maria-Fiore had been made a member of Muirfield without being able to play golf at all. This was delicious. If word got out that there was a new member of the prestigious golf club who did not have the first clue about the game, the committee would be a laughing stock. That would not be welcome, as Muirfield had only recently taken the decision to admit women members. Perhaps, thought Angus, the election to membership of an Italian nun would be a convincing signal that Muirfield was now committed to diversity, the next step on that progressive road being the admission of bad golfers or, as in the case of Sister Maria-Fiore, of people who could not play the game at all.

He looked at Sister Maria-Fiore and smiled. "You should try to play some time," he said. "You might surprise yourself. You might be rather good."

She gave a modest laugh. "Not me, dear Angus. I lack the co-ordination required." She looked thoughtful. "Of course, sportsmen – and sportswomen, too – have their patron saints to help them. Did you know that there is a patron saint for lacrosse players? St Jean de Brébeuf. I have a particular devotion to him, I must admit, because he put up with so much. He was a great friend of the Huron people in Canada. He learned their frightfully difficult language and was much concerned with their welfare. Then the Iroquois, bless them nonetheless, got hold of him and subjected him to the most appalling tortures. He survived everything – baptism with boiling water, having his nose twisted three hundred and sixty degrees and so on, *che Dio mi protegga*! But then they removed his stout and loyal heart from his body for culinary purposes. Nobody can survive that, I'm afraid."

"But why lacrosse?" asked Angus.

"No idea," said Sister Maria-Fiore. "But you do know, don't you, that St Andrew is the patron saint of golfers?"

"I can see why," said Angus. "St Andrews being the spiritual home of golf—"

"Indeed," said Sister Maria-Fiore. "Relics, you see. There are things that are of very great importance to us. They may seem ordinary, but they mean so much." She paused. "Such as the Stone of Scone."

Angus frowned. He wondered why she should suddenly have mentioned the Stone of Scone, the stone upon which the throne of England had perched since it was stolen from Scotland by Edward I. Then he thought: *stone*.

Angus stared at Sister Maria-Fiore. This was impossible. Surely not. And yet when it came to Sister Maria-Fiore dei Fiori di Montagna, nothing would surprise him. Could it be that she had somehow got hold of a piece of the Stone of Destiny? The Stone had been stolen back from the English by some spirited Glasgow students all those years ago, and there were persistent rumours that part of it, at least, had never been recovered. What if Sister Maria-Fiore had somehow got hold of one of these pieces, and was hiding it in Drummond Place Gardens? It seemed unlikely, but the whole point about Sister Maria-Fiore dei Fiori di Montagna was that she *was* unlikely – deeply so.

Angus fixed Sister Maria-Fiore with a conspiratorial stare. "Are you trying to tell me something?" he asked, his voice lowered.

Her reply was barely audible. "Yes," she whispered, looking over her shoulder as she spoke.

Angus muttered, "Edward the First – ghastly man."

"*Precisamente*," said Sister Maria-Fiore dei Fiori di Montagna.

# 29

## *Book Learning Makes Your Heid Sore*

In the far northern harbour town of Peterhead, a place not only girt by the cold waves of the North Sea but also buffeted by icy blasts from Norway and the Siberian steppe; a town that nonetheless puts on a brave face and calls its beach a lido; a town in which the figures for the annual catch of pelagic fish are the subject of intense debate in its draughty bars and cafés; in such a place Irene Pollock had now settled – part time, of course, as she still felt it her duty to visit Edinburgh regularly and play a role in the life of her two sons. (*Pair wee bairns*, people whispered. *Deserted by that mither of theirs, shameless Jezebel that she is* . . .) Not that Irene heard or cared about that sort of comment. She had found a new identity for herself, and she was content, which was more than could be said of those whisperers.

"It's important," as Irene once observed to Hugo Fairbairn, "that one has more than one dimension to one's life. I feel so sorry for people who have just one plane on which their life is experienced, Hugissimo – don't you?"

Professor Fairbairn, as he was more normally addressed, struggled to ignore the soubriquet. He was irritated by people who played with the names of their friends; Irene insisted on doing this with his own name – what was wrong with Hugo, after all? And why did he have to be promoted – with clear irony – by a superlative form that was normally the metonymous preserve of military dictators? There was a presumption, in his mind, that anybody who called himself *generalissimo* belonged in the *DSM-5*, the American Psychiatric Association's *Diagnostic and Statistical Manual of Mental Disorders*, used by psychiatrists everywhere to identify and classify the various unhappiness of their patients. A *generalissimo* would almost certainly fit the criteria for one of the personality disorders – possibly of the narcissistic variety.

"Not Hugissimo, *carissimo*," he muttered.

Irene affected surprise. "But I mean that as a compliment," she insisted. "Still, if people don't like an affectionate name, one should not persist."

"Just call me Hugo. That's enough."

"Well, Hugo," said Irene, "the point I was trying to make is that we can have more than one identity. People talk about wearing more than one hat. And I think that's something to which we should all aspire. Life is far richer if one is multifaceted."

Hugo looked away. One Irene was quite enough, he thought. He was fond of her and they were . . . well, he should be honest with himself and admit it: they were lovers – or had been, until they had drifted apart emotionally. Now she had found that fisherman and had entered what he considered to be her D. H. Lawrentian phase, it was all different. He was actually rather relieved: Irene was *intense*, and if the fisherman distracted her, then that made his own position easier. He would continue to see her in order to supervise her research, but he would no longer feel so involved with her. It was a pleasant form of bachelorhood, he decided, and he would make the most of it.

Irene's fisherman was the skipper of the fishing boat, the *Aberdeen Belle*, that had rescued her from the sea off Aberdeen beach after she had been swept out by an unexpectedly strong current. Fortunately, she had been spotted, and hauled out of the water and onto the deck by Graham, the skipper, and his shipmate, Doddie. They had taken her back to their home port, where she had been given dry clothing by Graham's mother, the matriarch of a sprawling Peterhead family. Irene found that she fitted in rather well, and was particularly appreciated for her hitherto unused ability to fillet fish. Within a short time, she found herself irresistibly attracted to Graham, and he, in his way, felt the same way about Irene. Chance, they both felt, had brought them together, and there was a point at which one should simply allow the tides of fate to lead them where they would. Besides, Irene had always wanted a strong, silent man, and Graham, who usually only spoke when spoken to, and who was known to lift two large boxes of fish without turning a hair, satisfied both of these criteria.

Rather to her surprise, Irene found herself intrigued by the wider family with which she was becoming involved. Firstly, there was Graham's mother, Ellie Mackie, née Scroggie. She had long been campaigning, sometimes unsubtly, for Graham to find a partner, and Irene, it seemed to her, was a gift from heaven, or at least from the sea. Any woman would have done for her son – so desperate was Ellie to see him settled – but to have one from Edinburgh, with all the cachet that involved, *and* one who was so good at filleting fish . . . well, that amounted to a clear overflowing of the cup.

Ellie herself had never been to Edinburgh, although she had visited Perth and Dundee, and had, as a young woman, spent four months in Glasgow, staying with a distant relative. She had seen pictures of Edinburgh, though, and had thought it a fine place that one day she might visit if she had the time. "The thing about Edinburgh," her aged aunt had once told her, "is that it gives Scotland a bit of tone. There are other places that let the side down a bit, but Edinburgh more than makes up for it. Folk take one look at Edinburgh, Ellie, and they start watching their manners. You can see it – you just have to look around, and it's there."

Irene's arrival was welcomed by the other members of the family, who took their cue from Ellie. Next door was Wallie Scroggie, who was the younger brother of Ellie, who was married to Mollie, who was the mother of Doddie, who worked with Graham on the boat. Doddie's father, Robbie, had gone off some years earlier with Ellie's cousin, Maggie, leaving Doddie, and his brother, Laurie, with Mollie.

Wallie Scroggie was pleased that Graham had found somebody like Irene. "I never thought you'd find a woman like that, Graham," he said to his nephew. "All that book learning makes your heid sore."

Not everyone, though, was pleased with Irene's arrival on their bucolic scene. Doddie and Laurie were sceptical. "That woman's trouble," Doddie hinted to Wallie. "Why's she not in Edinburgh? There has to be a reason. Did they get rid of her? Send her up here?"

Wallie told him not to be so suspicious. "You're right about being wary of Edinburgh folk, Doddie, but you have to give her a chance. Ellie likes her, and so does Mollie. Are you suggesting they cannae judge fit like she is?"

# 30

*Just the Local Women*

Although she enjoyed the novelty of her new life, Irene was not one to accept without question the ways of the community in which she now found herself. She was wary of commenting on Graham's mother, Ellie, partly because she barely understood the older woman's conversation. Graham had seen this, and tried to help by translating anything that his mother said: "What mother says is that it's a blustery day," he might say. "She says that she remembers a spell of blustery weather five years ago in which all her washing was blown out to sea."

Irene tried to reply directly to Ellie, but it was clear that the incomprehension was mutual, as Ellie would turn to look quizzically at Graham, and wait for a translation.

"Does your mother actually speak English?" Irene asked Graham.

He smiled. "Aye," he replied. "She speaks English right enough. She prefers the Doric, though. She has old-fashioned views about English, I'm afraid."

Irene was intrigued. "And what are those?"

"She says she can't tell whether somebody speaking English is lying," he said. "She says you can't lie in the Doric."

Irene laughed. "*Very* old-fashioned," she said.

"Aye, Mother isn't very modern," Graham admitted. "But she's had a hard life, you know."

"Yes," said Irene. "Living here can't be easy. All that . . . all that weather. And then there's the sea . . ."

"Aye," said Graham. "The sea. Always there. You look out the window and it's there. And the rain, too. The rain's there, too."

Irene was fascinated. Graham spoke with a deep voice, and his words, she thought, were pure poetry. *The sea. Always there . . .* You could only say that sort of thing if you really *knew* the sea, as Graham did. These were ancient currents in the blood. These were tribal memories going back centuries. This was the ancient wisdom of the people who had wrested their living from those waters and from this deep rich soil for generation upon generation. This was what she appreciated about these people: their rootedness, their depth.

At the same time, nothing was for ever, and human society had to evolve; it had to confront the injustices and cruelties of our social arrangements and adjust to a more egalitarian vision of what life could be. In particular, these men amongst whom she found herself had to understand that they could not continue to be men in the way in which they had been men for a very long time. These fishermen, these strong, courageous men who braved the North Sea to hunt the sliver darlings, had to understand that they could no longer justify going off fishing while they left their wives and girlfriends behind.

She asked Ellie, through Graham as interpreter, whether she had come across many women on fishing boats.

Ellie looked thoughtful. The women, she explained, usually worked on shore. They dealt with the catch – cleaning the fish and packing them in ice or in barrels. The herring fishery, she explained, had been a major part of the life of Scottish harbours for a long time.

"Mother says," Graham translated, "that if it hadn't been for the women, there would have been no fish sent off to the fish markets. There would have been no fish on anybody's table. It was the women who did all that work. They kept the whole fishing industry going."

"But what about going out in the boats?" Irene asked. "Why did the women not go off in the boats and leave the men on shore to gut the catch and carry the fish baskets?"

Graham looked puzzled.

"Ask your mother," prompted Irene.

Graham spoke to his mother in Doric. He shrugged at the end of his question.

Ellie hesitated. Then she gave a lengthy explanation to Graham, who nodded before he passed it on to Irene.

"Mother says nobody in their right mind would want to go out in the boats," he said. "She says that the women knew better than to go out there and tug on the nets and lose their fingers in the trawling gear. She says they were far better off sitting at home, making soup and reading the *Sunday Post*."

Irene shook her head. "Tell your mother she's got it wrong," she said. "That's an interesting view, but very outdated."

Graham hesitated. "Mother doesn't think she's outdated. Perhaps she knows how the women felt because she was one of them."

Irene smiled. "I don't want to argue with your mother, Graham. I'm sure that there are some things she knows about, but when it comes to these major shifts in the dynamics of human relationships, she might be just a bit out of her depth – just a bit."

Graham looked at her. He did not like to argue. He was more interested in deep, meaningful observation than the superficial cut and thrust of debate.

"We all have our own ideas of how the world is," he said at last. "Folk see things differently."

That was the end of that exchange, but the issue of male domination of the fishing fleet was not one that Irene was willing to let go. She decided that if she were to wait for new ideas to be discovered by the women of Peterhead themselves, she might have a long wait. The people around her – Ellie, Mollie and others – seemed to be content with their lot, but that, of course, was a matter of false consciousness. That needed to be confronted, and if an outsider had to do that, well, so be it.

She was aware that Wallie Scroggie's wife, Mollie, was on the committee of the local branch of the SWI, the Scottish Women's Institute. She had seen her reading a copy of the institute's magazine, and she had heard of a project that she had been involved in to help women refugees. Irene would never herself join an organisation like that – far too homely, she thought – but she realised that if she wanted to make contact with the women of the town and to encourage them to challenge unacceptable attitudes, then speaking at an SWI meeting might be just the way to go about it.

So, she approached Mollie.

"Would you like me to give a talk at your SWI?" she asked.

Mollie was surprised. "Good heavens," she said. "We're nothing special. We're just the local women."

Irene smiled. That was the problem. *Local women* – that was a typical, imposed, undermining description. That showed just how deeply rooted the problem was.

"You *aren't* just local women," she said. "Each of you is endowed with unique talents and an individual perspective. Each of you can do anything you want." She paused. "You could climb Everest if you wanted to."

Mollie gasped. "Everest? That's a Munro, isn't it? I don't know about that."

"Yes, Mollie, of course you could. So let me give you all a little talk, and we'll see what happens."

"That's awfie kind of you," said Mollie. "Next week? We

meet on a Thursday night. We take it in turn to make cakes."

Irene sighed. She was going to change all that. The women who made cakes on a Thursday night could look forward to being out in the boats, bringing home the catch. The men could make the cakes in their place, not that they would be any good at that, of course.

# 31

## *A Pirate Enlightenment*

Because she regarded it as Angus's preserve, it was unusual for Domenica to visit Big Lou's coffee bar in Dundas Street. She had always felt that the key to a good marriage was the preservation by each partner of an area that was theirs and theirs alone. That could be a place, an activity or interest, or even a friendship. Without such a retreat, a marriage could become claustrophobic, and the individuality of the people within it could wither. The inmost self, she believed, required a supply of oxygen that complete dependence on another may cut off. You had to have room to breathe, no matter how fond you were of your partner; no matter how comfortable the relationship.

In the case of her marriage to Angus, they both came to it with a past, which always helped. She had her career – as an anthropologist and member of the editorial board of an anthropological journal, and, over and above that, she had a previous marriage. That marriage had not been entirely easy for her. She had loved her husband, but the embrace of his family had quickly become a bit overpowering. He was from Kerala, in south India, where, when you married, you acquired in-laws to the *n*th degree – uncles, aunts, first, second and third cousins, and grandparents, including quasi, ersatz and putative grandparents. There seemed to be no end to the legions of others who took you to their heart once marriage was contracted. Marrying into an Italian family could be similar; the Italian ideal being the cohabitation of three generations of a family in a shared compound. Why live in isolation when you could be surrounded by children and noise; when you would never be without conversation, or the rough and tumble of family life?

Her Keralan family owned a small but profitable electricity factory in Cochi. Such businesses have their risks, and after her husband's accidental death, Domenica left India and returned to Scotland. She had not thought she would remarry, but when she and Angus met, she began to think again about sharing her life with another. Angus entertained her: he was never short of an anecdote or observation, and at times could even be prompted into writing poetry. Moreover, he was more than willing to pull his weight when it came to housework – something at which most artists do not excel. They rarely disagreed about anything, and even Cyril, who might have been expected to come between them, was accepted by Domenica. In return, Cyril acknowledged her, although occasionally in his dreams he and Angus were walking through sun-kissed fields, heavily populated by rabbits, and there was no Domenica to be seen.

Domenica encouraged Angus to have his own circle. For her part, she had friends with whom she occasionally played bridge, and there were various others who she had known since her schooldays. Angus saw these people occasionally, but did not expect to be invited to the dinners they had together or their group theatre outings. Domenica reciprocated, and she never suggested that she should accompany Angus to the Scottish Arts Club, where he would from time to time spend a convivial evening in the company of those she playfully referred to as "the Reprobates". They were harmless enough, being mostly people he had known since art college days, both men and women. They referred to one another by their surnames – a habit that had survived from student days when lists at the drawing class had been compiled on that basis.

There were some of his friends, though, whom they shared. Matthew was one of these – Angus saw him virtually every day at Big Lou's – and Elspeth, too, even if they saw her much less frequently. Domenica was fond of Matthew, but Bruce was another matter.

"Bruce is irrepressible," she remarked. "He seems to be able to take anything, even a lightning strike, and pop back up again in a thoroughly annoying way. That business with the Pictish Centre, for instance – he seemed not to care that it all eventually came unstuck. Matthew was upset, but not Bruce. Straight on to the next thing."

She looked at Angus, who shrugged. He accepted Bruce for who he was. He had improved greatly after the lightning strike, but now he seemed to have gone back to how he was before. Angus had always been sceptical about the extent to which people could change. "What they say about leopards and their inability to change their spots," he observed, "is, I'm afraid, quite true."

That morning, Domenica went to Big Lou's after Angus had returned from his morning coffee. She knew that late morning was a quiet time in the coffee bar, and that Big Lou would come over to sit with her at her table if there were no customers to attend to.

And that was what she found when she made her way down Big Lou's steps and pushed open the door into the café.

Big Lou greeted her warmly. "Well," she said, "here's yourself. I was thinking of you a moment ago."

"Positively, I hope," said Domenica.

"Oh, aye. Always positive. I was reading something about an anthropologist, you see, and I thought of you."

Domenica lowered herself onto one of the stools at the bar.

"Tell me about it over a—"

"Double espresso?"

"Exactly."

Big Lou turned to her coffee machine, speaking over her shoulder as she prepared the coffee. "There was a man called Graeber," she said.

Domenica knew who she was talking about. "David Graeber?"

"Yes," said Big Lou. "There was an article in the paper about him. He sounded quite a character."

"He was," said Domenica. "I met him at a conference in London once. He was an American, but he lived over here. He was larger than life. An amazing man."

"So I believe," said Big Lou. "He didn't like the way the world is."

"Who does?" said Domenica. "Everything's wrong about it." She paused. "David Graeber was a great opponent of globalisation and the people who have become far too wealthy through globalisation – the one per cent of the world's population that controls most of our resources."

"The fat cats?" asked Big Lou.

"More than that – the obese cats," said Domenica.

"And he wrote about pirates, too," said Big Lou. "I read about—"

Domenica smiled. "His book on the Pirate Enlightenment?"

"Yes."

"The Scottish Enlightenment, the Pirate Enlightenment . . . one makes sense, the other sounds a bit like an oxymoron."

Big Lou passed Domenica her coffee. "Do you think there really was such a thing as the Pirate Enlightenment?" she asked.

# 32

## À la Recherche des Pommes de Terre Perdues

Domenica did not answer immediately. She looked away, as if to marshal her thoughts on a complex subject. Then she said, "Pirate Enlightenment?" and gave Big Lou a sceptical look before her verdict was delivered. "Rather unlikely."

"That's what I thought," said Big Lou. "But of course, these days everyone is trying to turn things on their head. And if you were to say, 'Pirates couldn't possibly be enlightened because they were . . . well, brutes,' you'd get people speaking up on behalf of the pirates."

"Yes, they were brutes," said Domenica. "But then the whole world was pretty brutal in those days. Pirates, I suppose, were outsiders – outlaws. And outlaws could be expected to be ruthless, because they were given short shrift if caught. You *had* to be ruthless if you were to survive."

"Not enlightened then? Just ruthless?"

Domenica sighed. "I'm afraid not. I think that he – the author of *Pirate Enlightenment*, that is – was clutching at straws to support his hypothesis. He wanted to prove that there was an egalitarian society established in Madagascar by these pirates, and that the ideas behind it preceded Enlightenment ideas in Europe. In other words, he was trying to show that things that we think were invented here in Europe actually had roots further east."

Big Lou thought about this. "To stop us from getting too big for our boots?"

Domenica said that was one way of putting it. "Every civilisation, I suppose, thinks that it invented itself. But when you begin to look closely, there are often all sorts of influences, all sorts of links."

"And you shouldn't be too dismissive of others? Is that what you're saying?"

"Yes," said Domenica. "One shouldn't claim too much."

Big Lou frowned. "I've got a book back in the flat, *How the Scots Invented the Modern World*. Do you know it? It's about the Scottish Enlightenment and how it influenced the American constitution and the development of science, and so on."

Domenica said that she did. "Professor Herman's book? Yes. But remember one thing, Lou. He's an American. You couldn't write a book with that title if you were Scottish. People would think it . . ."

"Bragging? Would that be it?" Lou interjected. And then answered her own question. "I suppose it would be." She smiled at a memory. "Back home, we called it blawing."

"Scots words are so vivid," said Domenica. "You can just see somebody blawing, can't you? Blowing, I suppose – which is what boasting is."

"Aye," said Big Lou. "Or you might say that somebody was *crawing crouse*. You could say that." She paused. "There was a boy called Billy MacIntyre in my class at school. His father was a mowdie man – a molecatcher. Not full time, he just caught moles at weekends. Billy was always blawing about how he could do everything better than the other boys."

"And could he?" asked Domenica.

"Yes, he could. He won all the prizes. And then he went on to Aberdeen University and won all the prizes there."

"And his father? The mowdie man?"

"My father liked him," said Big Lou. "He said the mowdie

man had done something really helpful for him way back. He never told me what it was, but he said that we should be grateful to the MacIntyre family."

"I like the idea of inherited gratitude," said Domenica. "I like the idea of being thankful to a whole family for something that a previous generation might have done. He expected you to be grateful to Billy, I suppose. Even now . . . If you met Billy MacIntyre, would you be well disposed to him?"

"He studied medicine in Aberdeen. He became a dermatologist."

Domenica nodded. "We all have reason to be grateful to dermatologists."

Big Lou nodded. "I am. And I think he stopped blawing. So I heard, anyway."

"His father must have been proud of him," observed Domenica. "There's the molecatcher's son becoming a dermatologist." She looked at Big Lou. She thought of how she was connected to quite another Scotland from the Scotland that they could see by looking out at Dundas Street, with its galleries and cafés. Big Lou's Scotland was one of farms and tattie howking and mowdie men. Of hills. Of sheep sales. Of muddy tracks to byres; of fences that needed repairing; of DC Thomson and the *Press and Journal,* and Dundee and marmalade and Irn Bru, and Raith Rovers and . . . and, oh so much that was dear to her and so many others, and how could one not think about it and feel warm inside and proud, in a way, to be part of all that, and yet not to blaw about it . . .

The *mowdie man* . . . It came back to her, now, those lines from the poem that Albert Mackie had written about a molecatcher. The mole's small eyes, like beads, would touch every heart . . . but not the mowdie man's. She now told Lou about that, and Lou smiled. "True," she said. "Aye, that's true enough. And . . ." She broke off. A man had come into the coffee bar and was closing the door behind him. Big Lou rose to her feet. "Much as I'd like to sit and blether with you, Domenica, I've got a business to run."

"Of course," said Domenica, and she glanced at the man, who was approaching Big Lou's counter to place his order.

There was a hissing of steam as Big Lou prepared her customer's coffee. Domenica sat back and looked up at the ceiling. She enjoyed her chats with Big Lou, because they could lead anywhere – pirates, boastful boys, mowdie men – anywhere, really.

The door was opened again. This time it was Nicola. She saw Domenica at her table and smiled. "You're here," she said.

"Not often," said Domenica. "But I wanted to get out today."

"So did I," said Nicola.

"And how's wee Bertie?" asked Domenica.

"Fine. And Ulysses, too. He's settling in at nursery. And Bertie . . . well, you know what he's like. I know I'm his grandmother, and I'm biased, but—"

"He's a great wee boy," said Domenica. "We all think that. And that friend of his?"

"Ranald Braveheart Macpherson? Yes, he's doing fine."

"There's something touching about a friendship between boys, isn't there?"

"Yes," said Nicola. "It's . . ."

But she did not go on. She had seen the man who had come in just before her. And he had seen her. It was the cyclist who had spilled his potatoes over Dundas Street.

He smiled at her. "Nicola?"

"Yes. David, isn't it?"

"Yes," he said, adding, "Those potatoes you gave me. They were delicious."

She laughed. "They were just tatties."

"No, they were. I thought of you when I had them in a fish pie."

Domenica was puzzled. Potatoes? Fish pie?

# 33

## Don Pasquale

With his cup of coffee in his hand, David hesitated at the counter of Big Lou's coffee bar. The only table that was occupied was that at which Domenica and Nicola sat and he had already struck up a conversation about potatoes with Nicola. He hesitated – it was possible that Domenica and Nicola had come here for a chat, and would not welcome him, a virtual stranger, if he intruded. On the other hand, to sit down at another table might be interpreted as being unfriendly. He looked down at his cup. Normally he had a steady hand, but the cup and saucer now rattled slightly, as if from a tremor. He made an effort to stop it, and it settled down. He smiled at Nicola. She smiled back.

But it was Domenica who spoke. "I need to get back," she said. "I've got a mountain of ironing to do."

"Doesn't Angus help?" Nicola asked.

Domenica shook her head. "He offers. But he does other things. He does all the vacuuming. And he takes the rubbish out. And he sometimes cooks – but not very well. He pulls his weight."

Nicola nodded. She saw in her mind's eye a vast pile of clothes, piled up in Scotland Street, several storeys high. She saw Domenica standing before it, holding a laundry basket, looking defeated. *Metaphors*, she thought. There are metaphors everywhere, but she simply said, "Of course."

Domenica said quickly, "You stay. I don't mean to . . ."

She trailed off. She had picked up something, and she thought, *Yes, you can always tell when there is a current of affection.* She looked at Nicola. She knew about her history – that man in Portugal, the one with the impossible name, who had run off with his housekeeper, claiming to have been instructed to do so by the Virgin Mary herself. She knew all about that, because Angus had heard it from Stuart, who had been angry on his mother's behalf, but who had confessed that he had never liked his stepfather and that as far as he was concerned it was best for his mother to put Portugal behind her and return to Scotland. The Virgin Mary kept well away from Scottish affairs, he thought – and not without reason. She had more than enough on her hands having to respond to the Spanish and the Italians, who were always far more demanding than the less demonstrative and Protestant Scots.

Now Nicola said to David, "Won't you join us?"

Domenica glanced at her, not sure whether she wanted her to stay. Perhaps she had misread the situation; perhaps Nicola did not want to be left alone with this man whom she might not know very well, although it appeared that she had once given him some potatoes.

"I really must," Domenica said, and started to get up from the table. If Nicola wanted her to stay, she would press her to do so now, but she did not.

"Let's have lunch some time," said Nicola. "I'll drop in."

"Yes, please do."

David came to the table.

"I know that she's just going," said Nicola, "but this is my neighbour, Domenica – at my son's place in Scotland Street."

David smiled at Domenica. "I'm David," he said. "Nicola and I met the other day – in Dundas Street. I dropped a whole bag of potatoes from my bike. They went everywhere."

"I see," said Domenica. "I was wondering where the

potatoes came into it." She looked at her watch once again. "I really must . . ."

"Of course," said David, and sat down on the chair that she had vacated.

Once Domenica had gone, Nicola said to David, "She's wonderful, that woman. She's an anthropologist – quite a distinguished one, I believe. She's been all over the place and written several books. She was in the Malacca Straits not all that long ago. She stayed in a pirate community, apparently. She studied the pirates' wives. They loved her."

David raised an eyebrow. "Do pirates still exist?"

"Oh yes," said Nicola. "Off the Horn of Africa. And in places like the Malacca Straits, apparently."

"I see," said David. "I suppose we fool ourselves in thinking that the world is safe. It isn't – or large parts of it aren't."

He took a sip of his coffee. She noticed that he was looking at her over the rim of his cup – just a quick look, but she noticed it. She looked past him, at Big Lou, who had turned away from her behind the counter, attending to some task.

"Have you had one of Lou's bacon rolls?" she asked David.

He followed her glance. "That's Lou?"

"Yes. We call her Big Lou – everyone does. She doesn't mind."

"I haven't," he said, in answer to her question. "Next time, perhaps."

There was a silence. Nicola wanted to say something, but she was not sure as to what it should be.

At last David said, "I was at the opera last night. The Festival Theatre. Scottish Opera."

Nicola was relieved. She liked opera. They could talk about that. "What were they doing?"

"*Don Pasquale*. It's one of my favourites. Have you seen it?"

"A long time ago," said Nicola. "I like Donizetti. I saw *L'elisir d'Amore* once at Glyndebourne. It was the only time I've ever been there. It was a big treat."

"Picnic on the lawn? The whole thing?"

Nicola nodded. "I was taken by a cousin who lives down there. She came into some money and invited me. Champagne. Donizetti. It was pretty heavenly."

"You'd like this Scottish Opera production," said David. "It's set in a sort of nineteen-sixties *pensione*. That's what the Don does – he runs a *pensione*. It's done in the clothes of the time. It really works."

"It sounds marvellous," said Nicola, and then, "Are you keen on opera?"

"I love it," said David. He paused. "The other day—"

"Yes?"

"The other day when we met and had coffee together. I didn't ask you about yourself."

She shrugged. "We'd only just met. We were both in a bit of a hurry."

"I didn't ask whether you . . . whether you were married?"

She shook her head. "I was. No longer. It's a bit complicated."

"It always is," he said.

She could tell that he was pleased with her answer.

Then he said, "*Don Pasquale*'s on again next week. Would you like to go? I could get tickets."

She needed time, and so she replied, "*Don Pasquale*?"

And he, in turn, answered her with "*Don Pasquale*."

She thought: we can't go on saying *Don Pasquale* to one another, and so she said, trying not to sound too eager, "Why not?"

# 34

## Refuge

That morning, when the members of Bertie's class were disgorged from the schoolroom into the playground for their morning break, Bertie was quick to seek out Ranald Braveheart Macpherson.

"Quick, Ranald," he said, taking hold of his friend's arm, "we must go and find somewhere to hide. Olive is going to get me for her book group. Remember what she said yesterday? They're having a meeting this break-time."

Ranald looked anxiously over his shoulder. "But where are we going to go, Bertie?" he asked. "Olive will see us if we try to hide anywhere in the playground. You know what she's like."

Bertie lowered his voice to a whisper. "Where's the one place Olive can't go?"

Ranald Braveheart Macpherson frowned. Olive was ubiquitous – flanked by her lieutenant, Pansy, and her acolytes Lakshmi and Rose, the girls could easily comb the entire schoolyard. The obvious places to conceal oneself would quickly be eliminated by this eagle-eyed search team. It would be pointless trying to hide in the sports hut, where the games apparatus was stored – Olive was bound to look in there. But there were less obvious places of concealment, and now it occurred to Ranald that they might crawl under one of the cars in the teachers' car park. He suggested this to Bertie, only to be greeted with a discouraging response.

"I don't think that would be a good idea, Ranald," cautioned Bertie. "Sometimes the teachers drive away during break. I've seen them. They drive away if they feel they can't go on. I saw Miss Campbell doing that the other day. She came into the schoolyard muttering that she had had enough. Then she got into her car and drove away, although I think she only went round the block, because she was back in five minutes."

Ranald nodded. "My daddy sometimes does that, Bertie. Sometimes my mummy has to shout at him. If that happens, he gets into his car and drives once or twice round the block. He always comes back, though."

Bertie took the point. Ranald was right about the low threshold of tolerance that most adults seemed to have.

"Of course, we could do something else," Ranald said. "We could go into the main building and find a cupboard to hide in until it's time to go back to class. By then, Olive will have had her book club meeting and won't be able to do anything about it."

This was far too risky, thought Bertie. "We'd have to walk down one of the corridors to get to a cupboard," he pointed out. "I think the teachers have movement sensors in the corridors. That makes it possible for them to swoop on people."

Ranald did not give up. Olive was a major threat to his friend, and he would leave no possibility unexplored in his attempts to shield Bertie from her clutches. A further option now occurred to him.

"We could disguise ourselves, Bertie," he said brightly. "What if we found a long coat and I sat on your shoulders and put the coat on? We'd look tall – just like one of the senior school people. Olive would just see me. You'd be underneath, holding me up on your shoulders. That would fool her, I think."

Bertie considered this with the air of a senior officer in a POW camp assessing the escape plans of a subordinate. One did not want to throw cold water over the initiatives of junior officers, but one had to be realistic.

"I don't think that would work, Ranald," he said. "She would see your face, and she'd know it was you. She would realise that you were sitting on my shoulders. You can't fool girls that easily. They're very cunning, you know."

Ranald looked disappointed. He thought that he might propose digging a tunnel, but he suspected that such a plan would also fail Bertie's realistic criteria. He gave him a defeated look. At any moment, Olive or Pansy might appear, and then it would be too late: Bertie would be trapped, and would have no alternative but to be led off ignominiously to the book group and a discussion of *Pride and Prejudice*. He could do nothing to help Bertie, and he found himself reflecting on what a pity it was that Bertie had rejected his suggestion that he should pretend to have a heart attack and seek refuge in the Accident and Emergency department of the Edinburgh Royal Infirmary. Had Bertie done that, then he would surely have been out of the reach of Olive and her retinue.

Bertie repeated his question. "Where's the one place Olive can't go, Ranald?" he pressed. "And nor can Pansy. There's one really safe place."

Ranald was puzzled. "The staffroom?" he asked. "Only teachers are allowed in there. No pupils are allowed in because the teachers sit in there and say horrid things about all of us. They don't want us to hear what they really think."

Bertie had to agree that the staffroom was indeed a place where Olive's writ would not run. But that was not what he had in mind.

Leaning forward, he whispered in Ranald Braveheart Macpherson's ear, "The boys' toilets, Ranald. Olive can't go in there. If we went in there, we could sit under the washbasins and wait until it was time to go back into class. Olive could search and search and she'd never find us."

Ranald smiled. "That's really clever, Bertie. That would show Olive. And we'd never tell her where we were. We'd keep it a secret, so that we could go and hide there whenever we knew she was looking for us." He paused. "You're really clever, Bertie. You probably know that already, but I thought I'd tell you anyway."

Bertie was modest. "Not really, Ranald. You would probably have thought of the same idea if you'd had a bit more time."

Ranald appreciated this. Bertie never made him feel inadequate. In Bertie's company, he found that he could forget the burdens of life, such as his spindly legs. Bertie made him feel strong and brave – he was the best sort of friend that anybody could ever hope to find. He was kind, and unassuming, and he never let you down. It had been a fortunate day when he had met Bertie and he was confident that they would remain friends until they were really old – even as old as thirty-five or so. Ranald would do anything for Bertie, and Bertie, he knew, would do anything for him.

# 35

## *Olive Olivissima*

Flanked by Pansy and Rose, Olive emerged from the classroom, and when she saw Bertie talking to Ranald, she stepped forward decisively.

"So, there you are, Bertie," she crowed. "Thank you for waiting for me."

Bertie looked about him. He toyed with the idea of running away, but he remembered Ranald Braveheart Macpherson's warning that Pansy was known to be a fast runner. He glanced at Ranald, who was staring glumly at his feet.

"They weren't waiting for us, Olive," said Pansy accusingly. "They were thinking of running away. You can always tell. When boys have that look on their face, it means that they're planning to run away."

"From their responsibilities," chimed in Rose. "They run away from their responsibilities, just like you always said, Olive."

"That's possible," said Olive. She could afford to be magnanimous, and so she added, "I don't think Bertie's as bad as some other boys I could name." She stared directly at Ranald. "For instance . . ." She trailed off, and affected a look of puzzlement. "For instance . . . what's your name again?"

This was too much for Bertie. "He's called Ranald Braveheart Macpherson, Olive. You know that jolly well."

Olive was all innocence. "Oh, do I, Bertie? So you know what I'm thinking, do you?"

Bertie was silent.

"So, that's the famous Ranald Braveheart Macpherson," Olive continued. "That's a big name for such a weedy boy. Sorry, Ranald, no offence, it's just that it's best to be honest about these things."

Bertie sprang to his friend's defence. "Ranald isn't weedy, Olive. He's quite strong. Stronger than you or Pansy."

Pansy gasped. "Did you hear that, Olive?" she exclaimed. "Did you hear what Bertie said?"

Olive pursed her lips before responding. "I think I did, Pansy. But there are times when it is best to rise above crude insults, especially from boys who don't know what they're talking about. Such things are beneath our contempt."

Pansy, though, felt that there was a point of principle here. "You shouldn't let him get away with things like that, Olive." She turned to Bertie, who noticed, for the first time, that Pansy had eyes that were almost yellow. It was like looking into the eyes of a cobra, he thought. Perhaps Mr Attenborough should come and make a film of Olive and Pansy in the playground. He was used to danger.

"You'd better watch out, Bertie Pollock," hissed Pansy. "We could report you for sexism. You can't say things like that about girls – not any longer."

Ranald now spoke for the first time in this stressful encounter. "Bertie didn't say anything rude," he protested. "You were the ones who said I was weedy."

"Well, you are," snapped Rose. "It was Bertie who said that boys are stronger than girls."

"I didn't," said Bertie. "All I said was that Ranald was stronger than you. That's all."

Olive burst out laughing at this, and was followed by Pansy and Rose. "That's very funny, Bertie," she said. "I know you didn't mean it, because it's so obvious that both Pansy and I are much stronger than Ranald Brave Pants, or whatever he calls himself." She paused. "But we shouldn't waste our time arguing about such trivial things. We have our book group, Bertie, as you may remember. Ranald can go and play by himself while we have our meeting. Or he can play with Tofu and Larch, if he's as strong as you say he is."

Bertie gave Ranald a despairing glance, but Ranald had already peeled himself away and was making his way across the playground to where a small knot of boys were engaged in some innocent pursuit. The battle was over as far as he was concerned, and he did not want his continued presence to make the situation more difficult for Bertie.

"Well, that sorts that out," said Olive, in a businesslike manner. "Now let's go and sit on that wall over there and have our book club."

With the treaty of capitulation all but signed, Bertie accompanied the three girls to the low wall at the edge of the playground. Lakshmi, the other member of the book group, was already there. She gave Bertie a welcoming smile, which did not surprise him, as she was, in his mind, by far the most reasonable of the girls.

Olive called the meeting to order. "We only have another eight minutes," she announced. "We wasted a lot of time this morning, but there we are. Now, Jane Austen: you can begin, Bertie."

Bertie was not at all sure what to say. "Why me?" he asked.

"Because you're the newest member," said Olive. "These are the rules, Bertie. You have to accept that there are always rules and there's no point in pretending that they don't exist, even if you don't like them."

"I never said that I didn't like rules."

Olive glared at Bertie. "You're wasting precious time, Bertie. Tell us what you think about the book."

"I haven't read it," said Bertie. "How can I talk about a book I haven't read?"

Olive sighed. "You are so literal, Bertie Pollock."

"Seriously literal," echoed Pansy.

Olive now shook a finger at Bertie. "I think I know why you didn't read *Pride and Prejudice*, Bertie. "It's because Jane Austen is a girl – that's the reason, isn't it? You think that you can refuse to read books by girls, don't you?"

Bertie shook his head. "I don't think that, Olive. I really don't."

"I'm going to have to tell Miss Campbell, Bertie," Olive continued. "This school has a policy that forbids sexism. You know that as well as I do, and yet . . ." She shook her head, as if she found it difficult to comprehend the depths of Bertie's transgressions. "And yet you still say things that Pansy and I find offensive."

Pansy agreed. "Deeply offensive," she said.

Bertie said nothing. Was this what really happened at book clubs? He stared down at the ground. If they thought this, then why did they not ask him to leave the book club – which was exactly what he wanted.

"However," said Olive, "we'll bear in mind that this is the first time you've been at our book club, Bertie, and that you need to learn how to behave. We're here to support you, you know."

"Yes," agreed Pansy. "We're on your side, Bertie – you know that, don't you?"

# 36

*Light, Lenin, etc.*

*Light*, thought Matthew, as he drove back home that evening. The most difficult thing of all is light.

He thought this as he rounded the corner that came just after his road – the road to Biggar – suddenly split into two. His road was the high one, the road that hugged the side of the Pentland Hills and eventually led to West Linton and beyond. The other road, the one he never took, dipped down sharply, before levelling out and leading to the Bush Estate, where agricultural and veterinary students were trained, and where Dolly, the first cloned sheep, had made her debut. Dolly had been such an ordinary-looking creature – the lot of most sheep, naturally – but had briefly enjoyed the scientific limelight. Dolly was the beginning, people thought; soon we ourselves would emerge from test tubes, designed by scientists to embody the qualities that people in the future would want to have. Of course, it was nothing like that, and humanity was still very far from straightening its crooked timber. Yet Dolly herself, who died of old age – a fate denied to the overwhelming majority of sheep – was transported to Edinburgh and placed in a glass box in the National Museum, secure in her historical status. Just like Lenin, who was treated in much the same way.

Dolly, Lenin . . . As Matthew drove, the images followed upon one another, as thoughts do in our ordinary, stream-of-consciousness lives. He had visited Russia as an eighteen-year-old, in his last year at the Edinburgh Academy, when he had gone as a member of a school trip to Moscow and St Petersburg. They had stood in a slow-moving queue for hours before being admitted to Lenin's tomb, and then suddenly they were in the inner sanctum and Lenin was there before him, illuminated in the darkness, lying prone as he had done since 1924, even if, during the Second World War he had been spirited away to temporary safekeeping in Siberia when the Germans drew close to Moscow.

As they approached the sarcophagus, Matthew realised that in all his eighteen years he had not seen a dead body before. And now here was Lenin, soaked in chemicals, they said, somehow preserved against the dissolution that faced ordinary mortals. His classmate in front of him in the shuffling line of visitors had whispered, "He's deid," and had turned to Matthew and grinned. Matthew had not encouraged him. They had been warned that they were to be silent and respectful, and that they should not put their hands in their pockets while in the tomb, as the Russian authorities considered this an insult to the great man's memory.

They had passed by, and were on the way out when somebody behind them, a woman in a long, drab overcoat, had suddenly started to wail. It was an expression of grief, as heartfelt as any that might accompany any real, recent bereavement, and the sound of distress echoed against the solemn walls of the tomb. A couple of security guards appeared from the wings, and went to the support of the woman, who might otherwise have dropped to the floor.

The boy who had whispered "He's deid" turned to Matthew in astonishment. "How many years ago was it? And still . . . Jeez. Can't she get over it?"

Matthew had been embarrassed, and had said nothing. This was real. There was a dead body just a few yards away. People moved on, more hurriedly now, past the stricken woman, who was now being comforted by the guards. A young woman in what looked like the uniform of a first aider appeared and was crouching beside the woman, who was now seated in a folding stool that somebody had produced.

Once outside, Matthew and his friends had looked at one another, uncertain as to what to say about what they had seen. Their teacher, a history master, had said, "This is still all very raw for them, you know. Remember that there were seventy years of communism. People here believed for seventy years and then suddenly it was over. That poor woman was crying for all of that, perhaps. Perhaps her parents had given everything to a system that then suddenly simply walked away."

Matthew had known what he meant. He felt sorry for that woman. And now he remembered her, all these years later, as he took the corner on the road and the expanse of hill to his right climbed up to a wide evening sky. Light: it was all about light, which is what Vermeer understood. He thought of his picture of the woman pouring milk, where the light shone on the milk; where the whole room was filled with a light that the artist had only suggested. You can't paint light, he thought; it's just there. You can't paint empty air – all you can do is paint the things that are there, surrounded by the air; you can paint what the light *does* to those things. He thought of the *View of Delft*, and of the little square of light that Vermeer had depicted on a distant section of wall. That was just a tiny fleck of paint, but it was the most important fleck there was in all Dutch art. Just that minuscule square of yellow.

Now the road rose again, and the country opened up to his right. In the distance were the Lammermuir Hills, a line of attenuated blue. They always seemed so soft, he thought, as if they would prove, if one approached closer, to be a mirage, an idea of hills, rather than something real. Matthew loved them. He loved everything here – this road, this small forest clustered around a farm road-end, these sheep grazing on the lower slopes of the hills, this rooftop now just visible off to the right which was his rooftop, where Elspeth, whom he loved so dearly, was waiting for him, as were those three little boys who were his flesh and blood and to whom he was their omnipotent Daddy, who would urge him to kick a football with them for hours on end, and tell them silly jokes, and read to them their bedtime story when they were in their dressing gowns, and for whom he would do everything he possibly could, although he knew that the thing he most wanted to do for them, he could never do. He could not protect them from what the world was becoming. He could not protect them from the collapse of this exhausted world, from the bitterness of the struggle that was going to ensue over resources and water and a patch of land to stand on.

He drew up outside the house, and put these thoughts behind him. The boys were waving to him from the window. They were clearly excited.

# 37

*Twenty-two Sausages*

Each impatient to be the first to speak to their father, the triplets – Tobermory, Fergus and Rognvald – struggled to elbow each other out of the way.

Matthew sought to calm them. Where did this seemingly limitless energy come from?

"*Dinnae fash*, boys," he said in Scots, as they grabbed with small hands at his clothing. "I'm not going anywhere. There's plenty of time to tell me whatever it is you want to tell me."

"I'm going to tell him," Fergus said. "It's my turn."

"No, it isn't," protested Rognvald. "It's my turn." And added, "You stink, anyway."

"I do not!" shouted an affronted Fergus. "*You* stink."

"Nobody stinks," said Matthew.

Tobermory was ever the mediator. "They both stink the same. Nobody stinks more than anybody else, except me. I don't stink, do I, Daddy?"

Matthew laughed. "I told you, boys: nobody in this house stinks. And it's rude to tell people that they stink. We don't talk that way."

Elspeth appeared. She gazed fondly at Matthew. "Can you take over? They're a bit hyped up. They've been waiting for you for ages."

"We were doing a hanging in the gallery," Matthew said. "Jane got some of the measurements wrong. We had to start all over again."

"Which show is that?" Elspeth asked. "You did tell me, I think, but I've forgotten."

"It's a four-person show," Matthew said. "It's called *People Who Can Paint*. It's groundbreaking."

Elspeth frowned. "Why groundbreaking?"

"The title says it all," Matthew explained. "These are contemporary artists who know how to paint. They're very unusual as a result – now that the art colleges have given up teaching students drawing and painting."

Elspeth groaned. "So they're self-taught?"

"Yes," said Matthew. "Almost entirely." He paused. "I don't want to end up sounding like Angus. He's always going on about the Turner Prize, but—"

Elspeth bent forward to plant a kiss on his cheek. "You'll never sound like Angus. He's dyed in the wool; you're so . . . so progressive."

Matthew laughed. "I struggle to keep a straight face when people call themselves progressive. Are they really? Does anybody have a monopoly on progressiveness? Are change and progress the exact same thing? What if what you have at present is better than what is being offered in the future? Do you still have to be progressive?"

Elspeth frowned. "But at least progressives want things to get better. Do conservatives want that too?"

"No," said Matthew. "Or maybe, yes. I suppose conservatives might want improvement, but disagree with progressives as to how you get it." He paused. "I'm not conservative, you know – or I wouldn't describe myself as such. I'm *moderate*."

"Of course you are," said Elspeth, not really believing what he, or she, was saying. She stood on her tiptoes and kissed him.

"Why is Mummy licking Daddy's face?" asked Fergus, his nose wrinkling in disgust.

"*Kissing*, darling," said Elspeth.

Matthew grinned. "Well, anyway," he said. "What are the boys all worked up over?"

This brought about a hubbub of conversation.

"There's a dog," Matthew made out.

That had come from Tobermory, who quickly added, "It's a secret."

It took Matthew no more than a second or two to work out what was happening.

"Next door's?" he asked Elspeth.

She nodded apologetically. "Yes, he's the same one that was here before."

Matthew raised an eyebrow. "You haven't been encouraging the poor creature, have you?"

"He's called Ralph," gushed Tobermory. "Remember him? He came to see us before, and he ate all those sausages. He's really clever."

Matthew looked at Elspeth. Had she been encouraging the boys to believe they could keep Ralph?

"You do know that he belongs to somebody else?" he said to Tobermory.

"He used to," said Tobermory. "He's ours now, Mummy says."

"I didn't exactly say that," Elspeth insisted. "But—"

"We can't," whispered Matthew. "It's theft – or as close to theft as makes no difference."

Elspeth disagreed with this. "We did nothing to entice him," she said. "He came of his own free will – driven by hunger. He just turned up. How could I send him away?"

"You've fed him?" asked Matthew.

"He ate twenty-two sausages," Tobermory interjected.

"Poor thing," muttered Elspeth. "He was clearly fed up with his vegan diet." She paused, and then went on, "He's a refugee. We can't send him back to them. He wants to be a *dog*, Matthew – not an ideological statement."

Matthew hesitated. No home, he thought, should be run as an autocracy. "You really want to keep him?" he said at last.

There were squeals of enthusiasm from the boys. Elspeth merely nodded.

"All right," said Matthew. "But what if they . . ." He nodded in the direction of the neighbours' house.

"We'll keep him inside," said Elspeth. "We can take him out for walks on the other side of the house. They won't see."

"It won't be easy."

"We'll manage," said Elspeth.

Tobermory took his hand. "Come and see him, Daddy. He really wants to see you."

They went into the sitting room. At the far end of the room was a dog's bed, made out of a large wooden crate that had been cut in two. In childish letters, DGO had been painted on the side.

"I did that," said Tobermory.

"It's lovely," said Matthew. DGO . . . It could win the Turner Prize if cut out and framed. The resulting work would be entitled *Dog*, and would be praised for its subversion of our expectations. That was what art had become. It was nothing to do with beauty or harmony; it was about saying, *Don't think that things are as you think they are*. *Dog* – DGO – could be worth thousands – millions even, if Sotheby's could be persuaded to market it. After all, a banana taped to a wall with duct tape had been sold at auction for $6.2 million – and then its new owner had eaten the banana. It was all about the attribution of value to the valueless.

And I'm part of that world, Matthew told himself. After

all, any work of art, even a fine one, a Peploe or a Poussin, could be reduced to a small quantity of paint on canvas, or a few tracings of lead on cartridge paper. It was rarity that counted – rarity and belief.

Ralph looked up and wagged his tail. He was replete. He had once again eaten a large number of the Duncan family's sausages. As far as he was concerned, life was perfect. Sausages and sympathetic, sausage-eating people: what more could any dog want?

Matthew crossed the door to stand by the ersatz bed. He bent down and stroked Ralph's faithful head. "You're safe," he whispered.

Ralph looked into his eyes. The affection of centuries flowed between them. He sniffed at the air, filing away the scent of Matthew, that was linked now in the depths of his mind with pleasure, and with kindness, but most of all with permanence.

# 38

## *The Association of Scottish Nudists*

Ever since she had been a small girl, living on the farm known as Snell Mains, Big Lou had kept a diary. Every volume had survived, and she would read excerpts from time to time, randomly selected, marvelling at how uneventful her girlhood had been. A typical entry was this one, from when she was ten and still at the local primary school: *Friday: Tommy Anderson ate Billy Armstrong's pie without asking him. Jennie MacDougall caught her foot in a drain. Daddy says he hopes there's not too much rain, as he doesn't want the tatties to rot until we've had time to howk them out of the earth. One of the dogs ate a frog and was sick.*

She remembered little of this, although she could recall Tommy Anderson, who came from a farm a few miles away and who bore an extraordinary resemblance to Oor Wullie, a popular cartoon character usually pictured sitting on an upturned bucket as he ruminated on the issues of the day. Oor Wullie belonged to a Scotland of fond memory, a Scotland that was becoming fainter, more distant; a Scotland of values and courtesy for which there seemed to be less and less time in a present laden with suspicion and distrust of others. What we had back then was so precious, thought Big Lou, and yet we did not know it. But that was the same for everyone, everywhere – the fellowship that people loved, the human, intimate sense of connection and mutuality, the bonds that tied us one to another, were withering under concerted onslaught.

She had kept up the habit of writing a diary entry each evening. As she grew older, the terseness of the earlier entries was replaced by a more relaxed and discursive style. Whole paragraphs were devoted to passing thoughts and impressions. Public events were recorded with reference to what was said about them in the *Press and Journal* or the *Scotsman*. There was the occasional note, too, of regret at what had *not* happened, which was frequently as important, if not more important, than what had actually occurred. There was some sadness and disappointment, particularly on the emotional front, because Big Lou had been unlucky with men – until the arrival of Fat Bob, of course, who was a good and deserving man, unlike some of her earlier boyfriends.

She and Bob were suited to each other and were getting on well, but still maintained separate flats. Bob was living in Longstone, which was convenient for the gym that he attended and also on the right side of town to reach the workshop near Bathgate, where he and his friend Eddie had their shed construction business. The demands of that business varied, but it had proved successful and there were days when Bob and Eddie worked until ten at night in order to keep on top of orders. That meant that Bob could only manage to have dinner with Big Lou on two or three nights a week. As it happened, this suited Lou, who cherished her independence and who did not think relationships flourished if people were in each other's pockets all the time. She had her interests, and Bob had his. He enjoyed weightlifting and, in the summer, participating in Highland Games; she enjoyed reading and experimenting in the kitchen with new recipes. They did some things together, and had recently joined a tango class at the Counting House. Bob had been reluctant, but had overcome his reservations and was proving to be a promising dancer.

Big Lou did not show him her diary, although there was

no real reason for her not to do so. The diary contained nothing that would embarrass him; perhaps it was just a lingering childhood belief that diaries were strictly private. She knew that if others read what she wrote, she would somehow be more inhibited. As it was, the diary amounted to a conversation with herself, unrestricted by concerns as to how others might react.

That evening, Big Lou sat down to her diary shortly after nine. Finlay, the boy whom she fostered and whom she would – if all went well – adopt, was already asleep. He had been at a lengthy ballet lesson and had come home exhausted, too tired even to make much conversation over the dinner they had shared. Bob was working late – until midnight, he said – although they would see one another, he promised, the following day, when he would take the three of them to a Chinese restaurant. Once Finlay went to bed, the flat in Canonmills was quiet.

Big Lou wrote in her diary:

A normal sort of day – like most of my days, I suppose. I opened up a few minutes late, because I walked up Dundas Street rather than taking the bus. Everyone is counting their steps these days – using one of those watches. They say you should take at least ten thousand steps a day. Ten thousand! How many do I take at the moment? Two, at the most, I imagine.

Nicola dropped in. We had a bit of a conversation and then a man came in. I had not seen him before, but it appeared that she had met him. There was some story about him dropping a bag of potatoes from his bicycle in Dundas Street. I had things to do, but I noticed there was chemistry between the two of them. It was unmistakeable. That man is interested in her. And why shouldn't he be?

She's an attractive woman and it's never too late. She deserves a bit of romance in her life, I think, because she has to look after Stuart and the boys. I wonder, though, if he's going to be it. You can't trust men. I trusted them, and look what happened. Bob, of course, is different, I know that, but when you think of all the greasy chefs and Elvis impersonators out there . . .

We had those two in again – the chairman and the secretary of the Association of Scottish Nudists. They came in looking more than usually down in the dumps about something or other – they are never short of disagreements and disputes with their committee. I wonder what it is this time. They sat there for at least an hour – on one cup of coffee a head – muttering to each other and shaking their heads.

I wanted to shout at them: *Come on! Stop being so miserable. Enjoy life.* Of course, I said nothing. It's not for the person who makes the coffee to express an opinion.

I don't like listening in to other people's conversation, but at one point I couldn't help but hear what they were saying. They were talking about an application they've made to the Lord Lyon to grant the Association a coat of arms. Apparently, there are difficulties . . . Something to do with what the heraldic artists are prepared to paint. Odd. Why should that be an issue?

# 39

## A Bare Shield

Big Lou had heard only a snippet or two of what passed between the Secretary and the Chairman of the Association of Scottish Nudists. She had formed the impression, though, that all was not well in the Association – and she was right. It had been a very long time since the affairs of the Association had been anything but troubled. The Secretary had served for almost twelve years, and he could not remember a time when there had not been some form of sniping at the office-bearers. He had long been inured to snide comments and even overt attacks, but every so often these wore him down to the point of considering giving up altogether. If people wanted to haul him over the coals for issue after issue, then they might care to take on the role themselves. That would show them, he thought. It's easy to criticise, but not quite so easy to keep the metaphorical ship of state on a firm course.

Some of the challenges had been easily dealt with – others had been considerably more problematic. That latter category included the attempt by Glasgow members to take over the Association, under the guise of a campaign to rectify the imbalance in voting rights between Edinburgh-based nudists, who had several votes each, and those with a Glasgow address, who had one vote, or, in some cases, none at all. That had been fought off successfully, but it had brought in its wake an asset-stripping plot that would have seen the sale of the Association's expensive premises in

Moray Place and its relegation to some cramped office near Meadowbank stadium. That would never do: the Association was a prestigious organisation, and it needed a good address to command the respect it deserved. There were plenty of people who were prepared to snigger at the Association, but when they realised it was based in Moray Place, they had to take it seriously.

Moray Place was, in fact, an ideal location for the Association. The Secretariat occupied three floors of a five-storey house, originally the home of the Earl of Auchtermuchty, a Scottish aristocrat whose ancestor had come into possession of a number of confiscated estates following the unsuccessful Jacobite uprising of 1745. The first earl was Robert James Campbell, a kinsman of the Duke of Argyll, chief of the Clan Campbell. Robert James was a relatively modest tacksman, a tenant farmer, who had ingratiated himself with better-placed Campbells and, more widely, with Hanoverian interests. By dint of political cunning, he had acquired this number of confiscated estates and had eventually been ennobled. His nineteenth-century successor, the Earl of Auchtermuchty who bought the house in Moray Place when it came on the market, had made a modest fortune through trade between East Fife harbours and Dutch merchants. He spent some of his money on acquiring a collection of Dutch Golden Age paintings, including a Rembrandt and a Vermeer. These paintings, though, were sold in 1854, when the earl at that time, having made a large investment in Australian gold mines, had been defrauded by his partners. The house itself, though, remained in the hands of the Auchtermuchty family, now reduced to two estates – one in Fife and the other in Perthshire. In 1920 it became the property of an Edinburgh lawyer, Crombie Abercrombie, after the Auchtermuchty title became extinct. Crombie's heir, a horse-breeder in the Borders, had no interest in living in Edinburgh and it was he who eventually sold the Moray Place property to the Association of Scottish Nudists.

The Secretary enjoyed working in Moray Place, and was indifferent to the fact that he was cold-shouldered by some of the residents. If they did not like the idea of having nudists in their midst, then that, he thought, was their problem rather than his. He made a point of being a good neighbour, ensuring that other residents of Moray Place were invited to the regular getting-to-know-you parties that the Association held in the communal gardens, weather permitting of course. Few residents accepted, and none took him up on his offer of a cut-rate membership subscription for those who lived in Moray Place or Ainslie Place. A good number, though, indicated to him that they were sympathisers of the movement and that all that prevented them from becoming paid-up members was the deeply rooted inhibitions that were part and parcel of being brought up in Edinburgh. "It's not really that sort of place," one of them said to the Secretary. "We don't take off our clothes that readily in Edinburgh, I'm afraid, much as we'd secretly like to. It's just not us, really."

The Association had weathered various storms, particularly the takeover bid from Glasgow, and was now, the Secretary believed, in excellent health. It was that state of stability, in fact, that had prompted the Chairman to raise the issue of a coat of arms for the Association. "We can feel justifiably proud of what we have achieved," he said to the Secretary. "We need to fix our image in the public mind, and for that we need some sort of symbol. Just about everybody has a logo – we need to take it one step further and have a coat of arms. Plenty of public bodies have that sort of thing."

The Secretary had agreed, and the Chairman had gone on to explain what was involved. "I gather that the procedure is quite straightforward. You petition the Lord Lyon, and then if he gives you the nod, you get the arms designed by a heraldic painter. Then Lyon grants you the arms and they're registered."

"That sounds fair enough," said the Secretary. "I suppose we have to choose what goes on the shield."

"Yes," said the Chairman. "I've actually matriculated arms myself. I don't make a big thing of it, but I am, as they say, armigerous."

The Secretary was impressed. "Oh, yes?" he said.

"Yes. I must show you the actual grant one of these days. You get it on vellum. I have a lovely design. A rose to represent my interest in gardening, and a fish, because my grandfather was a great angler. And a sailing ship, because I'm a Watsonian, after all – same as you."

"We're everywhere," said the Secretary, adding, "Thank heavens."

They discussed the matter further, and a few weeks later they met one of the heralds, Adam Bruce, and discussed with him the devices that they might have on the Association's arms. Unfortunately, this was when the first problems arose. "I must point out," said Adam, "that Lyon is unlikely to approve any *revealing* design. Fig leaves are okay, but I'm afraid that anything without strategically placed cover might not be permitted."

The Chairman was dismayed. "But that's who we are," he protested. "We do not believe in fig leaves."

Adam sighed. "There are many things in which one may not believe, but yet which are unavoidable concomitants of life in society. Success in life involves navigating one's way past such obstacles, you know." He paused. "Why don't you consider having what we call a bare shield? That's one with nothing on it at all."

The Chairman glanced at the Secretary. It was so unfair. Everything was stacked against the Association of Scottish Nudists, it seemed: social attitudes, weather, biting midges – everything.

# 40

## *Edinburgh Isn't Bourgeois*

That morning, in their flat overlooking Scotland Street, half listening to the eight o'clock news bulletin, with its catalogue of misfortunes, Angus Lordie made breakfast for Domenica. Usually her breakfast consisted of low-carbohydrate muesli, fortified with additional seeds and nuts, but on the occasions when Angus prepared it, he always added scrambled eggs and smoked salmon to the menu – a combination, he claimed, that was as familiar and as firmly ordained as eggs and bacon, or haggis and neeps, or any of the traditional pairings in culinary culture.

Domenica enjoyed these breakfasts, even if she confessed to a certain guilt over the smoked salmon. "I've never got over regarding it as a luxury," she said. "When I was a girl, nobody I knew ate smoked salmon. Nobody. It was the sort of thing people ordered at the North British Hotel when they went there to celebrate an important occasion. Now people have it for their office lunch – along with cream cheese."

The mention of the North British made Angus smile. "The NB," he said. "I always think of that Robert Garioch poem about the NB. Do you remember it? There's a man at the end of Princes Street who sees a group of prominent local citizens coming out of the NB Grill. They're laughing fit to burst, he says. And then they all get into what he calls a 'muckle great municipal Rolls-Royce' and disappear off towards Calton Hill. And he says that although you and I can't join in that sort of thing, it gives our town some tone . . . It's spot on."

"Garioch was so witty," Domenica said, adding, inconsequentially, "He lived just round the corner, didn't he? Nelson Street?"

"Yes," said Angus. He wanted to return to the issue of smoked salmon. "People's tastes have become rather fancy these days. Bottled water imported from France or Italy. What's wrong with the local $H_2O$? Smoked salmon. Caviar."

"Not caviar," said Domenica. "Lumpfish roe. It's different. Petit-bourgeois caviar."

Angus winced. "Bourgeois is such an insult, isn't it? Remember how we use to be worried that people would accuse us of being bourgeois. It was a deadly insult in my art college days. And now—"

"Now, here we are," said Domenica.

"We aren't bourgeois," Angus protested. "Edinburgh isn't bourgeois – or at least this part of it isn't. We're—"

Domenica suppressed a smile. "Slightly bohemian?" She paused. "Mind you, let's remind ourselves of one thing: every society *needs* its bourgeoisie. The bourgeoisie keep things on an even keel. They save up their money. They teach their kids to count before they send them to primary school. They also teach them manners. They pay their taxes and cut the grass. Never destabilise your bourgeoisie – or your farmers, for that matter. Look at what happened when the Russians destroyed their farming class. Famine."

Now she looked at the plate Angus placed before her. "I shall supress any guilt I feel and enjoy this," she said. "I won't think of the cages and the pollution. Nor the sea lice that infest farmed salmon."

"Best not to," said Angus.

"Although I'm not saying one should go through life *not* worrying about all these things," Domenica continued. "Too active a moral imagination can lead to paralysis. You can end up doing nothing – because everything you do has an impact on the world about you. Eat beef and help to destroy Amazonian forests. Fly down to London and expand your carbon footprint. It's painful just to think about it."

Angus sighed. "Everything has a cost. I suppose we have to do our best to minimise it. Human life takes a toll on nature – it just does. There are too many of us."

Domenica took a mouthful of scrambled egg and smoked salmon. "I'm glad you said *us*. Sometimes people say *them* when they complain about the size of the human population – or when they feel threatened. *There are just too many of them.* I've heard people say that. They never think that they themselves are part of the problem."

Angus smiled. "I knew somebody called McGregor," he said. "He had seven children. We sometimes chided him for that. We accused him of irresponsibility in having so many children in an overpopulated world. You know what he said in his defence?"

Domenica waited.

"He said that the number of McGregors was actually declining. He said the Clan Gregor Society had proof of this from their shrinking mailing list. As a result, he felt no compunction in having all these children."

Domenica smiled. "There's something wrong with that reasoning," she said.

"The problem," said Angus, "is that he believed that it was a good thing in itself to keep up the number of McGregors. That's the problem. But that's a view that might only be held by McGregors, who naturally feel that they are a good thing."

Domenica considered this. "But they have to think that," she said. "If you stop thinking you're a good thing, you lose your sense of self-worth." She paused. "I'm not sure that it's helpful to make people ashamed of who they are. Is it healthy to be ashamed of who you are – of your history?"

"We should acknowledge our flaws," said Angus. "We need to face up to unpalatable truths – such as the fact that this country became rich through plunder."

Domenica looked down at what remained of her scrambled eggs and smoked salmon. "I hadn't imagined that we would start the day with a discussion of history and identity," she said, and added, quickly, "Not that I want to avoid such subjects."

Angus smiled. "I suppose these are things that most couples don't discuss. In most marriages, the conversation is more—"

"Prosaic?" suggested Domenica. "With questions like: what are you going to do today? That sort of thing?"

"Yes," said Angus.

"And what are you going to do?" asked Domenica.

Angus looked at his watch. "I'm going to meet Sister Maria-Fiore dei Fiori di Montagna in fifteen minutes," he said. "In the gardens."

He had told her about this, but it had slipped her mind. Now she remembered. "Oh, my goodness," she said. "I'd forgotten. And you said I could come with you."

"I'm sure she won't mind," said Angus.

"Did she really—"

Angus cut her short. "She did. She told me quite explicitly. She has a section of the Stone of Scone hidden in the gardens. And she's promised to show it to me."

Domenica shook her head. "I always thought there was something ridiculous about that woman."

"Oh, deeply," said Angus.

"I think she's a bit touched," Domenica went on. "A bit, you know . . ."

Angus said that she could be right. Sister Maria-Fiore was,

by any standards, a bit . . . He searched for the right adjective. *Fey? Peculiar?* Or, quite possibly, *unlikely?*

He stopped and frowned. An idea had occurred to him. What if Sister Maria-Fiore dei Fiori di Montagna was not what she claimed to be, but a cunning imposter? Somebody had once made the suggestion – which Angus had abruptly dismissed at that point – that Sister Maria-Fiore was no social-climbing Italian nun, but was actually from *Glasgow*.

# 41

## By the Way

"There you are," said Sister Maria-Fiore dei Fiori di Montagna. "There you are, *amico caro* . . . lurking, *per così dire*."

Angus tried to smile, but found it difficult. She was one to accuse *him* of lurking: *she* was the one who lurked in the gardens. How often had he seen the nun, in the characteristic tartan habit she had taken to wearing, skulking near, or even *in*, the rhododendron bushes?

"We weren't lurking," he protested. "We were waiting to see you – as arranged."

Sister Maria-Fiore cast a glance in Domenica's direction, as if to see whether she echoed this protestation of innocence.

"I hope you don't mind my tagging along," Domenica said. "Angus told me . . ."

She did not finish.

"I have no objection," said Sister Maria-Fiore, with the air of one conferring a favour.

Really! thought Domenica. This is too much. This woman is condescending to me in *my own gardens*. And in a *tartan habit* . . .

Sister Maria-Fiore, blissfully unaware of these uncharitable thoughts, continued, "Husband and wife are one in this life. Just like me and the Lord."

Angus stared at her. What exactly was she claiming? Had the Trinity suddenly been expanded to include Sister Maria-Fiore as a fourth component? He opened his mouth to remark on this, but thought better of it, and simply smiled weakly, as if some amusing reference had been dropped into the conversation.

"Of course, discretion is required in this particular matter," Sister Maria-Fiore continued. "Technically, I am in possession of stolen property, you'll understand. And that's—"

"Reset," Angus interjected. "That's what it's called in the law of Scotland."

Sister Maria-Fiore lowered her eyes. "I would never break the law," she said. "One of our vows touches upon that, you know. When we join the order, we implicitly promise not to contravene any provisions of the Italian Penal Code – amongst other things."

Angus nodded. He wondered about promises of poverty and humility. How could Sister Maria-Fiore square her vows with the lifestyle she had so enthusiastically embraced – with her membership of that golf club at Muirfield, for example, or the private dinners she held in the Long Room at the New Club, or the expensive-looking SUV in which he had seen her driving around with her friend Antonia Collie? Antonia had private means, he understood – most people whose sole occupation was researching the lives of obscure Scottish saints would need a private source of income. Their commodious flat in Drummond Place was not exactly a hardship posting, he imagined – they had bought it rather than taken a lease, and that would have been an expensive business. But this was not the time to speculate, and so he confined himself to asking her how she had come into possession of this fragment of the Stone of Scone.

"You'll know the history?" Sister Maria-Fiore said.

Angus nodded. The story of the Stone of Scone was something he had learned as a boy. He remembered his primary school teacher showing the class a picture of the stone in its position under the throne in Westminster Abbey. "That, boys and girls," she had announced in her arch Jean Brodie accent, "is the ancient Scottish stone on which the kings and queens of Scotland were crowned, until our neighbours . . ." And here she paused, assuming an expression of deep disapproval. "Until our neighbours, that is, the dear English, chose to remove it from Scotland and put it under their own throne in London many centuries ago. This was an act which the people of Scotland quite rightly regarded as unforgiveable. Great was the regret felt by the people when they saw their stone so treated. Great was their sorrow. Strong men wept. Little children lay awake in their beds at night, sleepless at the thought of their loss. One does not purloin the cultural symbols of those with whom one happens to share an island. It is not a friendly act, in any interpretation."

Now Sister Maria-Fiore lowered her voice. "And you will be aware, of course, of the act of those great patriots who determined that they would no longer countenance this continuing insult to Scotland?"

Angus nodded, as did Domenica.

"They were young men and women," Sister Maria-Fiore continued. "They were students at the University of Glasgow – that courageous Ian Hamilton, bless him, and his fearless companions. So brave, so brave. And so successful, too. They removed the stone from under the noses of the English and brought it all the way back to Scotland in their noble Austin A10 or whatever stout-hearted car it was."

Angus nodded again. "It was quite a gesture," he said.

Sister Maria-Fiore was enjoying herself. "The English, bless them, were furious. Such admirable people, of course, but slightly inclined to take themselves a bit too seriously when it comes to lumps of stone. There was a great manhunt

– a bit like the pursuit of dear Prince Charlie – may his immortal soul rest in peace – all those years ago."

Angus glanced at Domenica. She was a firm believer in rationality: this dreamy vision of Scottish history was a universe away from her idea of the past. Scottish history, she thought, was not about bagpipes and romps in the heather. It was not about symbolic lumps of stone placed under ancient chairs. It was about a struggle of ordinary men and women to make a decent life in the face of odds stacked against them. It was about dispossession – the theft of land. It was about people in shipyards and mines battling to get by on what little they had while the wealth of the country was controlled by distant others. Scottish history was about ordinary life in a cold country.

Domenica seemed to hesitate. Then she said, "Interesting, Sister Maria-Fiore. All very interesting."

Sister Maria-Fiore flashed a smile. "I can just imagine those young people, can't you? They struggled to lift this great stone as they brought it back to its home, and, unfortunately, they dropped it at one point and it broke. Ian Hamilton talks about that in that book of his."

"I seem to remember that," said Angus.

"But what is not generally known," Sister Maria-Fiore continued, "is that there were three pieces – and one of these pieces was brought to Edinburgh by those courageous, if Glaswegian, students. They wanted to get it out of Glasgow, as the Scottish police were now circling and arrests were imminent. You'll remember that eventually the poor students had no alternative but to hand the stone over, which they did."

Angus remembered.

"Well," Sister Maria-Fiore continued, "they decided to hold onto the third piece and hide it under the very noses of the Edinburgh establishment. And where would the best place for that be? In the Edinburgh New Town, of course. Right here in Drummond Place Gardens, by the way."

Angus froze. It was not this disclosure of the fact that a piece of the Stone of Destiny was in Drummond Place Gardens that made him draw in his breath – it was the fact that Sister Maria-Fiore dei Fiori di Montagna, this Italian nun from Tuscany – allegedly – had used a classic Glaswegian expression – *by the way*. They all said that, he thought – all the Weegies said that, all the time. It was almost a shibboleth, a sign of belonging – and she had said it.

"By the way," he remarked, "did you just say *by the way*?" He paused, and decided to be direct. "You aren't from Glasgow, by any chance?"

Sister Maria-Fiore seemed unfazed. "Never been there," she replied, adding, "by the way."

# 42

## *Off to Morningside*

It was about this time that Bertie was vouchsafed one of the most remarkable adventures yet of his short and entirely blameless life. It was not that nothing had ever happened to him – it had. There had been that extraordinary episode when he had gone on that school orchestral trip to Paris when, through a failure on the part of the conductor to count the children correctly, he had been left behind in France. That had worked out well, of course, as he had busked in the streets, been befriended by a group of students from the Sorbonne, and participated *con brio* in a seminar on deconstruction. Then, while boating off the shores of Argyll, he had been swept out to sea, briefly, landing on the Cairns of Coll, from which he was eventually rescued. He had also been lost, again for a brief period, in the Pentland Hills – on two occasions, once when a thick mist, a haar, had descended and he and his father had ended up in a remote farmhouse, and on another when, at a school camp, he had been unfortunate enough to be part of a group led by Olive that became lost in the hills as a result of incompetent map-reading. For most seven-year-olds, that would be enough – even more than enough to dampen any appetite they had for adventure, and to persuade them to follow a generally risk-averse path, but Bertie had taken all this in his stride. There was, it seemed, a divinity that hedged small boys who were open to unusual and challenging experiences.

This began with an invitation from Bertie's friend, Ranald,

to a Friday-night sleepover in the Macpherson house in Albert Terrace, on the south-facing slopes of Morningside, a well-set suburb on the other side of town from Scotland Street. Bertie had passed the invitation on to his grandmother, who, having consulted Stuart, gave her approval. Nicola liked Ranald, and was pleased that Bertie at long last had a friend who might protect him from Olive and her gang of co-conspirators. Nicola had seen through Olive on their first meeting, and had correctly assessed her as being every bit as bad, in an apprenticed sort of way, as Irene herself. In Nicola's view, the more time Bertie spent with Ranald Braveheart Macpherson, the better, as there seemed to be nothing objectionable about him – unlike that dreadful Tofu, the thuggish Larch, or the unpredictable Socrates Dunbar, who only recently had made his unwelcome appearance on the edge of Bertie's school circle.

"I have spoken to Daddy," Nicola said, "and he has agreed that you can go to the sleepover at the Macphersons' house."

Bertie beamed with pleasure. "Thank you so much, Granny," he said. "And will it be all right if I stay over there until six o'clock on Saturday evening? Ranald says that his daddy will bring me back on the twenty-three bus."

Nicola had said that this was perfectly all right. "I'll pack your small rucksack for you, Bertie. I'll put in your pyjamas and your toothbrush. You must promise me you'll clean your teeth. And there'll be spare socks too."

"And my compass, Granny," Bertie said.

"I doubt if you'll need that, Bertie," Nicola said with a smile. "We all know where Morningside is. But if you feel more comfortable with it, by all means take it."

"There's a boy at school who got lost," said Bertie. "He ended up in Leith and they had to rescue him. I'm not making this up, Granny. If he'd had a compass, it might never have happened."

Nicola had suppressed a smile. Bertie was such a wonderful mixture, she thought. On the one hand there was the little boy with his extraordinary ability to read – and understand – books well beyond the comprehension of the average seven-year-old. On the other was the innocent, with his enthusiasm for all the impedimenta of boyhood: compasses, Swiss Army penknives, football cards, jars of tadpoles – Bertie had a Junior Darwin kit – and so on. The mixture was such an odd one, but it seemed to her to be just right for her remarkable grandson. If only there was some miraculous way of preserving him just as he was, of keeping him seven, which was exactly the right age for him.

With his rucksack duly packed with items necessary and unnecessary, Bertie was delivered to Albert Terrace by Nicola that Friday evening. She did not linger, as she noticed through the front window that a Scottish country dancing gathering appeared to be taking place inside. Ranald's mother greeted her warmly and invited her to help make up an eightsome for the next reel, but Nicola explained that she had to get back to help Stuart with Ulysses' bedtime.

Ranald escorted Bertie to his room, one wall of which was dominated by a large picture of Robert the Bruce surrounded by exuberant Highlanders.

"We're going to have a lot of fun tomorrow, Bertie," Ranald said. "My daddy has to go to a meeting at a big hotel in town and he says we can come with him. I think they're planning an uprising. My mummy's going to her support group meeting and so we can't stay here. But we'll have lots of fun in town."

"That's good, Ranald," said Bertie.

"The hotel is that big one at the end of Princes Street," Ranald explained. "It's called the Balmoral."

"I've seen it," said Bertie.

"And we can go off to the hamburger stall in Princes Street Gardens," Ranald continued. "My daddy won't notice."

"I like hamburgers," said Bertie. "My mummy used to stop me eating them, but now that she's gone to Aberdeen, I'm allowed to. And pies too. My granny has a pie factory in Glasgow and we get heaps of pies from there."

Ranald nodded. "Your life's much better, isn't it, Bertie?" he said. "I bet lots of people in Edinburgh are really pleased that your mummy's gone to Aberdeen."

Bertie said nothing.

"They really hate your mummy," said Ranald. "My mummy does, anyway. She says that your mummy is a witch. I didn't say that, Bertie – I'm just telling you what my mummy said. She said that if we were in the seventeenth century they would have burned her at the stake. She said that she was sorry things had changed. That's what I heard her say, Bertie – I'm just telling you." Ranald paused. "She calls your mummy Lady Macbeth, Bertie."

"She isn't Lady Macbeth," Bertie muttered. "It's jolly unkind of people to say things like that."

"Oh, I think so too," said Ranald. "I'm just telling you what other people say. And anyway, let's go and play outside. My daddy's made a swing. We can try that." He paused, and then said, "Don't worry too much about your mummy, Bertie. I'm sure she's not half as bad as everybody says she is."

Bertie smiled. Ranald was so kind – and he felt grateful that he had him as his friend.

# 43

## *Campbell Kilts*

The Balmoral Hotel, to which Ranald Braveheart Macpherson's father took the two boys the next morning, had been a celebrated landmark at the end of Princes Street since its construction at the tail end of the nineteenth century. It had begun life as a station hotel, perched, as it was, above the platforms sheltering under the glass roof of Waverley station below. William Hamilton Beattie, the architect who envisaged this great wedding cake of a hotel, showed an enthusiastic eclecticism, delighting in French Renaissance touches as well as Dutch-inspired windows. In the design of Jenner's department store further along Princes Street he had excelled himself in architectural intertextuality, modelling the building on the Bodleian Library in Oxford.

And the eccentricity had continued. The clock in the main tower, easily visible along all the main approaches to the station, was set several minutes fast, as it still is today, with a view to ensuring that those hurrying to catch a train would discover, to their relief, that they had those several minutes in hand.

For many of the guests, though, minutes off the clock would be neither here nor there. This was the case with the late Queen Mother, once a loyal patron of the hotel, just as it was for Stan Laurel and Oliver Hardy, who waved to milling crowds as they arrived to take up residence. Or for lesser notables throughout the years, including a succession of prime ministers, for whom the North British, as it was, or the Balmoral as it became, was a convenient base in Edinburgh.

"I'm going to be a bit busy," said Ranald's father, as he settled them in a small sitting room on the hotel's ground floor. "But there's a game of Snakes and Ladders over there, I see."

"We'll be fine, Daddy," Ranald assured his father, giving Bertie a conspiratorial glance as he spoke. "You don't have to worry about us."

"I've told the people at the desk to look in on you from time to time," said Ranald's father. "And I'm just down the corridor in the meeting room. You can call me if there's anything you need."

"We won't need anything," said Ranald Braveheart Macpherson quickly. "You should go and have your meeting now, Daddy. You mustn't worry about us."

Once his father had left, Ranald turned to Bertie and outlined his plans. "We'll wait half an hour, Bertie," he said. "Then we can go to the hamburger stall in Princes Street Gardens. And we can go and look at trains in the station. We might even get on one if we see that it's going to Glasgow."

It was an enticing vision of freedom, but Bertie was cautious. "We'll see," he said. "We should stay in Edinburgh, though – just to be on the safe side."

Ranald agreed, even if somewhat regretfully, and the two boys sat down to a game of Snakes and Ladders. One or two other guests came into the room, but nobody lingered or paid any attention to the two small boys huddled over their board game. That is, nobody paid any attention to them until a rather anxious-looking woman in a grey trouser suit appeared in the room and immediately fixed them with an accusing stare.

Striding across the floor to stand above them, she said

reproachfully, "You two boys are holding everybody up. Didn't they tell you to go and get into your kilts? Everything's laid out for you. Now, you come with me – you can play Snakes and Ladders any day of the week."

"But—" began Ranald.

"Don't you but me, Ranald," scolded the woman. "You'll do as you're told."

Ranald was surprised that she knew his name, and felt that he should not argue. This was the voice of authority, and he felt in no position to argue with it.

"Come along now," chided the woman. "We don't have all day."

As they set off behind the woman down a long corridor to a lift, Bertie whispered to Ranald, "Who's this lady, Ranald? Do you know her?"

Ranald shrugged. "I don't know, Bertie. But we'd better not argue with her. She says that we're late already."

"But late for what?" asked Bertie.

Once again, Ranald shrugged. "Who knows, Bertie?" he said.

Bertie was puzzled. "She knew your name, Ranald," he said. "You heard her, didn't you? She called you Ranald."

Ranald frowned. "Maybe she's thinking of another Ranald," he said. "Maybe she's mixing me up with somebody else."

Bertie did not think that likely, but said nothing. Now they were at the doors of a lift, and the woman was ushering them into it. "Hurry up, boys," she said. "We'll have to be at St Giles' in twenty minutes. We can't waste a moment."

They emerged from the lift on the sixth floor, and were immediately led into a suite of rooms off the corridor. This was buzzing with activity: women were adjusting dresses, hats, and posies and bouquets of flowers. At the centre of the room was a young woman in a bridal outfit, being fussed over by several bridesmaids.

The bride turned to them and smiled. "Oh, there you are, boys. I'm glad that Mrs Forbes found you – we were getting worried."

Mrs Forbes laughed. "They were playing Snakes and Ladders, Ginny."

"A good way of calming the nerves," said the bride. And then, to the boys, she said, "I'm sorry we haven't met before. Charlie arranged all this, didn't he? Unfortunately, he's come down with flu and has had to stay up in Inverness. But he said you'd be all right with the other groomsmen." She paused. "Which one of you is Ranald Macdonald?"

Ranald was right, Bertie thought. There was another Ranald altogether. He pointed at Ranald.

"And you're?" asked the bride.

"Bertie."

"Well, you'd better get into your kilts. Everything is in the room next door."

In a smaller room they found kilts, jackets and sporrans laid out neatly on the bed. Ranald Braveheart Macpherson looked at Bertie. "I think this is a wedding," he whispered. "What shall we do, Bertie?"

Bertie looked thoughtful. "We don't want to spoil it for them," he said. "I think we probably just have to stand there and hold things."

Ranald agreed. "She's jolly nice, the bride, don't you think?"

Bertie nodded. "She deserves to get married," he said.

Ranald glanced at the kilts, and his face fell. "Bertie," he said, his voice breaking with emotion. "Campbell tartan. Look, Bertie. The kilts are Campbell tartan."

Bertie bit his lip. He could tell that Ranald was gravely upset.

"If my dad sees me in a Campbell tartan kilt, Bertie," said Ranald, "he'll have a heart attack. You know what the Campbells did, Bertie? You know, don't you?"

Bertie tried to calm his friend. "It was a long time ago, Ranald," he said. "You have to move on."

"Where to?" asked Ranald.

Bertie was about to answer when Mrs Forbes came into the room. "You're very idle little boys," she said. "You have five minutes to get into your kilts. Starting from now."

# 44

## *In the Thistle Chapel*

Bertie and Ranald Braveheart Macpherson travelled up to the High Kirk of St Giles in one of the two sleek wedding cars that had been waiting outside the hotel. In the car with them were two of the four bridesmaids, dressed in voluminous yards of chiffon, and Mrs Forbes, who was now revealed as the bride's aunt and wedding co-ordinator. As the cars turned the corner at the top of the Mound, the cameras in the hands of milling tourists were directed at them through the windows of the vehicles.

"Really!" Mrs Forbes muttered. "These people!"

Had she looked further up the Lawnmarket, her disapproval might have doubled. The ancient street, with its echoes of centuries of Scottish history, had been allowed to become an open bazaar, selling the products of distant foreign factories, painted in garish tartan: plastic models of the Loch Ness Monster; tea-towels emblazoned with the image of Robert Burns; thistle-topped porridge spurtles; children's nylon kilts in Black Watch tartan; no depths were left unplumbed.

But her gaze was directed elsewhere, past the tolerant statue of David Hume towards the doors of the cathedral itself. And there the wedding guests could be singled out, even at this distance, by the hats, the kilts, the flurry of silk caught in the slight breeze from the east – from the Firth and beyond, from Norway.

The cars drew up. The last guests hurried into the cathedral.

The tourists pointed and chattered. The bride, barely visible underneath quantities of voile, stepped out on the arm of her father, a stout, bandy-legged man in a kilt. Camera flashes dazzled. The bride's father looked away. He was a potato farmer from Angus. What was wrong with the local kirk, he had demanded of his daughter. Nae tourists there. Could they not do a good enough wedding? But it was the groom who had prevailed: he came from Edinburgh, and he had persuaded his fiancée to make this an Edinburgh occasion. His family was well connected, and both the New Club and Muirfield had emptied for the occasion.

"I think this is definitely a wedding," Ranald whispered to Bertie.

Bertie nodded, but did not say anything.

Mrs Forbes was fussing around the bridesmaids, and Ranald decided to make conversation, to put Bertie at his ease. This whole situation, after all, was his fault – or his father's fault, perhaps – and he felt he should try to do something.

"Do you think this is where you'll get married, Bertie?" he asked.

Bertie looked about him. "I don't think so, Ranald."

"Mind you," Ranald continued, "it'll probably depend on Olive, don't you think? She may want St Giles'."

Bertie shook his head. "I'm not going to marry Olive, Ranald. I never said I would."

Ranald looked apologetic. "She says that you did, Bertie. It's not me making it up – she told everyone you were engaged."

"But we're not engaged," Bertie protested. "Olive can marry somebody else. She can find somebody else who wants to marry her."

Ranald considered this. "But that's not the way it works, Bertie. It's not up to the boy – it's girls who decide. They see this boy and they say *I'm going to marry him*, and they do.

The only way you can avoid it – if you're a boy – is to join the Foreign Legion. That's what my dad says. I heard him. He told one of his friends that he tried to join the Foreign Legion but my mummy got him before he managed to join."

Mrs Forbes interrupted the conversation. "Ready now, boys," she said. "You walk behind the bride and hold her train. This is it here. You take that bit, Ranald, and you hold here, Bertie."

The bridal party entered the cathedral. The organist paused and then, with appropriate stops full out, plunged into Jeremiah Clarke's *The Prince of Denmark's March*. Slowly, the bride, her red-faced father, Bertie and Ranald, and the four bridesmaids began to make their way up the aisle. Heads turned; necks craned; exhalations of admiration were like a gentle wind amongst the cathedral's great pillars.

To Bertie and Ranald, it seemed an eternity, during which, at any point, the real pageboys might stand up in the congregation and denounce the usurpers. But no such thing happened, and eventually the bride and her father stopped, and the two boys were able to abandon the bridal train and retreat into the wings.

"We can get away now, Bertie," whispered Ranald. "Nobody's looking at us."

Bertie hesitated. He was a considerate boy, and he did not want to do anything that would spoil the bride and groom's day. At the same time, he and Ranald had performed the duties that had been set out for them, and he did not think that anybody would miss them very much if they were to absent themselves. He decided to agree to Ranald's suggestion.

"There's a door over there," he said to Ranald, pointing to a door underneath a commemorative plaque. "Let's try that."

As quietly as he could, Bertie pushed at the large oak

door. It did not resist, and as it opened an adjoining chapel was revealed.

"Look at all those flags," Ranald whispered, pointing at the standards suspended above the row of stalls.

Bertie knew exactly where they were. "The Thistle Chapel," he announced in awed tones. "This is where the Knights of the Thistle have their meetings, Ranald."

Ranald looked worried. "What if they catch us, Bertie?"

Bertie reassured him there would be no adverse consequences. "The Knights of the Thistle are harmless," he said. "They're nice people, Ranald. They're just people who've done important things."

"Is it a club?" asked Ranald Braveheart Macpherson.

"I think so," Bertie replied. "There are all sorts of clubs in Edinburgh. Lots of grown-ups don't have all that much to do, you see. There's the Royal Company of Archers, Ranald. They have a big clubhouse near the Meadows. It's called Archers' Hall."

Ranald Braveheart Macpherson remembered that club. They had seen the Archers shooting their arrows on the Meadows in some sort of competition, and one of their stray arrows had hit Ian Rankin in the arm while he was walking along a path (he had been very nice about it). That was the sort of thing that happened when people who should know better played around with bows and arrows.

"Grown-ups are a bit odd, aren't they, Bertie?" said Ranald.

Bertie nodded. Ranald was absolutely right. But he had no time to think about that now: he had seen a door in the side of the chapel and a small sign saying *Tunnel*. Edinburgh was full of clubs, but it was also full of tunnels. This one, with any luck, would enable them to leave the Thistle Chapel and St Giles' without being seen by Mrs Forbes, the bekilted potato farmer, the bridesmaids, or any of the congregation.

"Let's go down those steps, Ranald," said Bertie. "It's our best chance, I think."

# 45

*Neptune's Dram*

While Bertie and Ranald Braveheart Macpherson were in the middle of their adventure in Edinburgh, considerably further north, in the ancient fishing town of Peterhead, Irene Pollock, now ensconced in the home of her new rescuer and lover, Graham Scroggie, the skipper of a medium-sized trawler, had embarked on a journey that represented the summation of days of cajoling and planning. None of that had been easy, but now at last, as she looked out past the bow of the *Aberdeen Belle*, which she wanted to temporarily rename the *Melanie Klein*, she was able to reflect on the personal victory that she was on the point of achieving for progressive opinion not only in the north-east of Scotland, but for the whole country. It was a sweet moment of triumph – and it was only just beginning. No fish had yet been caught, but the sea ahead of them was calm, a wide blue plain, inviting under the benign July sunset, a place of teeming pelagic fish waiting to be caught by the all-female crew of six volunteers.

There had been resistance from both men and women. The men had been the most difficult, and Graham Scroggie had initially greeted Irene's suggestion that women should be given the opportunity to take the boats out with undisguised hostility.

"Why?" he said. "What difference does it make? The point of the fishing industry is to catch fish, isn't it? Does it matter *who* catches them?"

Irene sighed. She was in love with Graham – she would not deny that – but there were so many respects in which he was a good fifty years behind the times. And now she struggled to explain things that elsewhere had been accepted as blindingly obvious.

"I'm sorry, Graham," she said, "but it matters a great deal. This is an issue of *rights*, you see. Women have the right to do any sort of job they want to do." She paused, and gave him a look of mock reproach.

Graham listened. He was a courteous man, and he did not consider himself to be unduly old-fashioned. "But it's hard work," he said quietly. "I'm not sure that a lassie could do it as well as a man, know what I mean? You need to be tough."

"But women *are* tough," said Irene. "Women do all the work that men do these days. There are women firefighters. That's tough work. Go out to the oil rigs and you'll find women doing all sorts of jobs. Women can be roustabouts at the bottom or rig managers at the top."

Graham frowned. "Michty," he said.

"So you see," Irene continued, "women can do any sort of job. And there are women who are deckhands on trawlers – not many, perhaps, and none, obviously, on your trawler. But that really needs to change, Graham. You have to move with the times."

Graham looked doubtful, but he had learned not to argue with Irene. Now he simply raised the issue of who might go out from Peterhead. "Do any of the local wifies want to go?" he asked.

Irene took a deep breath. "They are not *wifies*, Graham," she said. "That sort of language is completely unacceptable."

Graham cowered. "I didn't mean it insultingly. Some of the womenfolk call other women wifies – I've heard them."

"False consciousness," snapped Irene.

"But do they want to go?" Graham pressed.

Irene was ready for this. "I've spoken to a number of them," she said. "And I can tell you, Graham, that they do – at least they do now." She paused, and allowed herself a self-congratulatory smile. "I have persuaded them."

Graham said nothing. He wanted to ask whether any of those who'd agreed to go would know what they were doing. He assumed, of course, that he would be at the helm and that Irene and her friends would be the crew. Now came Irene's bombshell.

"I shall be skipper," she said. "Mollie proposed me for the role, and I accepted."

Graham stared at her. "You?" he asked.

"Yes," said Irene. "I shall have a bit of assistance. Nellie Mackie has experience of boats. She was with Caledonian MacBrayne for years. She knows about navigation and the . . . the steering . . ."

"Helming," muttered Graham.

"Yes, helming," agreed Irene. "She will stand beside me. We'll be very careful. We'll only go out on a fine day – to begin with – and we won't go far."

Graham stared at the ground. He was formulating a plan that would enable him to avoid a direct row with Irene, and, at the same time, ensure that life and marine property was not put at undue risk. Wallie had a boat that he shared with a cousin, Jimmie Scroggie, and Jimmie's son, Geordie. They could stand by, and when, as was bound to happen, the *Aberdeen Belle*, with its new skipper and crew, got into difficulties, they could nip out and take over. He would not tell Irene about this, of course, but they would be watching closely.

"All right," he said. "If it means so much to you – take the *Belle* out and catch some fish."

Irene beamed. "You've made a very wise decision, Graham," she said. "I should have known that underneath it all, you were a new man."

"Oh, aye," said Graham, hoping that none of this would get into the local paper, the *P&J*.

"And I expect that we'll come back with a good catch," said Irene.

Graham struggled. "Aye . . ."

"One thing, though," Irene went on. "If we do the catching, you and Wallie will do the gutting, I take it."

Graham's voice sounded strangled. "Aye, well—"

"Good," said Irene quickly. "And a further thing. I'd like to use a different name for the boat for this special trip."

Graham frowned. "You cannae change a boat's name," he said. "It's bad luck."

Irene had her answer prepared. "I've read about that superstition," she said. "And I believe that if you offer compensation to Neptune in the form of a bottle of whisky poured into the sea, you can do it. It's only going to be temporary."

Graham's eyes widened. "A bottle of whisky? You're going to pour it into the sea?"

Irene nodded. It was a ridiculous superstition, she felt, but she knew that Mollie and Nellie, as well as Jennie and the other members of the crew, would like this to happen.

Graham shuddered. He had an Aberdonian soul, and the idea of pouring good whisky into the sea caused the deepest possible offence.

"Couldn't we use Irn Bru?" he asked. "Or even tea?"

Irene shook her head. "It has to be whisky," she said.

"Oh well," said Graham, only conceding defeat with some reluctance. "A bottle of Bell's, perhaps. From the Co-op. Only Bell's, but still . . ."

Irene shook her head again. "Glenmorangie," she said. "I've already bought it – from the housekeeping. Twelve year-old."

# 46

## *A Miraculous Draught?*

Watched by half a dozen pairs of eyes, the *Aberdeen Belle*, sailing under the temporary name, the *Melanie Klein*, slipped out of Peterhead and into the open sea. Irene had suggested that there should always be more than one person at the helm, in accordance with the sharing ideals for which she had always striven, so now she and Mollie jointly set the fishing boat on its projected course. Out on deck, the other crew members watched the receding shore with a mixture of satisfaction and trepidation. Fortunately, the sea was quite flat, undisturbed by even the slightest breeze, and the sky, unusually for that part of the world, was devoid of cloud.

Mollie had explained to Irene about the sounder, on the screen of which the eyes of both of them were firmly fixed. At the outset of the voyage, the sea below them had been represented by an empty blue, but now, when they were not much more than a nautical mile offshore, a large, irregular ball of white, ragged at the edge, appeared on the screen, midway between the surface and the seabed some twenty metres below.

"Fish," said Irene, authoritatively.

Mollie agreed. "Aye," she said, "those are fish right enough."

The shoal was immediately below them, and Irene throttled back the engine to bring the trawler to a halt.

"You can get the girls to lower the nets," Irene said.

Mollie went outside, where she spoke to Annie and Katie, the two deckhands who had been charged with the task of catching the fish. They began to lift the net off the deck while Irene and Mollie watched.

Annie raised a hand. "A wee problem," she said. "Look – a muckle great hole."

Katie stared in dismay at the large hole that was revealed in the middle of the net. "We'll catch no fish with that," she shouted.

Irene came out of the wheelhouse. With Annie and Katie at her side, she examined the gaping void in the middle of the net.

"We might as well go right back home," said Annie.

Irene's jaw set in a look of pure determination. To return to the harbour would be an admission of defeat. They had barely been out for an hour, and already they were staring defeat in the face. The men would love it, she thought; their return would merely confirm what they had thought all along – that the women were incapable of catching fish by themselves.

She looked about her and saw two rolls of strong blue twine used for securing odds and ends on the deck. Then the next thing she took in was a couple of brooms used for sweeping the deck. In a moment of blinding insight, she saw the solution to their problem.

"Mollie," she said, turning to her fellow helmswoman. "You're an expert knitter, aren't you?"

Mollie accepted the compliment modestly. "Some fowk say that, aye," she said. "I'm nae better than many others though."

Irene explained what she had in mind. Using the two broomsticks as giant needles, could Mollie knit the blue twine into a large patch which could then, in turn, be knitted to the edge of the hole and thus repair the net? Was that possible, did she think?

Mollie frowned as she considered the proposition, but then her frown broke into a broad smile. "It'll be nae different from mending my man's breeks," she said.

"*Precisamente*," said Irene.

The knitting task was soon begun. As Mollie knitted, the great ersatz needles sending a loud clicking noise over the calm waters of the sea, on the shore the men trained their binoculars on the trawler, puzzled as to what was going on.

"It looks as if somebody's knitting," said Wallie.

The others laughed. "The lasses must have given up on fishing," said Billy Mackie. "Awfie funny, isn't it, Wallie?"

"No surprise there," said Graham.

The repair did not take long. As Mollie worked, the whole crew enjoyed a mug of tea brewed up by Annie and a piece of Dundee cake that Katie had baked only that morning. Then, when the net was ready, it was lowered into the water, down to the depth at which the sounder had revealed the presence of fish. After a few minutes during which the trawler drifted gently in the current, all hands hauled on the ropes that brought up the net. It was a hard task, as the net was bulging with a glistening silver mass of fish.

"Mackerel," exclaimed Annie.

"Aye," said Mollie. "There they are. Simple."

They landed the fish, tipping them into long, wooden fish boxes.

"We might as well go home now," said Irene. "This is a good enough catch to keep the men busy for a while."

The whole crew laughed. They relished the thought of the men having to roll up their sleeves and begin the dirty, slippery work of gutting the fish.

"We should go off to the pub," suggested Annie.

This idea met with general approval.

And when they nosed their way back into the harbour, lining the trawler up neatly and not even needing to employ her thrusters, Graham and his friends watched in astonishment. They could see the fish boxes with their glistening catches; they could see the look of quiet satisfaction on the faces of the various members of the crew.

Irene handed the keys of the trawler back to Graham, who received them in a state of mute astonishment.

"We could have caught more," she said, nodding in the direction of the fish boxes. "But it's important to know when to stop."

Graham opened his mouth. For a few moments it seemed as if he was about to say something, but he did not. He stared down at the ground, a defeated man.

Irene said, "I hope you've learned a lesson, Graham."

He opened his mouth again, but a discouraging look from Irene made him shut it again.

Irene smiled. "You should take more care of your nets," she said.

Graham nodded meekly.

Irene looked at her hands. She felt strangely alive. She was leading an authentic life – there could be no doubt about that. She was here amongst these people who needed only a little bit of leadership to free themselves of the whole stultifying edifice of small-town Scottish attitudes. This was just a beginning – a hint of what could lie ahead, as she brought about a transformation that would sweep the Highlands before making its way back to Edinburgh and Glasgow. This was just a beginning. Fishing was nothing – a procedure so simple that even a man could do it. Talk about the miraculous draught of fishes . . . No, it was skill.

She looked up at the sky. Soon she would go back to

Edinburgh, where she could continue with the work that she was doing here. There was so much to be done in Edinburgh, but she had a missionary's zeal and would tackle whatever work was given to her cheerfully and without complaint. Irene was not one to give up.

# 47

## Being Bruce

Nor was Bruce the type to yield too quickly to an adverse turn of events. He had encountered difficulties of every sort, ranging from social embarrassment to direct lightning strikes, and had emerged undefeated. The instances of social embarrassment were, of course, for the most part minor, but, when remembered at odd moments, could still bring a warm feeling to the back of the neck. That awkward evening, for instance, when he had gone to the annual dance of the Edinburgh South Conservatives in his kilt, but had forgotten to wear any underpants, still made him cringe, even if it was the sort of thing that was too easily done. The only way of saving face in such circumstances was brazenly to assert that the omission was deliberate. That applies to all wardrobe malfunctions: the *déshabillé* should simply say, "But that was intentional", at which point any embarrassment will evaporate. It is no fun laughing at an intended effect.

Bruce had always been self-confident. When, as a young boy dressed in his Anderson tartan kilt, he had been taken by his mother to the Crieff outfitters, T. Palmer Valentine, he had drawn crowds of admiring women. A few years later, as a teenager, he had become accustomed to having an eager and extensive following of girls whenever he appeared at the school sports day, or took to the field as the captain of Morrison's Academy rugby team. These girls were referred to as the *Brucies*, and were known to exchange photographs of

Bruce they had discreetly snapped as he strode onto the sports pitch.

He took all this in his stride. Bruce knew that he was good-looking, and it seemed only appropriate to him that women should admire him. He admired himself, after all, and so he understood why others should do so too. More than that, he felt sympathy for women who gazed at him with such dreamy longing: how hard it must be to live with unrequited yearning. He would do what he could to throw a few scraps of comfort in the direction of these admirers – a smile, perhaps, or even an occasional wink – but he knew that this might only stoke unrealisable hopes. But what more could he do? There was only one of him, and there were so many young women.

The confidence that Bruce felt in his appearance spilled over into his working life. Bruce had previously been employed as a surveyor, but had decided that working for others was not how he saw himself. Some people, he said, are destined to spend their working lives as cogs in a piece of machinery: not him. "I'm a natural mover and shaker," he had once remarked to a girlfriend. "I'm a guy who gets things done."

"Oh, Bruce," she had cooed. "You are, big time!"

That would be a heady plaudit if laid at the feet of most young men; for Bruce, though, it was an incidental compliment like any other, only to be expected. Yet the reality was somewhat different: his business career, for one given to moving and shaking, had not been conspicuously successful. That did not deter him, though, from following up on such opportunities as presented themselves. And now, as he stood at the door of the small basement flat he had recently acquired in India Street, he reflected on the challenge that lay ahead. He had paid a substantial sum for a dark and poky two-bedroom flat in need of considerable refurbishment. In a rare moment of candour, the selling agents had refrained from using the arch expression "in need of a bit of TLC", and had warned that the purchaser would have "a great deal of work to do". In a different location, that would have depressed the price, but not here, not in the heart of the Georgian New Town, within spitting distance of Heriot Row, and only round the corner from Moray Place. Anything, even in the most modest purlieus of such streets, could be expected to command a substantial price, no matter its condition. This had happened, and Bruce had been obliged to offer seventy-five thousand pounds over the already inflated asking price in order to acquire the flat.

He had not begrudged that premium. He knew that if his projected renovation went according to plan, he would easily double, if not treble, his money. Of course, there were some who might say that what he planned was frankly unacceptable, but there were always people who seemed determined to crush initiative. That was a real problem, he thought – people who thought of reasons why one could *not* do something, rather than think of ways of doing it. These people were everywhere, discouraging innovation, pouring cold water on enterprise. Look at the people who objected to the Christmas German Market on Princes Street. What a bunch of spoilsports, said Bruce. They had objected to cutting down trees in Princes Street Gardens; they objected to what they described as noise and vulgarity; they railed against the selling of half-glasses of sweetened glühwein at absurd prices, or plaster models of Santa, imported all the way from China, but marked with the description "Designed in Germany". What was wrong with that? Bruce wondered.

And why had these same objectors been so up in arms over a perfectly reasonable plan to convert the Scott Monument into an immersive experience? What's the issue there? Had immersive experiences existed in Walter Scott's day, could any of these people say that he would not have been perfectly happy to license it? Scott had been in debt, and surely would have welcomed any means of repaying his creditors that was easier than penning the Waverley novels.

But now Bruce put aside such thoughts as he unlocked the door to which he had an hour or so ago been given the key. Once inside the flat, he moved from room to room, switching on the lights in each. Edinburgh basement flats can be dark, and this one was markedly so. Yet the important thing, as Bruce had often remarked to clients in his estate agency days, is to see beyond what you see. A dingy, neglected property could become something quite different with a lick of paint applied judiciously. Discouraging kitchens could be transformed by a few well-placed cupboards; uninviting bathrooms could become something quite different with the installation of the right lighting and a new basin. There was a lot that could be done relatively simply and without breaking the bank.

This flat, he thought, was different. Yes, it needed smartening up with the usual redecoration, but his plan went considerably further than that. By changing the address to the flat, he would change everything. A dingy basement flat in India Street would, after minimum structural intervention, become a highly desirable lower-ground flat in Heriot Row. It was all so easy, so utterly obvious.

Bruce waited for the arrival of his builder friend, Tony. They were to meet in the flat that morning, and Bruce would show him exactly what he had in mind. And if Tony was willing, they could even make a start.

Bruce smiled to himself. He was where he wanted to be – working with buildings – making a difference to the lives of the people who bought them. It was, he thought, a form of social work, almost like working for a charity.

# 48

*You Hear Something, Henrik?*

Tony was late.

"Sorry, Bruce," he apologised. "I know I'm half an hour late, but you know how it is. Things to do, my friend." He winked.

Bruce smiled. "Yeah, Tony, we've all got things to do. That's all right, old pal. Nae worries, as they say."

Tony grinned. "You're a pal, Bruce." He paused, and gave Bruce a playful punch on the right shoulder. Bruce returned the punch, and they both laughed. Then Tony aimed a friendly kick at Bruce's shin. Bruce dodged the kick, responding with a poke in Tony's ribs.

"You're putting on weight, Tone," said Bruce. "My finger almost disappeared in the avoirdupois."

"You're one to talk," responded Tony, putting an arm around Bruce's shoulder and shaking him. "But it's good to see you, man. Jeez, it's been ages."

"You still going out with . . . what's her name, the one with the face. Remember?"

Tony laughed, then winked again. "That's the one, Bruce," he said. "Know what I mean?"

Bruce smiled. "High maintenance?"

"You got it," said Tony. "But I can't complain." He looked at his friend. "You fully recovered from the lightning?"

"Totally," said Bruce.

Tony gave him an enquiring look. "No long-term effects?

Know what I mean? Nothing like that?"

Bruce shook his head. "Nothing. *Nada*."

"Jeez," said Tony. "You're walking along and suddenly – *kapow!* – and you get fifty thousand volts up your neb and you're knocked into next Christmas. Not for me, old pal. I do *not* want to be struck by lightning. Okay for some – not me."

"There's a very small risk," said Bruce.

"Yeah, sure, but when that risk comes up, boy . . . No thank you." Tony looked around. "Let's get serious. You bought this dump, Bruce? You paid actual money for it?"

Bruce laughed. "I'm going to make a killing, Tony. Serious wonga."

Tony looked doubtful. "It's very dark. People like to see where they're going. This place, you'd get lost going to the bathroom, know what I mean? You'd have to send out search parties."

"It's a basement flat," said Bruce, in a slightly irritated tone. "You have to look beyond these things."

"Yeah, sure," said Tony. "But you still need light. *Let there be light*, as the Big Guy said." He looked around again. "I suppose you could put in some spots up there on the ceiling. Maybe something movement-sensitive so that they switch on when you come into the flat and prevent you from falling over yourself. Could work."

Tony looked up at the ceiling. Then he crossed the room and peered into a built-in cupboard. He gave a non-committal grunt. Then, turning to Bruce, he said, "I've got new speakers. Fantastic."

"Oh, yes? I'd forgotten – you're into hi-fi, aren't you?"

Tony nodded. "You know what they cost me? Twelve thousand. And that was second-hand."

"A lot of bass?" asked Bruce.

Tony rolled his eyes. "You put them on and it's like an

earthquake. These are speakers you *feel*, not listen to. If you turned them up full you'd get a letter from the British Seismic Survey people – I'm telling you."

"Great," said Bruce. "Good stuff."

Tony nodded. "I met this Irish guy, see – and he showed me his speakers. They were taller than him – I'm not exaggerating. I thought: why does the guy want such big speakers? And you know what? I realised that he had big speakers because he was a really short guy. Sometimes the Irish aren't all that tall. I'm not saying all of them, but some of them. You get these Irish jockeys, you see, and they don't want to be tall. Jeez, they can ride." He paused. "Have you seen the Dutch, Bruce? You been to Holland? You seen the people there?"

"Tall?"

"You said it. They're all up there – all of them. Something to do with the dairy products they eat. They've been eating that stuff for yonks, Bruce. It's given them big bones. Huge. The Dutch are *huge*, Bruce. I'm not exaggerating. They look down on us. They say, 'You hear something, Henrik? You hear somebody talking down below?' And it's us, Bruce. I swear. That's how it is over there. Big time." He paused. "There are no Dutch jockeys. Have you noticed that, Bruce? It's a fact. No Dutch jockeys. True as God."

Bruce was distracted. There was business to discuss, but he was about to ask Tony a favour, and he had to listen. And Tony was all right, he thought. A bit of a lad, but who isn't? "I suppose not."

"No. And the women? Bruce, I'm telling you – they are seriously tall. If you're a small guy – say, an Irish jockey going to Amsterdam for a weekend – you have zero chance. You may as well stay in Bally-whatever-it-is. Dutch women won't *look* at you if you're under six foot. And they're on the lookout for elevator shoes. If a guy wears elevator shoes and a Dutch broad finds out, he's toast, that guy. That's true, you know. There was this guy from Glasgow who thought his elevator shoes would help his chances in your actual Netherlands. Did they? I think you know the answer, Bruce. Poor guy. Ended up in a canal. He might as well have gone to Paisley for the weekend."

Bruce decided to move the conversation on. "Let me show you what I have in mind," he said, leading Tony into the room at the side of the flat. This was the room with the small window that looked onto the basement wall outside. Up above could just be glimpsed the trees growing on the gardens side of Heriot Row.

Bruce explained his plans. "If we take out that window and put in a door instead," he said, "what do you end up with? A Heriot Row address – that's what."

Tony crossed the room to examine the window – a tiny opening. After a minute or two of tapping the wall, he turned to Bruce.

"Are you mad, Bruce – as in *mad*? This is a supporting wall. We can't touch it. End of story."

Bruce's jaw dropped. "End of story?" he stuttered.

"Yes," said Tony. "End of story. Game, set, match. *Finito.*" Then, seeing Bruce's expression, he added, "Sorry, pal. Edinburgh's a UNESCO heritage area or whatever. You interfere with that wall, the building falls down, and you get the UN onto you. I'm not making this up. No can do."

# 49

## *In the Tunnel*

Bertie and Ranald Braveheart Macpherson stood at the doorway marked *Tunnel*. Behind them, in the main body of the kirk, they heard the choir and the wedding congregation embarking upon "Guide Me, O Thou Great Redeemer". The words were indistinct, though *I am weak but thou art mighty* might have given them some of the courage needed to follow the steps down into the subterranean reaches of St Giles'. They began the descent.

"It's very dark, Bertie," said Ranald. "Do you think—"

Had Bertie not begun to answer, the escapade might have ended right there as doubts consumed both boys. But Bertie started to reply, and did so in a tone intended to stiffen Ranald's resolve. "We'll be quite all right, Ranald," he said. "Your eyes get used to the dark, you know."

Ranald was not convinced, but he was conscious of the fact that Bertie had always been the brave one in their friendship, and he was unwilling to appear weak. So he said, "I suppose this will be just like all the other Edinburgh tunnels."

"It will," said Bertie, his voice betraying the uncertainty that he felt at setting off on a journey the end of which was completely unknown. He knew about some of the hidden streets under the Old Town, including Mary King's Close; he knew about the old railway tunnel that connected Waverley Station and the former marshalling yards at the end of Scotland Street. He hoped that this tunnel, of which he had never before heard, would link up with the Scotland Street tunnel and therefore bring them back to thoroughly familiar territory. But he could not be sure. What if it went quite another way, and brought them out in a completely unfamiliar part of Edinburgh?

Bertie was on the point of admitting these doubts to Ranald, when his friend suddenly announced that he was not in the slightest bit afraid. "I don't mind the dark," said Ranald. "Some people are frightened of it, but not me."

Bertie, although only seven, was wise enough to know that when somebody said that they were not frightened of something, it was, in many cases, as good as a frank admission that the thing of which they were allegedly not frightened was, in fact, something of which they were deeply afraid.

"You don't have to be ashamed to say that you're afraid of the dark, Ranald," he said. "Nobody should be ashamed of that sort of thing."

"But I'm not afraid," said Ranald. "I promise you, Bertie – I'm not afraid of not being able to see where we're going."

"Good," said Bertie, his voice still tremulous.

"You're not afraid, are you, Bertie?"

In the almost complete darkness, Bertie crossed his fingers on both hands. You could tell fibs if you crossed your fingers – everybody knew that. He had seen the truth of that proposition a few days ago when he had watched a politician on television claiming never to have promised not to raise taxes. There had been a rise in taxation, and the politician in question had appeared for interview on television with two fingers on his right hand noticeably crossed. That was not a sign of trustworthiness, Bertie thought. It was a general rule that those who said they would never tell a lie were less trustworthy than those who admitted that they were human, like the rest of us, and that while they might not resort to direct lies, occasionally omitted to say things they should perhaps say.

Now he said to Ranald, "Me afraid, Ranald? What's there to be afraid of?"

That was not a direct answer, but Bertie felt a certain responsibility for Ranald Braveheart Macpherson, and he did not want to say anything that could sap his friend's already fragile morale.

Ranald shivered. "There could be ghosts down here, Bertie. Edinburgh's full of ghosts."

Bertie tried to sound robust. "Ghosts don't exist, Ranald," he said. "Nor do bogles."

Ranald was silent, but then he said, "What's the difference between a bogle and a ghost, Bertie?"

Bertie considered this. They were now a hundred yards or so down the tunnel, in almost complete darkness, although a small chink of light filtered through from some source ahead of them. "A bogle," Bertie said, "is a sort of ghost, but a bit nastier, I think. It's a creature that lives here in Scotland – in a place like . . . like . . ." He almost said *like this*, but stopped himself just in time.

"They don't exist, Bertie?" asked Ranald. "Are you sure about that?"

"Yes," replied Bertie. "There's no such thing as a bogle, Ranald."

Ranald said nothing, and they continued to make their way along the tunnel. The walls were smooth and the pavement firm underfoot. The air was slightly musty, but the tunnel did not feel as if it had not been used for a long time.

"I wonder who comes down here," Ranald Braveheart Macpherson mused. "Do you think it's the Knights of the Thistle, Bertie?"

Bertie considered this. "Probably, Ranald."

"Do you think we might see some of them?" Ranald asked.

"I don't think so, Ranald. I saw a picture in the newspaper of them arriving at St Giles' by taxi."

They continued in silence. Then Ranald said, "Bertie, can you hear something?"

They stopped.

Bertie strained his ears. He heard Ranald's breathing, and he heard his own heart, hammering now within his chest. Apart from that . . . Ranald grabbed his arm. "There, Bertie," he whispered.

At first, Bertie thought it was Ranald's imagination, or, indeed, his own. But then he realised that there was a sound, and the sound was that of footsteps on the stone floor of the tunnel. They were still faint, but unmistakeably getting closer.

"We're finished," said Ranald Braveheart Macpherson in a quivering whisper. "I've had a good life, Bertie. And thank you for being my friend."

The silence returned, and then they heard the sound of voices somewhere, drifting down the tunnel. "This way, First Minister – after you . . ."

"Don't give up, Ranald," whispered Bertie. "Let's run."

Pushing, half dragging Ranald with him, Bertie made his way as fast as he could along the tunnel, which now sloped sharply down towards Princes Street. There was a glimmer of light from the occasional, half-hearted wall light, but they were mostly surrounded by darkness. Bertie became aware that Ranald was crying, as when they stopped to get their breath, his friend's sobs filled the air. Behind them, still indistinct but growing steadily louder, came the ringing footsteps.

They continued to run, and in a short while the tunnel began to slope upwards. Without their knowing, it had reached the Waverley end of the Scotland Street tunnel, and it was along this that they hurtled, tripping from time to time, but picking themselves up with the easy ability that small boys have to recover from falls. And then, suddenly, they saw a circle of light ahead of them. This spurred them on.

They heard a bark, and then another one, and these familiar canine sounds seemed to come from the opening mouth of the tunnel.

There stood a small dog with a distinctive gold tooth. Cyril.

A few minutes later, emerging into the old marshalling yards, with Cyril brimming with enthusiasm at their feet, Bertie looked up in gratitude at the sky. He felt like Tam O'Shanter at the end of his mad dash from Cutty Sark, delivered from the threat of something that may not exist, but which is no less frightening for that.

# 50

## Naughtiness and Envy

The arrangement that Nicola had made with David was that they should meet at Big Lou's before making their way up to the Festival Theatre for the matinée production of *Don Pasquale*. The performance would end at five thirty, David said, and that would mean they could go for dinner somewhere nearby, provided, of course that Nicola did not mind eating that early. "We have a word for a late breakfast," he said. "We're quite comfortable with *brunch*, but we don't have a word for a meal that's such a late lunch that it becomes an early dinner. *Linner*? Or possibly *Dunch*?"

"Either would do," said Nicola. "But *dunch* sounds a bit better, I think."

"Good. So we'll do dunch after *Don Pasquale*."

Nicola was surprised at how much she anticipated this date with David – and it was a date that she was going on, she told herself – a real date. This was not a trip to the Festival Theatre with just any friend; this was an outing with a *man* whom she had met on the street – in the middle of Dundas Street to be precise. How often did you go to matinée performances of an opera with a man you had met in the middle – quite literally – of Dundas Street, amidst a scattering of potatoes?

She tried to remember when she had last gone on a real date. It must have been with Abril, before they married, which was how many years ago? She stopped trying to remember because any thought of the passage of years tended to depress her. We have only a brief time on this earth and the years ran so quickly . . . How did Domenica put it? She was always quoting Auden, and there had been a line from one of his poems she had mentioned that Nicola thought particularly memorable. *The years shall run like rabbits* . . . That was how he put it – and he was right. They did. Our time was so short – a tiny instant in the cosmic scale, barely registerable in the context of the fire and fury of the galaxies in which we, such minuscule, insignificant creatures, found ourselves. *Carpe diem*, as Horace advised.

She had gone to a collection of Auden's poems on Stuart's bookshelf – left behind by Irene, probably; she did not imagine that Stuart read much poetry – to find the reference to these fleet-footed years, and had located it. But as she leafed through the book she had come across a poem that reminded her of her impending assignation. The title had caught her eye – "Heavy Date" – and she had read it there and then, caught in the poet's skein of observations about love, as he looks out over the city in anticipation of his date.

Love requires an object, Auden said – and went on to suggest that almost anything would do – as a boy he had loved a pumping engine, and had thought it "every bit as beautiful as you". Nicola wondered whether that was true, and decided that it probably was – or was true to an extent. Perhaps Auden was right in saying that what really mattered was that we should love *something* or *somebody* – that we should allow ourselves to experience love in essence rather than in particularity, and not yearn after perfection. That was probably unattainable, anyway – and the sooner we learned that lesson, the easier would be our romantic experience. Crying for the moon, Auden went on to say, was "naughtiness and envy", which, once again, was probably true. Love that which comes your way, rather than what you would like to find.

She arrived at Big Lou's fifteen minutes early – an indication, she admitted to herself, of nervousness. It was like being back at school, being sixteen, and waiting to meet – what was his name? James Fairbrother – waiting to meet him at the café near Burt's Hotel in Melrose, looking anxiously at her watch, hoping that nobody saw her and realised that she was waiting for James, who had his many admirers, as he was one of the most popular boys in the school. Here she was, in her fifties, feeling sixteen again, which was ridiculous. And yet, she said to herself, we never really change much *inside*. It's as easy to feel awkward at fifty as it is at sixteen, because we're still *us* inside, throughout our lives, with all the weaknesses and anxieties to which the young self was prone, even if we might manage these better as the years went by.

Big Lou was surprised to see her. "I didn't expect you," she said, adding, quickly, "Not that I'm not pleased to see you. It's just that you seem to have your hands so full these days with the bairns."

"That's true enough," said Nicola. "But Stuart is very considerate. He makes sure that I get time to myself."

"He's a good man," said Big Lou. "It's such a pity . . ." She stopped herself. She was about to say that it was such a pity that he had married Irene, but she realised that this could be tactless. Nicola was, after all, mother-in-law to Irene. Family issues were best left to those involved, even if friends and acquaintances had strong views.

Nicola smiled. "I have no time at all for Irene, Lou," she said. "I don't mind telling you that. I've never been able to stand her. You needn't worry. In my view she's . . . well, you may imagine what I think."

Big Lou was relieved. "I don't like to comment on people,"

she said. "But I've always been prepared to make an exception in Irene's case." She paused. "And that pair wee boy, wee Bertie. What a start in life. And yet he's somehow weathered the storm. He's a braw wee man, right enough."

"Bertie *is* a treasure," said Nicola. "We all love him to bits."

Big Lou noticed as Nicola glanced at her watch. "You off somewhere?" she asked.

Nicola hesitated. But she decided that she did not want to keep anything from Lou – who would not wish to trust this stout-hearted woman with their confidences?

"I'm meeting a man," she said. "Then we're going to *Don Pasquale* at the Festival Theatre."

"Ah," said Lou. "*Don Pasquale*. The poor Don. He shouldn't have married at his age." She stopped herself, and blushed. "I'm not saying that people who are getting on a bit shouldn't go out with people."

Nicola laughed. "Don't worry, Lou. I'm not sensitive. I know it looks ridiculous – going out on a date at my stage in life – but . . ."

"Exactly," said Big Lou. "But . . ."

There were so many *buts* in this life; each a potential justification, an entirely necessary anodyne.

# 51

## È finita, Don Pasquale

Big Lou looked over Nicola's shoulder. The front door of the coffee bar opened onto a set of steps descending from street level. Next to the door was a window through which it was possible to watch the arrival of customers, or at least to see their disembodied legs before they reached the door.

Big Lou nodded towards the entrance. "Your friend, I think."

David pushed open the door. Nicola turned round, raising a hand in salute. He smiled, slightly bashfully, she thought. Perhaps it was as awkward for him to go on a date as it was for her. She wanted to reassure him, to let him know that she, too, was on tenterhooks.

He joined her at the bar. "I'm probably late," he said. "Have you been waiting for ages?"

It was Big Lou who replied. "Two minutes. We've been talking."

David looked at his watch. "We probably shouldn't linger. There's no hurry, but we may have to wait some time for a bus. You never know."

Nicola was surprised. It had not occurred to her that they would go on a date by bus. There was no reason why one should not, of course, but it struck her as slightly incongruous.

David picked up her hesitation. "Or we can get a taxi," he said hurriedly. "I could phone for one."

Nicola shook her head. "No, a bus will be fine."

"The twenty-three . . ." David began.

"Get off at the McEwan Hall," said Big Lou. "Then it's a five-minute walk to the Festival Theatre." She paused. "*Don Pasquale?*"

David nodded. "You know it?"

Big Lou sighed. "*Com'è gentil la notte a mezzo April!* I love Donizetti. Anything Italian does it for me."

David agreed, then glanced again at his watch. "We should perhaps . . ."

Nicola rose from her stool. "Of course."

They walked to the bus stop. Further down the road, a bus trundled up Dundas Street. It was a twenty-three. They boarded it, and took a seat at the back. To begin with they were alone, but at a stop further up the hill, a woman got on the bus and took a seat opposite them. She was somewhere in her early forties, Nicola thought. She was wearing a faded cotton dress and a tailored beige linen jacket. Her features were fine. An intelligent face, thought Nicola.

Nicola looked at her, and their eyes met. Then the woman transferred her gaze to David, before looking back at Nicola. Embarrassed by the scrutiny, Nicola looked away. Through the window of the bus, she saw the sky bisected by the white line of a vapour trail. She wondered whether the jet on high was heading east or west. It took a few moments for her to get her bearings before she realised that it was east. It was from Canada, perhaps from Montreal, and was flying over Scotland towards Copenhagen or Berlin. She thought, we are just a patch of green down below, with blue all about us. They don't know anything about us.

The woman noticed. She said, "Think of those people up there. Think of them."

Nicola nodded. "A tiny metal tube. So high."

"Yes."

David followed their gaze. "Bernoulli's Principle. That's what keeps them up there." He paused. "You know that?"

"Not really," said Nicola.

"No," said the woman.

David pointed up at the vapour trail. "Bernoulli proved that air that moves fast is at less pressure than air moving slowly. So if the wing increases the pressure of the air below it while the air above is at lower pressure, you get lift. The wing's lifted up, you see. That's what's keeping that plane up there."

"Oh," said the woman.

Nicola was not sure what to say.

Then David said, "We're going to the opera."

The woman looked interested. "Which one?"

"*Don Pasquale*," answered David. "The Festival Theatre."

The woman said, "I've always wanted to see that. I've missed it. I didn't even know it was on." She paused. "Do you think there'll be tickets?"

"There are always returns," said David. "People go down with colds. They change their minds. They have to babysit. You can always get a ticket."

"Do you think so?" said the woman.

David nodded. "I do." And then he said, "Come with us, if you like."

Nicola caught her breath. This was their date, and he had just invited a complete stranger to join them.

The woman hesitated. "I think I will. Do you mean it?"

"Of course."

He could have consulted me, thought Nicola. He could have given me a glance to see if I objected – that was all. But he did not.

The woman laughed. "I feel highly irresponsible. I'm

meant to be going to a lecture at the National Library. But I'm going to go to *Don Pasquale* instead."

Now David turned to Nicola. "You don't mind, do you?" he said.

Nicola struggled to control herself. She wanted to say: *I mind very much*. But she did not. Instead, she said, "Why should I mind?"

It occurred to her now that this had never been a date. This was simply a trip to the opera by two people who independently wanted to see *Don Pasquale*. That was all it was. And if that was the case, then she could quite reasonably have a sudden change of mind. She could say that she had forgotten that she had to do something else, and that she would need to get back to Scotland Street. She could so easily do that.

"It's a wonderful production," said David. Then he added, "I'm David, by the way. And this is Nicola."

The woman introduced herself as Janet.

"And let me guess your star sign," said Janet.

"Whose star sign?" Nicola blurted out. What was this? "Mine or his?"

"Both," said Janet. "His first." She gave him a penetrating glance. "Leo – right?"

David burst out laughing. "Spot on," he exclaimed.

"Could be coincidence," muttered Nicola.

"Oh no," retorted Janet. "You can always tell." She paused. "And you're Aries? Am I right?"

She was, but Nicola remained tight-lipped.

"I see," said Janet. "I suspect I was right."

"It's amazing," said David.

"You don't believe in all that nonsense, do you?" said Nicola.

David shrugged. "Who knows? There could be something in it."

Nicola stared out of the window. She could never go to the opera with a man who saw the slightest element of truth in astrology. She just couldn't. She made up her mind. "Oh dear," she said. "I've just realised something. I'm meant to be picking up Ulysses from nursery. I always do that on a Friday."

"But today's Saturday," said David.

Nicola ignored this. She turned to Janet. "You can have my ticket, if you like."

Janet frowned. "But . . ."

"No, I mean it," said Nicola.

"You're really kind," said Janet.

The bus had reached the McEwan Hall. "I'm not going to get off," said Nicola. "I'll stay on. I can change at Tollcross."

David stood up. "I hope you don't mind," he said. He looked embarrassed, and it crossed Nicola's mind that he simply had not thought it through. But it was too late to unpick the disaster.

"Of course I don't."

She gave her ticket to Janet, whose offer to pay she brushed aside. "I don't need any money," she said.

She looked out of the bus window, marked as it was with the grime of the city, like a layer of regret. They rose to disembark, and she uttered the goodbyes that politeness required, but said nothing more. As the bus moved off, she wanted to cry. This was as bad as being sixteen again, waiting for James Fairbrother in the café near Burt's Hotel. He'd never turned up. Something about rugby practice. Something like that. It was a long time ago, and it's hard to remember all the details of yesterday's disappointments.

*È finita, Don Pasquale*, she thought.

# 52

## *Most Patient of Dogs*

In their house at Nine Mile Burn, Matthew and Elspeth had been woken up that day even earlier than usual. The boys usually slept until shortly after six, the light of summer mornings being kept out of their room by heavy blackout curtains. But now, at half past five, they were wide awake, the curtains had been opened, and sunlight was streaming into their bedroom.

They knew that their parents did not like to be woken until at least six thirty, but on this particular morning they were unable to curb their enthusiasm. In the warmth of the kitchen, installed in what had once been a fruit crate, the newly adopted Ralph had spent a night of dreamless, contented sleep. Now, having crept along the corridor from their room, the boys tiptoed into the kitchen to be reunited with the dog that had so unexpectedly and miraculously come into their lives. They had plans for Ralph's day that included lessons in retrieving sticks, a run through the woods, where there was a good chance he might encounter a rabbit, and a lesson – at Tobermory's insistence – in the climbing of trees. Rognvald was adamant that dogs could not be taught to climb trees, no matter how intelligent they otherwise were, but Tobermory could not be persuaded to abandon the project and continued to try to push Ralph up onto the lower branches of a sycamore tree in which the boys had erected a make-do treehouse.

Matthew and Elspeth had watched from their bedroom

window, laughing at the seriousness of the boys' efforts. But they had marvelled, too, at the dog's tolerance. While Ralph clearly lacked the fundamental ability to climb trees, he nonetheless tolerated the indignity of being half lifted, half pushed onto a low overhanging branch.

"He is the most patient of dogs," Matthew observed. "Look at him – most dogs wouldn't stand for that sort of thing. He's letting them get away with it."

"Yes," agreed Elspeth. "And that's not the only ordeal he's had to put up with. I saw Rognvald trying to ride on his back. He just stood there, accepting everything."

"He's saintly," said Matthew. He looked thoughtful. "Do you think that an animal might be a saint – in the sense of having a moral, good nature?"

Elspeth gave this some thought. She agreed that Ralph seemed particularly friendly. "He's a very gentle, sweet-natured dog."

"But are these moral qualities?" asked Matthew. "Is friendliness in a dog something for which the dog deserves moral credit?"

It seemed to Elspeth that the answer was obvious. "Yes, of course. Dogs can express goodness, just as they can show hostility. They can show love. They have a moral universe." She paused. "And what's the most common compliment paid to a dog? *Good dog.* That's what we say." She looked at Matthew. "Why do we say that if we don't recognise goodness in dogs?"

Matthew hesitated. "I never agreed with Descartes on this. He said that dogs are just machines."

"Well, Descartes was wrong. If dogs are just machines, then so are we."

Matthew grinned. "Aren't we?" His grin faded. "I don't mean that, of course."

The arrival of Ralph had been a big thing for the boys, as was Matthew's yielding to their entreaties that the dog should be allowed to stay. But this decision, reached out of sympathy for the dog's evident desire to leave his owners, and also because the boys were so keen to keep him, gave rise to certain practical problems. The first of these was the concealment that would be necessary. The neighbours had yet to come in search of Ralph, but it was only a matter of time before they did so. After all, the first place anybody would look for a missing pet must surely be next door.

Matthew was not sure what he would do if Robert and Maureen were to knock on the door and ask him whether he had seen their dog. He had never found it easy to lie; in fact, he found it almost impossible. Inevitably, he blushed, and would begin to stutter if he deviated at all from the truth. It seemed that he was constitutionally unable to dissemble, which would make him a very bad candidate for any profession where anything other than the strict telling of the truth was required. I would not be a very good spy, he said to himself. Nor a good party politician, either.

He could, of course, merely say nothing if any question were to be asked about Ralph. He might say "Ralph? Of course, he . . ." and leave it there. That was an ancient response to an unpopular or awkward question – simply to avoid the issue. Sometimes it worked, although sometimes it made an interrogator dig in. If rats were to be smelled, then somebody would eventually do just that and he would be left in the impossible position of having to explain why they had given Ralph sanctuary.

It would be possible, of course, to brazen it out – to say that it was clear that the dog was happier where he was, and that was the end of the matter. That was the *best interests* test, and it worked in custody disputes over children. But dogs were different: people *owned* dogs in a way in which they did not own children. The proponents of animal rights, of course, disputed that: they took the view that we were carers, rather than owners, of domestic animals – a theoretical position for which there was some justification and that was, to an extent, recognised by the law. If you mistreated an animal, the state could take it away from you: there was nothing radical in that. And yet that principle did not recognise any preferences in the animal itself: the wishes of the dog were neither here nor there in such a context – only objectively discernible mistreatment would suffice to overturn the claims of ownership.

Now, as the boys brought that morning a bounding and enthusiastic Ralph into their parents' bedroom, Matthew made up his mind as to what he would do next. He would have to sit the boys down and stress to them that if they wanted to keep Ralph, they would have to be very careful indeed. They could play with him outside, but only on the far side of the house, away from neighbourly eyes, or in the trees, where there was shelter enough for security.

"Whatever happens, boys," he said, "the people next door must not see him. If they do, I'm afraid that will be the end of Ralph."

"Will they kill him, Daddy?" asked Tobermory.

"Of course not," said Matthew. "But they will take him away – and Ralph himself does not want that."

"So, he's going to be a secret dog?" asked Fergus.

"That's a good way of putting it," said Matthew. And thought: *a secret dog* – yes, that made sense. And the pleasure one might get from having a secret *anything* was sometimes greater than the pleasure we derive from the overt.

# 53

## *Neighbours Drop In*

It lasted one day. The boys listened to their father's pep talk about the need for discretion, and each of them, in turn, voluntarily crossed his heart and hoped to die should he be so careless as to reveal the presence of Ralph. They made suggestions – all of which made Matthew smile. Fergus asked whether they could dye Ralph so that he appeared to be a different dog – or even paint him, if dyeing were to prove too difficult. If he were painted white, and black spots were to be added, then surely he could pass for a Dalmatian, and would thus be able to lead a less concealed life. Rognvald wondered whether Ralph could be kept permanently in the attic, where there was plenty of room for him to take regular exercise. "He'd get used to the dark after a while," Rognvald suggested. "And nobody would hear him if he barked up there."

Fergus considered this, and then came up with the counter-suggestion that Ralph might stay indoors during the day, and then be let out at night when he would be undetected by the neighbours. Was it possible, he asked, that a vet might be able to remove his bark, or at least make it not quite so loud?

In the event, Ralph spent a considerable amount of time outside that day, mostly in the woods, but also being taken for a walk up the lower slopes of the Pentlands, well out of sight of his former home. But when Matthew returned, Elspeth greeted him with the worrying news that the invitation he had issued to Robert and Maureen, and that they had both forgotten about, was, in fact, for that very night – and they were due to arrive for dinner at seven thirty. She had remembered just in time to prepare a vegan menu, using recipes that she had downloaded from the BBC cookery website. *Water soup* was to be followed by an amuse-bouche of *carrots on horseback* and then, as the main course, *soya surprise* would be served with kale and distressed pumpkin. "Thank goodness I had all the ingredients," she said. "Now everything's ready except for . . ."

He was thinking the same thing. "Except for Ralph?"

"Precisely. What do we do? We can't let him wander about while they're here."

Matthew scratched his head. "The attic?" he said at last. And then, warming to the idea, added, "We could put camp beds up there for the boys. Then they can keep him company. We won't hear from any of them."

Elspeth hesitated. The attic was remote, cold and rather dusty. Would the boys be warm enough up there?

"They'll love it," said Matthew. "We can tell them that it's camping. It'll be a big adventure for them."

It was agreed, and the boys were informed. As Matthew had predicted, they were excited by the idea, and a great deal of time was spent in marshalling flashlights, water bottles and emergency supplies of one sort or another. Then, accompanied by their father, who agreed to read them a bedtime story by the light of a headtorch, they trooped up to the attic and were installed on three small camp beds. Ralph was given a blanket on the floor, and a large dog-chew at which he had already started worrying away.

Robert and Maureen arrived shortly before seven thirty, unannounced in their almost completely silent electric car. Matthew welcomed them on the drive and could not resist commenting on the fact that they had chosen to drive rather than to walk across the fields.

He chose his words carefully. "Much safer to drive, rather than walk," he said. "One might stumble, I suppose, when walking across the fields. People do."

Robert looked at him suspiciously. "Our electricity is almost entirely green. We charge the car from our solar panels."

Maureen backed him up. "We're almost entirely off-grid, you know. It's the only way."

Matthew pretended to be impressed. "That's great," he said. "People go on about the carbon footprint of new electric cars – you'll know what they say about the resources used to build them – the lithium and so on. But I think they're still worthwhile – and their torque is terrific, isn't it? I can well understand how people are taken with their torque." He paused. "Tesla certainly know how to torque the torque."

Robert glared at him. "Our car comes from China," he announced.

Matthew raised an eyebrow. "Not exactly next door," he said. "But there we are. Do you know the Leonard Cohen song, 'Suzanne'? One of the lines there sticks in my mind. He sings about eating oranges that come all the way from China. When he wrote that, such things were pretty exotic, but now . . . Well, here you are in your entirely Chinese car, driven by electricity from your Chinese solar panels."

Matthew stopped himself. He had not intended to be rude, and it was probably his jumpiness over Ralph that lay behind these digs. Now he said, "Let's go inside and join Elspeth. She's spent a lot of time on making dinner. And I could show you the view from the patio on the other side of the house. We've a good view of the Lammermuir Hills. I never tire of sitting there and gazing at them. It's why I love this place so much – that view."

"It's nice," said Maureen.

'Yes," agreed Robert.

They went inside, where Elspeth greeted them, after wiping her hands on a tea-towel.

"I brought you some chocolates," said Maureen, handing her a wrapped-up box.

"Fairtrade," said Robert.

Elspeth looked surprised. "Oh, what do you want in exchange?"

Matthew laughed. "No, *Fairtrade*, Elspeth. It means the cocoa people are paid generously. I like that idea."

"Of course," said Elspeth, blushing. "Thank you so much."

"Let's go and look at the view," said Matthew.

Maureen looked about her. "Where are your boys?" she asked.

"In the . . ." Matthew stopped himself from saying *in the attic*.

"Upstairs," said Elspeth. "Fast asleep. They get very tired dashing around with . . ."

"With each other," said Matthew quickly.

Was this how it was going to be? he asked himself. Was this how it was going to be – all night?

# 54

## *You Mince-Heid!*

They sat down at the table, the ill-matched four of them: Matthew, Elspeth, Maureen and Robert. It was a strange feeling for Matthew – to be entertaining a couple whom he did not like, while trying, as far as he was able, to maintain an air of neighbourly civility. As Elspeth served the water soup, he went over in his mind the possible reasons for his discomfort. He was not a person of fixed views, and in general was tolerant of those with whom he disagreed. Nor was he an extremist of any stripe: he was broadly in tune with the zeitgeist, while avoiding the more aggressive notes of bigotry, vitriol and intolerance that were a hallmark of contemporary public debate – such as it was. What he did not particularly take to was the tendency to sit in judgement of others who might not match one in one's own attachment to a strong position on a range of environmental and social issues. In a liberal society, he thought, there would be room for those who were out of step with majority enthusiasms, and it was fundamentally wrong to set out to shame them because they had a different view or because they did not utter with sufficient vigour the shibboleths of the times. Robert, he felt, did just that.

"Great soup," said Maureen, after she had taken her first sip of the light green concoction that Elspeth had served.

Elspeth thanked her. "It's the first time I've made it," she said.

"Watercress?" asked Robert.

Elspeth shook her head. "Mostly water," she said. "But there's a bit of cucumber and celery."

"I love celery," said Robert. "I worked on a celery farm in France when I was a student. Six weeks. I fell in love with a girl who was working there too. She was a long-distance swimmer."

Matthew thought: *I do not want to hear about that.* He looked at the soup. Elspeth had done her best, but he found it far too insipid. And what had they to look forward to? Carrots on horseback? He wondered what that would be like; it did not sound particularly promising. And he had never liked soya, no matter what people did with it.

"She was studying in Paris," Robert said. "Her father had been in the 1968 riots. I could never imagine my own parents rioting. I was so impressed. The French have a far more exciting life than we do."

"Hah," said Matthew.

"She did not return my affection," Robert went on. "She said I was too English. I explained that I was Scottish, and she simply shrugged. You know how the French do that Gallic shrug of theirs."

Matthew noticed that Maureen was listening to this steely faced. It was another point against Robert: husbands should not discuss former girlfriends in the presence of one's spouse, and nor should wives discuss their old boyfriends.

"She married a man who fixed telephone wires," Robert said. "He was one of those people you see climbing up ladders. He was called René."

"How interesting," said Matthew.

And that was the point at which Ralph began to bark.

It was not all that clear – not at the beginning – and Matthew was able to mask the sound by clearing his throat as loudly as he could manage. As he did so, he glanced at Elspeth, who was sitting quite still, as if caught in the headlights of a car.

Robert frowned. "Was that a dog?" he asked.

Matthew shook his head. "No, I didn't hear anything."

Ralph barked again – a muffled sound drifting down from the attic, but unmistakeable.

"I didn't know you had a dog," said Robert, fixing Matthew with an intense stare.

"We don't," said Matthew. "And that wasn't a dog. Or at least, if it was a dog, it was on the television. The boys must be watching a television programme. You sometimes get dogs on television."

Robert gave him a scornful look. "You don't need to tell me that," he said.

'Like Lassie, the wonder dog," Matthew continued. "Remember her? *Lassie fetch help!* And away she'd go. Lassie was terrific."

"Schmaltz," muttered Robert. "Pure schmaltz."

Matthew drew in his breath. This man was *appalling*. You did not accuse your host of talking schmaltz – even when he was. Lassie was definitely schmaltzy, but you did not have to spell it out at the dinner table.

The door was suddenly pushed open, and Ralph bounded in, quickly followed by Tobermory, dressed in his astronaut pyjamas.

"Oh, Daddy," Tobermory burst out. "Ralph escaped. I tried to stop him, but I couldn't."

Robert sprang to his feet. "That's our dog," he exclaimed. "You've found him!"

Tobermory stared at Robert. "We didn't find him – he found us," he said. "He lives here now – Daddy said he could. He says that Ralph doesn't like you."

Robert took a step forward to Ralph, and bent down to

embrace him. Ralph looked at him for a moment, then let out a warning growl.

"Don't growl at Daddy," interjected Maureen. "It's Daddy, Ralph – Daddy."

Ralph growled again.

"I don't think he wants to have too much to do with you," said Matthew. "I think that dog has voted with his feet. Or paws, rather."

"Don't talk nonsense," snapped Robert. "Ralph loves me." He addressed the dog directly. "You love your daddy, Ralph, don't you? And your mummy over there – you love her too."

Ralph growled again, and then, as Robert took another step towards him, he lunged forward and nipped him sharply on the ankle. Robert gave a shout of pain. "Bad, wicked boy!" he screamed.

"Yes," Maureen joined in. "Bad, bad boy. Say sorry to Daddy."

Ralph did no such thing. He growled softly and moved closer to Matthew, who gave him a comforting pat.

"I really don't think he likes you," ventured Matthew. "Something to do with his diet, perhaps?"

Robert shot Matthew a poisonous look. "You've alienated his affections, you . . . you mince-heid!"

"Me a mince-heid?" asked Matthew. "You're a mince-heid, if anybody's a mince-heid."

"What's a mince-heid?" asked Tobermory.

Robert felt his injury – the dog's teeth had broken the skin at several points. He looked up. He drew in his breath, and aimed a kick at Ralph. He missed, though, and ended up kicking Elspeth.

"Did you just kick my wife?" demanded Matthew.

"Mind your own business," snapped Robert. And then,

to Maureen, he said, "We don't have to stay and listen to all this."

"Quite right," she said.

"These things don't always end with dignity," whispered Elspeth to her son.

"Will Daddy hit him?" asked Tobermory.

"There are lots of things Daddy would like to do," replied Elspeth. "But don't worry – he never does them."

"Is Ralph staying?" whispered Tobermory.

Neither of his parents said anything, but the answer was obvious.

# 55

## *Becoming Irish, Part 1*

If that day had been significant for Matthew and his family, the following day was to produce an equally important salience in Bertie's life. Bertie had put up with so much in his seven short years so far, most of it engineered by his mother, Irene: saxophone lessons, yoga classes in Stockbridge, Italian *conversazione*, and, of course, psychotherapy with Dr Hugo Fairbairn, as he then was, author of that classic of child psychotherapy, *Shattered to Pieces: Ego Dissolution in a Three-Year-Old Tyrant*. These slings and arrows came at him not only at home, but at school, too: there had been the additional burden of dealing with Olive, Pansy, and, of course, for a short and particularly difficult period, the exceptionally bossy Galactica MacFee. And those were just the girls: equally trying were the boys, of whom Tofu was the most egregious example. He was ably assisted by the pugilistic Larch and, more recently, by the unpredictable Socrates Dunbar. In all of this, only Ranald Braveheart Macpherson was there to support and encourage Bertie – to give him a vision of the friendship that helped him to deal with the vicissitudes of life.

But in any list of tribulations, there is always one that seems to be such a gratuitously unfair burden – the proverbial straw that breaks the overladen camel's back. This now seemed to have arrived in Bertie's life in the shape of Irene's decision that Bertie should get an Irish passport, which he could do on the strength of a maternal grandparent. An application had been made for this, supported by all the necessary paperwork, and sent to the Irish Passport Office in Dublin, the government department charged with extending the benefits of Irish citizenship to a wide diaspora. Irene had gone through all the bureaucratic hoops but, not satisfied with those stipulated by the Government of Ireland, she had created an additional one. This was a plan to ensure that Bertie should not just be a paper Irish citizen, entitled to move through EU queues at airports, but should be made fully aware of his Irish heritage. To this end she planned for Bertie to have a two-hour lesson each Saturday morning on the subject of Irish culture, to be given by an Irish postgraduate student at the University of Edinburgh, Eamonn Flynn. That morning, the first of these lessons was to take place, Stuart having reluctantly given in to Irene's demand that he should be there to introduce the tutor to Bertie and to provide coffee for Eamonn at half-time.

Nicola was quietly fuming. "This really is the end," she muttered. "That poor little boy having all sorts of Irishness thrust on him. That woman is the end – the absolute end."

Stuart had simply looked down at the floor. "I know what you mean, Mother, but she's entitled under our agreement to have some input into Bertie's education. I have to go along with her on some things."

Nicola muttered something – in Portuguese. Having been married to a Portuguese wine producer had its advantages – one of which had been the acquisition of an ability to express herself fairly volubly in the dialect of Portuguese used on the banks of the Douro. This was sometimes more expressive than the textbook language.

And now, at ten o'clock sharp, as arranged with Irene and confirmed by Stuart, Eamonn Flynn, a young man of twenty-six, a graduate of the University of Cork (BA) and Trinity

College, Dublin (MPhil) and now a PhD candidate at the University of Edinburgh, knocked on the door of the Pollock flat at 44 Scotland Street.

Stuart tried to look welcoming as he opened the door. It was not this young man's fault, he told himself: he had simply answered Irene's advertisement and would have no knowledge of the background circumstances. For Eamonn Flynn, no doubt, this was no different from any other student-type employment, such as being a coffee bar barista (or *avocato*, in Scotland). What was it they said about messengers? That you shouldn't shoot them?

Eamonn introduced himself. "I'm a wee bit early, I'm afraid. I didn't want to be late."

Stuart led him into the kitchen. "Bertie will join us in a moment," he said. "He's just tidying his room."

"It's rather an unusual request," Eamonn ventured. "Teaching Irish culture is . . . well, a bit difficult. There's so much. There's history and geography and literature and music . . . well, rather a lot, when you come to think of it."

Stuart nodded. "I agree. It's his mother's idea, actually . . . She lives up in Aberdeenshire, as you may know."

"She told me that," said Eamonn. "Awful cold up there, I believe."

"Freezing," said Stuart.

"And a lot of fish," added Eamonn. "Which is a grand thing, I suppose. Nothing wrong with fish."

"No," said Stuart. "Fish are . . ." He searched for the right expression. "Fish are a good thing, I suppose." He paused before continuing, "Fish are a great thing in Ireland, aren't they? I remember a line of Yeats – 'the mackerel-crowded seas'. A very vivid line, I thought."

Eamonn laughed. "The Spanish have put a stop to that, but let's not go there."

"Yes," said Stuart. "There are an awful lot of places we're encouraged not to go these days."

He looked at Eamonn. "What are you going to talk to Bertie about today?" he asked.

Eamonn shrugged. "I thought I might just tell him a bit about Ireland in general. A bit of Irish history, perhaps."

"Ah," said Stuart. "There's a lot of history in Ireland, isn't there?"

"Yes," said Eamonn. "But it's quite simple, really. All you have to remember is that the Irish were having a grand time, speaking Old Irish and making poteen, but the English came and spoiled it for us. Then we kicked the English out and the Church took over, and spoiled it for everyone all over again. Then we kicked the Church out and Brussels came and spoiled it for people by saying we had to charge company tax and so on. It's an awfully difficult business being Irish, so it is."

He said this with a straight face, but eventually could not prevent himself from laughing. Stuart joined in. "Sure, you're a great fellow," he said, in an attempt at an Irish accent.

"Don't come the stage Irishman with me," said Eamonn, with mock bellicosity. "My thesis subject is the plays of J. M. Synge. I know all about those boyos."

They both laughed again. And at that point Bertie came into the room.

"Sure, it's yourself," said Eamonn, with a wink.

Bertie looked puzzled. This was just another thing. He took a deep breath. He imagined that becoming Irish was rather like going to the dentist. You closed your eyes and told yourself it would not go on for ever.

# 56

## Bertie's Theory of Ice Cream

"So, Bertie," said Eamonn. "Here we are. Are you looking forward to talking about Ireland?"

Bertie was on his own in the kitchen with Eamonn, Stuart having retreated into his study to allow the tutorial to take place without him.

Bertie looked at Eamonn. He was an honest boy and found it hard, if not impossible, to lie. Tofu found it very easy, as did Larch and Socrates Dunbar – and Olive, too, he suspected. In fact, it seemed to Bertie that everybody lied effortlessly and without remorse – except him, that is.

"Not really," he said, adding, "If you don't mind."

Eamonn grinned. "I don't blame you," he said. "When I was your age, I spent most of my time riding my bike and catching frogs. Have you ever caught a frog, Bertie?"

Bertie shook his head. "Tofu has," he said.

"Tofu?" asked Eamonn. "Is he a boy in your class?"

Bertie nodded. "Yes, he catches frogs and then puts them in girls' desks. He did that to Pansy, and she screamed and screamed."

"That sounds fun," said Eamonn. "We'd call that *craic* in Ireland. Do you know that word, Bertie. Do you know what somebody means if they say that the craic was good?"

Bertie did not.

"It means a good time," explained Eamonn. "It's an expression we like to use in Ireland. As a general rule, the craic is good in Ireland – not so good in England, I'm afraid, but there we are. The craic can be good in Scotland, but there are an awful lot of moaners in this country, sure there are."

"My granny says that's because of the Reformation," said Bertie. "She said that John Knox was a real old misery-guts."

Eamonn smiled. "I believe he was, Bertie. Knox didn't have much craic, poor fellow."

There was a brief silence. Then Bertie said, "Will I feel any different when I'm Irish?"

The question took Eamonn by surprise. "Probably not, Bertie. Although you might have a bit more fun. We enjoy ourselves, you see, rather than bickering with each other as some people do in Scotland – no offence, Bertie."

Bertie inclined his head. "I think that you should enjoy yourself – if you can. I don't think you should be unhappy."

Eammon looked at him with interest. "Do you now, Bertie?"

"Yes. I think that you should enjoy what you have, while you have it. Because things don't last for ever, you know."

Eamonn could not conceal his admiration. "You're the real wee philosopher, Bertie."

"It's like ice cream, Mr Flynn," Bertie continued. "When you have an ice cream, you need to eat it. You could sit there and look at it, but it melts. So, you should enjoy it straight away. You should also share it, if you can. If there are people who haven't got any ice cream, you should give them a lick of yours."

"Of course you should," said Eamonn.

"Yes," said Bertie. "Because ice cream tastes better if it's shared."

Eamonn's jaw dropped. This was a seven-year-old boy. This was not David Hume or Adam Smith, or even John Rawls. This was Bertie Pollock, to whom he was meant to be teaching Irish culture at the behest of that pushy mother of his. But any instruction on his part would be otiose, he decided. This little boy knew who he was and what he should be. *Ice cream tastes better if it's shared.*

Now Bertie had a question. "What do you do, Mr Flynn? What's your job?"

Eamonn wondered how to describe it. "I'm studying for a PhD, Bertie. Do you know what a PhD is?"

Bertie nodded. "It's a doctorate of philosophy, Mr Flynn. My mummy is trying to get one up in Aberdeen. And most grown-ups in Edinburgh have one, I think."

Eamonn grinned. "Well, I suppose this is the city of the Enlightenment. And do you know what my PhD is in?"

Bertie shook his head.

"It's in Irish drama," said Eamonn. "Irish people have written tons of plays, Bertie. Tons and tons. When you become Irish, you can be really proud of that. Sean O'Casey, for example."

Bertie waited.

"He wrote a wonderful play called *Juno and the Paycock*," Eammon went on. "There's a character in that play called Captain Boyle. He's a great man, the Captain is. He looks up at the sky and asks, 'What is the moon?'"

Bertie listened gravely. "Does anybody tell him?" he asked.

"No," replied Eamonn. "That's the problem. He never gets an answer."

Bertie looked sad. "Poor Captain Boyle," he said. "I know what it's like when people don't answer your questions."

Eamonn was silent. He looked at his watch. Only fifteen minutes had passed. "I tell you what, Bertie," he said. "Would you like to go to the Musselburgh Races? They're on today. We could see if your father would like to come. We could all go. Irish people love horse racing."

Eamonn left the room to speak to Stuart. When he came back, he was smiling broadly.

"Your Da says he'd love to go. We can all set off in ten minutes or so." He paused. "And I'm going to give you five pounds to put on a horse. Irish people love putting money on horses – it's a big bit of our culture."

"Oh, thank you, Mr Flynn," said Bertie.

He liked Eamonn Flynn. He liked the sound of Ireland. It was even better than Glasgow, he thought – which was really saying something.

# 57

*Crushed Avocado*

Sister Maria-Fiore dei Fiori di Montagna arose early that morning. In their shared flat in Drummond Place, just round the corner from Scotland Street, she and her friend, the hagiographer, Antonia Collie, had drawn up a carefully prepared rota to decide who did which domestic tasks. That week, while Antonia was in charge of cleaning and laundry, it was Sister Maria-Fiore's turn to do the cooking from Sunday breakfast to Saturday dinner. She much preferred this to vacuuming and dusting – tasks that, in the convent in which she had lived in Tuscany, had been relegated to novices. The Mother Superior, a scion of a prominent aristocratic family from Umbria, had firm views on hierarchy, and had expressed these in terms that were readily grasped by even the youngest and least sophisticated girls consigned to the convent by their *contadini* parents.

"There's you," said the Mother Superior – known fondly by the other nuns as *la Principessa*. "You are down at the bottom. Then above you there is me. Then, above me, is the Bishop; and above the Bishop there's the Holy Father – each one in his or her place. Then there's the Lord himself, who is the Holy Father's line manager, so to speak. There's no room for ambiguity or vagueness. That's how it works." She paused. "Do you all understand? Good."

It was a bit of a comedown for Sister Maria-Fiore to have to undertake menial housekeeping duties when she moved to

Edinburgh, especially after she began her meteoric rise up the social ladder. There was something fundamentally wrong with a trustee of the National Gallery – and a member of the New Club Management Committee – having to do the washing-up, even of her own dishes in her own flat, but Antonia had not been persuaded that they should hire domestic staff. "Who's going to pay for them?" she enquired, knowing that the only person with sufficient means in their flat would be herself.

"I thought we might find a volunteer," suggested Sister Maria-Fiore. "We could call her an intern. In Italy, I knew several people who staffed their houses with unpaid interns. It's work experience, you see."

Antonia was dismissive. "One may be able to do that in Italy," she said. "Not here, I'm afraid. Our young people don't take to work terribly well, even when you pay them. That's why all our hotels and bars are staffed by Eastern Europeans. They're thought of as very hard workers."

Sister Maria-Fiore considered this. "Do you think we might be able to get an Eastern European to do our kitchen work?" she asked. "On a work experience basis?"

Antonia thought. "I'm afraid we'll just have to roll up our sleeves and make do," she said.

And that is what Sister Maria-Fiore did, in spite of her misgivings, offering up her efforts as a penance for past sins, all of which were in the venial category and therefore nothing to feel too bad about: the occasional yielding to feelings of envy, for instance, or the passing on of a scrap of gossip, or impatience with some of the weaker brothers and sisters. These were all things that could be readily forgiven, although she tried, as far as possible, to avoid them. Some temptations, of course, remained strong, and they were almost impossible to resist. Sister Maria-Fiore enjoyed the occasional cigar, which she knew was frowned upon – and she would also sometimes find it difficult to walk past a betting shop without going in briefly to put a very small bet on a horse. That she tended to justify on the grounds that the betting shop employees would lose their jobs if nobody came in to place a wager, and so she was directly helping them as she indulged in her minor flutter.

That morning she had only a small breakfast herself – a bowl of muesli and two slices of Parma ham she had bought from Valvona & Crolla the previous day. For Antonia, though, who usually rose a bit later, she prepared a much larger meal. This included peeled kiwi fruit, crushed avocado on toast, a poached egg, and sourdough toast spread with Patum Peperium. On the table at Antonia's place was a copy of the *Scotsman* that Sister Maria-Fiore had slipped out to purchase from the local newsagent, along with the morning's post, which had come through the letterbox only a few minutes earlier. Antonia maintained a wide correspondence with historians in Glasgow and Aberdeen, and in such other centres where there was interest in the lives of the early Scottish saints – her principal subject of research. She also had various correspondents working in Byzantine history, which was her other main academic interest. One day she would write a life of Acacius, the father of the Empress Theodora. Acacius was a bear-trainer in the Constantinople Hippodrome; his daughter, Theodora, became an actress, and caught the eye of Justinian, who married her in spite of strong opposition from members of the senatorial class to those who earned their living on the stage. Antonia was convinced that many of Theodora's enlightened attitudes and diplomatic skills were attributable to her upbringing, and, in particular to paternal influence, but was having great difficulty in finding out anything about the life of this man, whose deeds appeared completely unrecorded. But that was the incentive to write such a book: if nothing is known about a particular figure, then a biography is all the more necessary.

Now, over her crushed avocado, Antonia looked up from her newspaper and asked her friend about her plans for the day.

Sister Maria-Fiore sat down to explain. "I'm going to transfer the stone. It will be more secure elsewhere."

Antonia considered this. "A good idea," she said at last. "Drummond Place Gardens are just too public for an artefact of such significance."

"That's exactly what I think," said Sister Maria-Fiore. "I've spoken to Big Lou about it. She says that her sister-in-law farms up near Aberfeldy. I'm going to leave it with Big Lou, who will keep it under her counter until her sister-in-law comes down to Edinburgh for some dental work she's having done."

Antonia approved. "That sounds like a reasonable plan," she said. "It may only be a fragment of the Stone of Scone, but it is of great significance. The English would love to get their hands on it again. They must be prevented at all costs."

"*Precisamente*," said Sister Maria-Fiore.

Antonia gazed at her friend in complete admiration. "You're wonderful," she said. "You really are."

# 58

## *A Site of Pilgrimage*

Immediately after breakfast, Sister Maria-Fiore changed into her tartan habit and left the flat. She was careful to check that there was nobody about – this was a mission that required close attention to what eyes might be upon her. There was nobody, apart from an unfamiliar couple walking a dog at the London Street end of Drummond Place and a delivery van parked outside a house a few doors along. Satisfied that she could make her way into the gardens without being observed, Sister Maria-Fiore hurried on her way. It would not take her long to retrieve the stone in its Toppings Bookshop tote bag, and to walk briskly along Northumberland Street to Dundas Street. She was looking forward to handing the relic over to Big Lou's care: the responsibility of looking after a piece of stone of such importance to Scottish history was daunting, and having it safely tucked away in Perthshire would be a weight off her mind.

There were one or two people in Northumberland Street, but nobody seemed to take more than passing notice of Sister Maria-Fiore dei Fiori di Montagna walking purposefully along with her heavy blue bag. One passer-by recognised her, and greeted her with a friendly *good morning*. She returned the greeting, but kept her eyes steadily on the pavement ahead: she did not wish to engage in conversation lest enquiry be made as to the contents of the bag.

Towards the end of Northumberland Street, just short

of the junction with Dundas Street, Sister Maria-Fiore stopped for a moment outside the Wally Dug, a well-known pub into which she and Antonia occasionally dropped on Friday evenings. She was a welcome presence in this bar, and would engage in lively conversation with a number of the locals before returning for dinner in Drummond Place. There was always much to discuss, it seemed, and her views were generally listened to attentively. Several of her aphorisms had, in fact, been noted down and were quoted on the food menu or inscribed on the walls of the toilets, with due attribution.

That morning, Sister Maria-Fiore noticed that several workmen were busying themselves outside the Wally Dug. She had been told that work was being planned in the pub – a stone floor, described as being a "floor of appropriate character", was being installed and several other changes were being made to the décor. This work must now be starting, she thought, as she saw one of the workmen unloading the new flooring material from a van parked nearby.

The foreman, a stocky man in dusty overalls, greeted her warmly. "Nice morning for a walk, Sister," he said. "If you feel like a drink, pop in and we'll fix you up."

"Bless you," she said. "The work that we all do, in our various ways, can produce not just a spiritual thirst."

"Aye," said the foreman. "That's true enough."

It was at this point that Sister Maria-Fiore heard a cry from Dundas Street. Looking up sharply, she saw that a woman had tripped on the pavement and was sprawled at the edge of the road. Without hesitation, she dropped her tote bag, gathered the skirts of her habit about her, and ran to the woman's aid.

The casualty did not seem to be badly hurt – beyond a few scratches – and was soon sitting up, being comforted by Sister Maria-Fiore.

"I was being particularly careful," said the woman. "But the pavement's so uneven just there."

"You're absolutely right," said Sister Maria-Fiore. "But the important thing is that nothing seems to be broken. Can you stand up, do you think?"

She helped the woman to her feet. She asked her whether an ambulance needed to be called, but the woman was quick to discourage this. "I'll be absolutely fine," she said. "If you wouldn't mind coming with me to the bus stop, I can get on a number twenty-three and go directly home."

Sister Maria-Fiore accompanied the woman to the bus stop. In the distance, they could see a bus beginning to lumber its way up the hill. In no time at all, it was with them.

"I think I should come with you," said Sister Maria-Fiore. "Just to be on the safe side. I'll see you to your door."

"You're very kind," said the woman.

The bus set off, and it was only when they were approaching the stop on Morningside Road at which the woman said they should get off that Sister Maria-Fiore realised that she had left her Topping's tote bag, with the fragment of the Stone of Scone, on the ground outside the Wally Dug.

She saw the woman to her door, and then went out to Morningside Road to catch a bus back to Dundas Street. She tried not to panic. Stones would not be expected to go far. But when she arrived back at the Wally Dug, she found that the bag was nowhere to be seen. She spoke to the foreman, who scratched his head. "What was in it?" he asked.

"A piece of stone," she replied.

He looked down into the pub, where the workmen had already laid a large section of floor – with a hundred small pieces of stone.

Sister Maria-Fiore was aghast. "Oh, my goodness," she muttered. "*Desastro!*"

The foreman was apologetic. "My Italian's not up to much, but I gather that means *disaster*."

"It does," she said.

The foreman winced. "I'm afraid we can't take that floor up now," he said. "I can give you another piece of stone, though – if you like."

Sister Maria-Fiore took a deep breath. She had always believed in the virtue of positivity. This was not an ideal outcome, but it could have been worse. At least this fragment of the Stone of Destiny was safe, and here it might be appreciated by those who might wish to come to view it. The Wally Dug could even become a place of pilgrimage – a shrine to an important part of Scottish history. It could have been far worse.

# 59

## *Love and Friendship*

Three days later, Domenica and Angus sat in their Scotland Street kitchen, attending to the buffet supper that they were to serve their guests that evening. It was shortly after five o'clock, and the evening sun was still strong and golden on the slate roofs of the New Town, on the trees in the Drummond Place Gardens, and on the distant hills of Fife. Most of the preparation had been done by lunchtime; now they were concentrating on the dishes that would need to be warmed up for the arrival of their guests.

"It seems so long since we last did this," said Domenica.

"Well, everything has changed," said Angus. "And that includes our social habits."

Domenica thought about this as she sprinkled pepper on a large tray of moussaka. Angus was right – to an extent; life had indeed changed – the old certainties, the routines, the expectations, the *feel* of the world – all seemed to have shifted. They themselves were still there, as were most, even if not all, of their friends, but somehow the *view* had changed; somehow a sense of things being in flux had taken over. So much had happened in the world – and at such a disconcerting pace. Rapid change disturbed us – it always did. And now, were we just children lost in a dark wood, deprived of our authority figures and our gods, whose absence was so painful to us? How fortunate, she thought, were those who believed in something beyond the material.

She glanced out of the window. Edinburgh was still there, as was Scotland. And shortly, she and Angus would be joined by friends with whom they had shared these occasions, these gatherings in Scotland Street, over so many years. Perhaps the doubt was purely within her; perhaps it was completely subjective, and others did not feel what she felt: sometimes we made the mistake of attributing our own feelings to others – that was a form of wishful thinking, and was such a natural thing to do.

She looked at Angus; she did not think that he felt this way at all, even if he acknowledged that social habits had changed. She sighed. The condition of humankind was a parlous one. For a long time, we had enjoyed the illusion that there was to be no terminus to our existence, that human society would always be here, and that our little bit of it, our civilisation, our local culture, would persist. But now those long-term assumptions seemed unduly optimistic.

And yet, what was the point of such thoughts? They might be useful in concentrating our minds on doing something about those threats we could do something about, but beyond that? The answer, it seemed to Domenica, was to live in the moment, but not hedonistically; not to abandon the ambition to lead a good life: to cherish what we had, and make such contribution as we could to the happiness of others. That shouldn't be too hard, she felt.

Angus had been thinking too: not about these great issues, but about the simple, immediate subject of friendship. The real issue for most people, he thought, was loneliness. From the moment we came into this world we needed to be with another: with our mother to begin with, and then, step by step, with others. We sought out friends to blunt the loneliness of existence, and then we deepened that search into a quest for love. We all wanted to be loved – we wanted that more than anything else. That was why love was the great theme of song, the most accessible and universal of all the arts. Our songs were almost always about love – overwhelmingly so – and love was what we thought about for so much of the time.

He thought of some of his friends. How had they fared in that human search for love? Stuart downstairs had been unlucky – it must have been trying beyond measure to be married to Irene, and since his liberation from her baneful influence, he had failed, it seemed, to find somebody who would love him. Perhaps he would do that soon, now that Irene appeared to have her fisherman lover up in Peterhead. Poor fisherman: what a fate to be linked with Irene, to have to listen to her every day! But perhaps that was what he had been looking for. There was no accounting for human taste: people found the most unlikely partners.

Then there was Nicola. He had heard of her recent disappointment – that date that turned out not to be a date at all. That man must have been highly insensitive, and she was better off without him. But it was disappointing for her; perhaps she would encounter somebody else, although perhaps not in similar circumstances. Of course, she had her pie factory in Glasgow – that was something. But material goods – even something as . . . as *lovely* as a pie factory – could never make up for a lack of love.

Matthew and Elspeth were coming. They were happy with one another, he thought, and of course they had their three boys. Children were a wonderful object for parental love. When you had a child, you embarked upon a love affair that in some cases simply never failed. There were no questions to ask, no doubts to be resolved: you just gave your love to your children and, if you were lucky, they gave it back to you. And that lasted for life.

Angus looked at Domenica, and she looked back at him.

He was in no doubt about it: he loved her, and he believed she returned his love. There was no need to talk about it – no need to say, at the end of each phone call, *Love you*, as some people did. He could never be so . . . so *external*. Love was a big, powerful word – bandy it about, and you cheapened it, deprived it of its force.

He and Domenica were content with one another, even if there were no surprises in their relationship. He knew what she thought about things, and she knew what his views were. She had heard him express his opinions on every conceivable subject, and he had heard her do the same. There was nothing wrong with that. The entirely familiar was a great consolation in life: familiar places, familiar friends, familiar music – all the things one recognised.

*May each day be the same*, he thought. That was a comforting thing to say to another, although the recipient of such a wish may not understand the benediction bestowed.

# 60

## *The Heart as Metaphor*

The sound of the party being held by Angus and Domenica filled the stairwell at 44 Scotland Street and drifted out, hospitable upon the breeze, across the cobbled junction with Drummond Place, and into the gardens. A passer-by looked up and smiled: for some, the fact that others are enjoying themselves is consolation enough for not having been invited.

Domenica sat in the kitchen, surrounded by her friends, while Angus attended to glasses, filling them with wine or zero-alcohol beer. For Bertie, who had been specially invited, along with Stuart and Nicola, there was a bottle of Irn Bru Zero, a drink newly on the market from which everything had been extracted, including the orange colouring of the original. This was also marketed as water, but under a slightly different label.

Domenica turned to her friend, Dilly, and asked her about Colonsay, the Hebridean island to which Dilly went in the summer. Had there been warm winds from the west, smelling slightly of seaweed? There had. Had there been days when the sea was absolutely calm, flat and silver, a mirror to the mountains in the distance? There had been several such days. Had there been the sound of children's voices on the beach, and wildflowers in the grass, and the MacBrayne ferry coming in from Oban, a dot on the horizon now but getting bigger by the moment? Yes, all that was there; all that had happened.

James Holloway, another friend who was always at their

parties, came and sat next to them. He spoke to them about an exhibition of the Scottish Colourists that James Knox had put together. It was important to see the Colourists in the context of what was happening in France and elsewhere. Domenica agreed. "We do not make much sense unless you look at those around us."

"Of course," said James. "You're an anthropologist. You do that instinctively. You're aware of the culture that shapes all of us."

Elspeth passed by, carrying a plate for replenishment. She said, "You must come and see us out at Nine Mile Burn. All of you. We mustn't lose touch."

"No," said Domenica, "we mustn't lose touch." And with sudden insight – one of those rare moments when we are vouchsafed a vision of *agape* – she realised how fortunate she and Angus were to live here, at this particular time, in this particular place. They had taken it all for granted, but she realised that they should not have done that. It was as fragile as it was precious, and it could easily be destroyed by so many dangers, indifference being in the vanguard of its enemies. But what was *it* – the thing she was thinking of? It was human community; it was being part of something; it was sharing a mutual attachment to some idea of the good, in an age in which bad manners were becoming the international norm. It was, in short, civilisation, that precious, precious concept that people disregarded now and seemed embarrassed even to mention.

James looked about him. Angus had come into the room, and now James remembered his duty. He always called on Angus for a poem on these occasions, and it was time to do that now. "Angus," he began, but did not have to say anything more. Angus nodded, and took a piece of paper from his pocket.

"Dear friends," he said, "you expect this, I know . . . and so here is something about the heart. Just that – the heart. I have called it 'The Heart as Metaphor'."

*"Few metaphors,"* he began, *"are as important, few as*
*Regular companions in our language, as uncomplaining;*
*The human heart begins its long duty at birth,*
*Seems unsurprised by what we ask of it.*

*For more than being that daily essential,*
*The heart is a subtle and familiar metaphor,*
*A way of talking about the world,*
*A way of telling others how we feel.*

*How easily, for instance, do we break*
*The metaphorical hearts of others*
*While following the promptings of our own;*
*In its sorrow, the heart resigns itself to fracture.*

*Hearts may be followed, regularly are,*
*Yet hearts are unreliable guides,*
*They lead us seductively down paths*
*They claim to know, but frequently do not.*

*You broke my heart, you found that out*
*But kept silent; I thought of you every day*
*Never forgetting unexpected moments,*
*Stored such things, of course, in my heart.*

*And always failed to utter the words*
*The heart would articulate, had it the chance;*
*The head may apply a rule of silence*
*While the heart would have it otherwise.*

*My heart is yours, it always has been,*
*Don't turn away and say you didn't know;*
*You did; the heart is a bad actor,*
*Finds it hard, you know, to dissemble.*

*It is a condition of the human heart*
*To be largely unfulfilled; that happens*
*Often in life and yet we start each day*
*Hoping the heart gets what it wants.*

*The heart has a photograph album*
*Quite of its own: often we may leave our heart*
*In Paris or the Tuscan countryside,*
*Some spot where we've known happiness;*

*My own heart has been left so many times*
*In some quiet Highland glen, rain-washed,*
*Or at a point where blue islands, distant,*
*Occur on the sea's horizon, afterthoughts*

*To the land I love so much it hurts:*
*Scotland claims my heart, I've given up*
*Fighting unequal battles that I'll never win;*
*Yes, Scotland: there goes my heart again."*

He stopped. Nobody spoke. Someone cried, but did so quietly. Bertie looked up at the ceiling, where the evening sun had traced a small unwavering line of gold.

THE END
(of this volume)